# CHILL FACTOR
## ICE STATION ZOMBIE 2

### JE GURLEY

1

Aug. 3, Washington, DC

General Terrence Scott began coughing as soon as he stepped off the MH-60M Blackhawk helicopter. Flinty dust kicked up by the backwash of the rotors tainted the sweltering, muggy Washington air that seemed uncomfortably heavy as he drew it into his lungs. The burnt-tar smell of hot tarmac assaulted his nostrils as the August heat rose in waves from the landing pad. The alabaster-white façade of the Pentagon building danced in the air like a mirage, a child's balloon floating in the air with no string. The heat was immediately stifling, but it was a welcome relief from the sterile, frigid air at *Resurrection City* in Oates Land, Antarctica. He could almost smell the sweat from the Capitol building across the Potomac as a divided Congress attempted to rip each other a new asshole, as if Washington needed any more assholes to add to its plethora of useless talent.

The general stretched his taut muscles, still aching after the weary two-day flight aboard the C-17 Globemaster from Antarctica. His damp shirt beneath his uniform jacket clung to his skin like toilet paper to a shoe heel. He hoped his deodorant lasted just a few hours longer. The six-hour rain delay in Christchurch, New Zealand, had eliminated any chance of even a quick shower before his meeting. He barely had time to eat. The reason for the meeting did not improve his foul mood.

A sudden wave of nausea swept over him. He stumbled and reached out for the side of the chopper to regain his balance. He glanced at the stub of his expensive *Cohiba Esplendido* cigar, frowned, and tossed it onto the tarmac at his feet.

"Damn thing must be tainted," he mumbled.

His journey to Antarctica had uncovered some unsettling results. Project *Resurrection* was not going as well as the Joint Chiefs had hoped. The project manager, Doctor Willis Cromby, was losing control of the situation. Cromby's outdated ethics refused to allow him to cope with what in Scott's opinion could be a God-given discovery. Perhaps it was time to replace him with someone a little more ambitious, like John Gilford. Cromby's ambitious assistant struck him as a completely ruthless and unscrupulous man, exactly the man they needed for the new, unexpected turn of events.

Scott had watched in awe as the AR-10 serum, designed to rejuvenate dead tissue and stimulate the growth of amputated limbs for soldiers, had brought back to life a dead soldier. He had then recoiled in terror, as the soldier became a mindless, ravenous creature, a flesh-eating zombie. Cromby saw it as a failure. Scott saw it as an opportunity. He knew squat about nanite technology. The idea that microscopic, self-replicating robots could crawl around inside the human body making repairs and encouraging certain cells to regenerate made his skin crawl. He rubbed absentmindedly at a persistent itch in his chest. According to Gilford, the nanites, while failing to remain focused on their original task, had animated the *truncus encephala* of the corpses, turning them into brainless animals with limited cognitive ability and an insatiable appetite. He rolled his tongue around the word – *truncus encephala*. It sounded like a damned venereal disease. On the trip back, he had looked up the term on the internet. It meant the brainstem, the part of the brain that controlled motor and sensory functions. He didn't need a medical degree to oversee projects like *Resurrection*. For that, he relied on people like Cromby. However, he could appreciate the military applications of the zombies Cromby had inadvertently created.

The most difficult part of any military operation was logistics. To deliver enough men to do the job required a means of transport, which reduced the chance of surprise and brought with it the added risk of immediate retaliation for the incursion. A single zombie or a small force of zombies, dropped in a strategic location could infiltrate the enemy, killing and infecting others as they went, increasing the number of casualties and of marauding zombies. Any losses would be minimal, since the attackers were dead already. It was an intriguing proposal he was taking back to his superiors, one he hoped brought him the recognition he deserved. At 62, he was near retirement age and wanted another star to add to his shoulder before going into oblivion.

He checked his watch – two p.m. His meeting with the Joint Chiefs of Staff was scheduled for two-thirty. If he paced himself, he could pass through the countless security checkpoints and walk through the door of the briefing room exactly on time. Punctuality was important. Arriving too early indicated over eagerness; being late spoke of a lack of regard for those who controlled promotions and he wanted that fourth star.

As he marched toward the Pentagon with his aide, Major Frank Belknap close on his heels, the general suddenly belched loudly. He stopped and patted his stomach. Another wave of nausea swept over him. He wiped the perspiration from his forehead with the back of his hand and turned to the major.

"Damned heat! It's too early for food poisoning to show up, isn't it?"

Major Belknap smiled reassuringly. His job was always to reassure the general. He had tied his future advancement to that of Scott's. "I doubt that you got food poisoning from a steak and baked potato at *W.T. Smithers*, sir."

"I hope the hell not. It's my damn favorite place to eat in Dover." A frown creased his brow. "I hope I didn't pick up a bug from that damned hell hole in Antarctica."

"It's just jet lag from your journey, sir. And the heat," he added quickly at a stern look from the general at his implied suggestion that Scott was getting too old for long trips. "I'll locate some antacids for your indigestion once we're inside."

Scott hoped Belknap was right and that it wasn't ptomaine poisoning. He didn't want to spew his lunch in front of the Joint Chiefs. He resumed his quick pace. Belknap automatically fell into step the perfunctory two paces behind.

The pair entered the briefing room at exactly 2:30. The Joint Chiefs were sitting around the conference table waiting. Only the Chairman, the Vice Chairman, the Director, and three others were present, what passed for a closed meeting for the JSC. He ignored their stares and dutifully took his seat at one end of the table, feeling somewhat like an interviewee for a job. The Chairman, General Theodore Winston Herbert III, wearing a uniform jacket with seams so crisp they could cut butter, fixed him with the piercing blue-eyed stare that had made him famous during the Congressional hearings over the Chicago mall terrorist fiasco that had cost over two hundred lives. Campaign ribbons and awards covered his chest like a mosaic flak jacket.

"General Scott, your message was frightening in its brevity. In the twenty-four hours since receiving it, we have," he glanced at his fellow Joint Chiefs, "made inquiries of Doctor Cromby_ -but have received no reply." Herbert tossed the pen he was holding on the table with such force that it bounced to the floor. His face grew stern. "Now, can you tell me what the hell is going on down there?"

Scott wiped his suddenly perspiring forehead and smiled weakly. "Doctor Cromby is… um…proving unreliable. He's afraid to push the envelope. His assistant, John Gilford, suffers from no such fears. He might make a good replacement. He and Doctor Gregory Malosi seem to have goals similar to ours. Gilford is eager to make a name for himself and Malosi is … well, Malosi is absolutely without moral principles. Project *Resurrection* has so far failed in its attempt to re-grow healthy tissue, but the new nanite serum, AR-10, has produced some rather startling results."

Admiral Alexander 'Mac' McMann, the Director, pushed his wire-framed shades up the bridge of his long nose, leaned forward, and rested his arms on the table. "Such as," he prompted. Scott knew the Admiral's vision was 20/20. He didn't need glasses and certainly didn't require shades in the confines of the office. The shades were a mere affectation. Wearing them, the Admiral thought himself a shorter version of General Douglas McArthur, his World War II idol. All he needed was a corncob pipe.

Scott cleared his throat, which had suddenly become very dry. He looked around for a pitcher of water but saw none. "Zombies," he said.

He secretly delighted in the murmurs that ran around the table and in the looks of astonishment from the Joint Chiefs. They continued until General Herbert slammed his fist on the table to quiet them. "Not another *Providence* disaster, I hope."

Scott winced at the reference to the loss of the attack submarine *USN Providence* and its crew of one-hundred-twenty-nine men two years earlier. "No, sir. The sailor who was the initial source of the zombie infection aboard the *Providence* is also the source of the AR-10 serum. It has since been refined. While it is unstable, I believe that with some carefully directed research, we can develop a method to control zombies for use as a military weapon."

Air Force General Trenton A. Stiles half rose from his seat. Stiles, a tall, lanky Texan with cotton-white hair and matching bushy eyebrows, was notorious for his outspoken manner and directness. He wagged a thin finger at Scott.

"Are you out of you friggin' mind, General Scott? It took every resource and calling in every favor that we had to keep the *Providence* disaster from public scrutiny. The Aussies are still pissed. If word ever got out that the U.S. military was actively attempting to develop zombies ..."

General Herbert raised his hand, stopping Stiles midsentence. He patiently waited until Stiles had resumed his seat. "The idea is not without risks, I agree, but let us not dismiss it entirely. After all, we have financed this project to the tune of two billion dollars of taxpayer money. Nanite technology has far-reaching applications." He looked at Scott. "You have prepared a report?"

Scott rubbed his eyes as Herbert's face began to waver. Ignoring his growing discomfort, he forced himself to focus as he reached into his briefcase for his carefully worded report. The manila folder felt strangely heavy as he lifted it from the case and held it out for his aide to deliver to the general's hands. Suddenly, a violent spasm in his hand caused the file folder's contents to scatter across the table. He ignored the shocked faces around the table and stared with mounting alarm at his trembling hand. He clenched and unclenched his fist, but the trembling remained, and a cold numbness was spreading up his arm. Breathing became more difficult, as if breathing through a clogged gas mask. As his chest grew tighter, he clawed his shirt open and stared down in horror at the black, blotchy, patch of skin just above his sternum. Angry black lines radiated like spider webs from the blemish, spreading upward toward his neck. He coughed and spewed dark, viscous blood across the long table and the manila folder. The Joint Chiefs began scrambling away from the table, as did his aide, Major Belknap.

Scott reached out his hand for help. "Please," he groaned.

The room spun. He fell over, face-forward into a pool of his own blood. His body began to convulse, his head beating a staccato rhythm on the table. Bones snapped in his nose and his fingers, a sickening popping sound like dead twigs.

As the room grew dim around him, he heard Admiral McMann's frightened voice suggest, "Maybe we had better get him to Walter Reed."

"I'm not touching him," General Herbert replied. "Major Belknap, call in the OD and get this man out of here. Get someone to clean up this mess."

As General Scott lay there, his mind slowly slipping into a deep pool of darkness from which he knew he would never return, he realized that the aches and pains had not been a precursor to the flu, food poisoning, or jet lag, but something much direr. He could almost feel the microscopic nanites careening through his body, dismantling good flesh and re-building it in the image of their creator – friggin' Willis Cromby. His lips would not move so he mentally cursed Cromby and his damned zombie serum as he fell over the edge of oblivion.

2

August 15, Oates Land, Antarctica

Gregory Malosi listened to the wind howling outside his small tent as he huddled over the tiny flame of his kerosene camp heater. He was low on food and almost out of fuel for the heater. For ten days, he had camped on a tiny patch of rock thrusting through the ice, avoiding *Resurrection City* and the death that stalked the base like the avenging finger of God. He doubted anyone remained alive. A few had fled the madness on snowmobiles but had little chance of reaching any inhabited Antarctic base. If by some miracle they did make it, they would be sowing the seeds of their own destruction.

He had arrived at the decision to abandon ship, so to speak on Day 5, numbering the days of the world's end from the initial outbreak. If God were exacting revenge for meddling in His handiwork, most of those responsible had been judged and punished. Doctor Willis Cromby was dead by his own hand, and John Gilford was either hopelessly insane or homicidal. Malosi had so far survived the invisible fingers of death and destruction, but perhaps that was because he placed no belief in any god. Rather, he put his faith in his revolver and a steady hand. Remaining at *Resurrection City* had become too dangerous. Men killed for imagined safety or for food. Zombies roamed the barracks, the labs, and stalked the open areas between buildings, killing and devouring anyone they caught. Malosi thought it both ironic and fitting that the whimsical name *Resurrection City* that everyone used when referring to their base of operations, had now become doubly appropriate. It had begun as a project designed to induce new growth in amputated limbs and damaged organs, especially nerves; now had it become Ground Zero for the resurrected dead. Hell on

Earth had been unleashed and it had all been General Terrence Scott's fault.

When General Scott had arrived from Washington on a surprise inspection, he had quickly made known his obvious lack of enthusiasm for progress on Project *Resurrection*. Through him, the Joint Chiefs expressed their concern that their two billion dollars had bought them nothing. Over Cromby's spineless objections and with Gilford's backing, the general had cajoled Cromby into administering the nanite AR-10 serum to a patient knowing its miserable rate of failure. Once again, it proved its ineffectiveness by killing the patient, and then resurrecting him as a bloodthirsty zombie. It would have been just another wretched failure if the general's biohazard suit hadn't developed a pinhole leak. To make matters worse, the technicians had not discovered the hole until Scott was already enroute to Christchurch on the first leg of his return trip to Washington. The military had chosen the old Australian base because of its remoteness. All their preparations had been for naught because one lousy, conceited general had insisted on wearing his uniform, medals and all, beneath his biohazard suit. The only consolation Malosi could see was that General Scott was probably long dead.

Before they had abandoned all hope of stemming the epidemic, the technicians had discovered that the mutating nanite virus had become airborne as well as transferred through zombie bites. They were all infected. They were all doomed. According to the reports of cities in flames and populations fleeing before communications ceased, the entire world was doomed. Malosi's only hope of survival was his belief that the dropping temperatures would render the zombies immobile. A quick trip back into *Resurrection City* for supplies and extra fuel for his snowmobile, and he could attempt the long trek to McMurdo Base. He expected no rescue there. He simply wished to place as much distance as possible between him and *Resurrection City* in case the military decided to sterilize the area with a nuclear strike.

Malosi packed his tent and few supplies and secured them to the sled behind the snowmobile. He experienced a short moment of panic when the vehicle didn't start on the first try, but on the third attempt, the engine turned over smoothly. Because he had chosen the least likely route from the base to avoid others, through narrow trails of snow and ice winding through spines of treacherous rocks, he covered the twenty miles to the base in just over an hour. He stopped the vehicle outside the base and walked the last few hundred yards to avoid attracting unwanted attention. He needn't have bothered. The base was silent and dead. Frozen corpses sprouted from the snow like a crop of death. Snow-dusted bodies lay in open doorways. He sat on his haunches watching the lab where John Gilford had established his safe haven from the carnage. A thin rill of smoke rose from a makeshift chimney sticking out an office window – Gilford. When Malosi had left on the fifth day after the first outbreaks, at least twenty men were still alive. Judging by the silence, it appeared that Gilford alone remained.

Malosi skirted the labs and went directly to the cafeteria in search of food. Bodies and parts of bodies lay in obscene positions of death in the dining room, some human, some zombies. Blood trails marred the linoleum floor where others had died. The large hall that had been the central hub of off-duty activity for restricted base personnel, where men and women had met for food, conversation, and games, was now a mausoleum dedicated to the folly of man's hubris. The scent of death seemed to fill the cold air, even though he knew it was mostly in his imagination. The dead bodies were pristine; free of corruption and decay by bacteria for as long as they remained frozen. He shook off his apprehension and hurried to complete his task.

He had decided to try to reach McMurdo Base. The death that stalked the planet had not spared McMurdo, but his chances of escaping Antarctica were better from McMurdo than from an invisible base no one knew about. The journey was a long one – almost 600 miles across rough ice, rocky terrain, and glaciers. He needed as much food and fuel as he could carry. He knew he couldn't carry heavy cases of food and cans of fuel back to the snowmobile. He would need to stage them outside the base and come back with the snowmobile. By loading quickly, he hoped to avoid facing Gilford. He had no qualms about killing his insane former colleague, but Gilford was a better shot. Discretion was wiser than revenge.

He made two trips from the storeroom carrying boxes into which he had loaded cans of meat stews, soups, vegetables, and fruit. He also added several bottles of vitamin supplements and a can of Rishi green tea, his favorite brand because of its high catechin content, an antioxidant. If his food supplies ran low or his diet became too unvaried, supplemental vitamins could keep him healthy and a good quality green tea, unlike coffee, needed no sweeteners. He also added a fully stocked first-aid kit.

The motor pool still had its complement of vehicles stored out of the weather, the keys safely locked away in a steel vault for security. The person with the keys had been one of the first to turn zombie, curtailing most attempts at escape. Malosi had been lucky. He had stumbled across a brand new Yamaha RS Venture GT, which one of the mechanics had been assembling in a storage shed. All it needed was a few finishing bolts and fuel. He filled four, five-gallon cans with fuel and ferried them to his collection. He decided to return for an extra snowmobile battery. That move almost cost him his life.

He walked around the front of the motor pool just in time to see John Gilford exiting the lab. He ducked behind a parked jeep, but in his haste, he kicked an empty oilcan. The can rolled in front of the jeep. Gilford stooped, eyed the can, and took his pistol from his coat.

"Who's there?" he shouted. "Come out or I'll shoot." He laughed wildly. "I'll shoot anyway." Gilford fired three shots into the jeep. One passed through the window and struck the wall inches from Malosi's head. He slowly withdrew his revolver and held his breath. Gilford cocked his head to one side and stared at the oilcan for a few moments longer, and then laughed and continued to the cafeteria. Malosi released his breath and rushed into the motor pool, grabbed the battery and fled the base, relieved that he had avoided a confrontation with Gilford.

He returned to the snowmobile but waited an hour to give Gilford time to complete his business and return to his sanctuary. At the last minute, caution won out over speed, and he decided to drive closer but not onto the base. Instead, he parked near the runway and made several trips between his stash and the sled. Satisfied he had greatly improved his chances for survival, he cranked the Yamaha and roared away, smiling as he thought of Gilford rushing out to chase ghosts.

3

Aug. 21, Amundsen-Scott South Pole Base, Antarctica

Only a certain breed of man could feel at home in the Antarctic. During the twenty-four-hour daylight of the Antarctic summer, the whiteness is so intense that it is almost blinding. The Polar Plateau is a featureless plain of ice and snow, built steadily deeper layer by layer over millions of years. With ice almost two miles in depth, the glacial coldness rises like a living creature, sapping strength and insinuating itself into every living thing. In fact, the only creature foolhardy enough to visit the South Pole is man. Bent on his exploration of the world around him, even the Poles have proven no barrier, but in March, the sun dips below the horizon one final time, leaving the land blanketed in perpetual gloom, broken only by the moon and the stars overhead. The wind, frigid enough to freeze flesh in minutes, moans in the darkness. For those used to the diurnal movement of the sun, the constant twenty-four-hour darkness of the Antarctic winter is unnerving and difficult to ignore.

Bradford Niles was such a man. Born in North Dakota, a veteran of thirty-one harsh winters, he relished the cold. Like North Dakota, the clear skies of Antarctica were perfect for his chosen field, astronomy. The South Pole presented whole sections of the galaxy invisible in the Northern hemisphere. The six months of darkness allowed him to scan the skies whenever he needed, and the dry atmosphere reduced absorption of the millimeter wavelengths collected by the telescope he used. Exhausted by a twelve-hour shift of mapping dark matter in the Magellanic Cloud Galaxies, his current project, he glanced at his watch and performed the mental calculations necessary to determine the time in his hometown of Bottineau, North Dakota. There, people would just be sitting down to Sunday breakfast on a warm summer morning. At Amundsen-Scott South Polar Station, it was just before two a.m. Monday morning, an eighteen-hour time difference with Daylight Savings Time.

In the reversed seasons of the Southern Hemisphere, North Dakota winter was the season of warm weather and perpetual daylight hours in Antarctica. During the months of September through February, the base housed up to two-hundred-fifty researchers and visitors. By March, most had gone, leaving only a few hardy researchers and the support staff of forty-eight. The office that he and his fellow overwintering astronomer, Daryl Overton shared, was on the second floor of Pod B, one of the two, U-shaped buildings that comprised the base. He glanced at the temperature gauge for Bottineau on his computer – eighty-five degrees. Outside the base, the temperature was hovering near sixty-five degrees below zero, a one-hundred-fifty-degree difference. He stretched his aching muscles and pushed away from his desk, too tired to continue. The remainder of the data could wait until later.

Still stretching his arms over his head, he stepped out into the deserted corridor. Except for the ticking of a clock and the soft whisper of water in the overhead pipes, all was silent. Walking the deserted corridors was like prowling an empty shopping mall after closing hours. He always felt that he should walk softly and whisper when he spoke. The sound of a ball bouncing drew his curiosity. He passed the row of managers' offices lining the hallway. They were mostly empty for the winter, and only a few night owls like him remained awake in the early morning hours. The sound was coming from the basketball court. Curiosity drew him downstairs to the gym.

He entered the two-story basketball court that also served as a meeting room for large events and found Mark Walls shooting hoops. Walls noticed him enter and tucked the ball under his arm.

"Ready for a little one-on-one?" Walls asked.

Brad grinned. While he was an outdoorsman, often hunting moose in the Turtle Mountains and fishing at Lake Metigoshe, he had never enjoyed participating in team sports except for watching a good hockey game and the usual Super Bowl event the base threw. Walls knew this and it had become a standing joke between the two.

"No thanks. What's wrong, Mark? Can't sleep?"

Walls took a jump shot from the corner of the court. The ball made a whishing sound as it sailed through the net without touching metal. He pumped his fist in the air in triumph.

"Nah. I'm running a program for the TDRS uplink. I'm killing time until it's uploaded."

The TDRS-F1 and Iridium System were two of the communication network satellites that kept the base in constant contact with the rest of the world. The old timers had told him about the early days of almost total isolation. Now, they enjoyed cable television and internet access for several hours each day while the satellites were high enough above the horizon, and twenty-four hour access via the newly installed fiber optic cable to Concordia Station.

"Problems?"

Walls looked thoughtful for a moment, and then frowned and shrugged his shoulders. "Who knows? I'm receiving no signal from any of the satellites. Could be a bug." He dribbled down the court for a layup. The ball bounced off the glass and missed the hoop. He cursed and chased after it. While Brad was computer savvy, he knew little about the science of telecommunications, Walls' specialty. He only hoped he didn't lose his link with the A.A.O. in Coonabarabran. The Australian Astronomical Observatory was allowing him to access data from the 3.9-meter A.A.T. and the 1.2-meter Schmidt telescopes, which, like the 10-meter telescope at Amundsen-Scott that he was using, were also studying the Magellanic Clouds.

"I guess I'll try to catch a few winks before breakfast," he said.

Walls yawned, and then glanced at the clock on the wall. "My program still has two more hours to run. I'll kill some more time, run a few final checks, and join you later for breakfast. Then, I'm going to smoke a nice Peruvian cigar, hit the sack, and sleep in all day."

To keep the air inside the base as pristine as possible, especially during the long Austral winter, all smoking was confined to one small room with a separate ventilation system, much to Walls' displeasure, but to Brad's delight. He had walked in one day as

Walls was smoking a *Miguel Grau*, his favorite Peruvian cigar. The pungent smell had gagged him.

"Smoking will kill you," Brad told him.

Walls grinned. "It's either cigars or sex, and there's not much of that down here."

Of the forty-eight people remaining at the base, only nine were women. Of these, two had already paired with each other, four were in semi-steady relationships with members of the staff, and one, Faith Mendez, was determined to sleep her way through the remainder. That left Nattie Mullins, one of the two sous chefs, and Elizabeth Strong, the base's medical officer. Nattie was a great cook and friendly, but she cursed like a sailor and looked like a toothless walrus. Elizabeth, Liz as she preferred, had politely brushed off countless attempts by male members of the love-starved staff to woo her. Brad found her attractive and friendly, but somewhat cool and reserved. Everyone had their favorite reason why such a woman would confine herself to the ends of the world. He suspected a bad relationship or a failed marriage, but no one knew.

"Faith might look you up," he said.

"Fat chance of that. She's still working her way alphabetically through the K's and L's. W comes a long way down the alphabet, my friend." He looked at Brad pointedly. "N comes up soon. You should be happy."

Brad shook his head. "Not me. I'm out of here in another six weeks, back to North Dakota to collate my research material."

Walls shrugged. "Never pass up free poontang."

"Nothing's free in this world, my friend. Remember that. Now wouldn't you hate to get back to that girlfriend of yours in Dallas with some Antarctic STD, like frostbite of the penis?"

Walls made a pained-face expression and grabbed his crotch. "Ouch."

"See you later," Brad said and turned to leave. Behind him, Walls began dribbling again; then cursed as he missed a shot. On his way out, Brad reached out and gently touched the South Pole logo, a white Antarctica surrounded by a blue sea set inside a white circle. It served as a reminder that he was truly there.

The winter quarters were located in one wing of Pod A. A second wing housed the summer crew but was presently shut down to conserve energy and used to store perishable food items in the just-above-freezing environment. His winter quarters room was located at the far end of the base on the lower level. As he started down the corridor, he heard one of the dryers in the laundry room spinning. Who would be doing laundry at such an un-Godly hour? To avoid yet another distraction preventing him from sleep, he backtracked and took the stairs to the upper level. Passing through the corridor outside the medical lab, the 'Hall of Fame' lined with photos of over-winterers, he smiled at the thought of his face being there soon among the others. He was so absorbed in the prospect of a little piece of immortality that he almost walked into an equally distracted Elizabeth Strong.

"Excuse me," she gasped. "I wasn't expecting to see anyone at this hour."

Brad was surprised to see her at such an ungodly hour. The medical lab usually kept normal working hours. He looked at her without appearing to stare. She wore a white lab coat over a gray warm-up suit that didn't hide her well-rounded figure. Her dark-framed glasses dangled from her neck by a silver chain. She had tied her long, blonde hair in a ponytail to keep it out of the way of equipment. From her California Girl tanned complexion, it was obvious that she had been utilizing the tanning lamps. His own pale skin made it equally as obvious that he had not.

"My fault," he said. "I was daydreaming. You're up late."

"I was completing an inventory of the medical supplies. I wanted to finish it today and get it out of the way for another three months. Any interesting stars tonight, Doctor Niles?"

"Please call me Brad. There are way too many doctors here."

She smiled at him. "Okay, Brad. In that case, you may call me Liz."

"I logged a new pulsar that might prove interesting, but mostly more of same. It's a slow, tedious process."

"Like inventory."

He chuckled; then realized that she wasn't joking. "Yes, that's what I'm doing essentially, inventorying the stars in the low millimeter wavelength." He glanced down the darkened corridor. "I'm on my way to bed now. Would you like to join me?"

Her expression hardened. "Excuse me?"

He immediately recognized his mistake and blushed. "No…er…no…I meant, would you walk with me to the dorm?"

The smile returned to her face. "Thank you, but I have to go downstairs to the laundry room first. I have some clothes in the dryer."

*The mystery of the dryer was solved.* "Okay. See you later."

He cursed himself for his stupidity all the way to his room. "She must think I'm crazy," he mumbled to the hallway walls.

During the summer, the base reached capacity of over two-hundred-fifty people. The summer quarters were smaller and often shared. Each of the overwintering crew enjoyed the luxury of a private room. His room was somewhat Spartan in furnishings. A bed, a desk and chair, and an extra folding chair for the occasional visitor were all he required. He welcomed the opportunity for privacy, especially when the base had been overrun with the summer crowd. He had arrived in mid-February to prepare the telescope and install the programs necessary for his research. The base had seemed as crowded as a bar on Super Bowl Sunday. He sometimes worked from his room using his laptop, but it was more convenient to use the lab's facilities. During the long, dark winter months, like most of the others, he preferred the company of his fellow Antarctic castaways to the lonely confines of his room. Though not normally gregarious by nature, the gatherings in the libraries or television rooms for idle conversation, card games, or a Saturday night pool tournament, quickly became routine.

For recreation, very important for morale in a secluded environment, the base had a two-lane bowling alley, an arts and crafts room, a computer room, a music room, a pool table, a library, a fully equipped gym, and a basketball court. It even boasted a large-screen television where he and the others had watched *The Shining* and *The Thing*, a long-standing tradition for those overwintering.

When he reached his room, snoring from the next room broke the deep silence of the night. He grinned. Anthony Pirelli, the station manager, denied snoring despite the numerous accusations.

Ignoring the snores and exhausted from his long shift, Brad collapsed on his bed fully clothed and fell fast asleep.

\* \* \* \*

The artificial station 'morning' came early. Roused by the noise of others up and about, Brad reluctantly forced himself from the comfort of his bed, showered, and shaved. During the summer, to conserve water, each person was allowed a two-minute shower twice per week. This made for a heady aroma in the base. With fewer people, his shower was slightly longer, but he had quickly learned early on to shower with haste. He dressed in his usual casual attire of jeans and t-shirt and headed to the galley. In stark contrast to his earlier early morning walk, the aroma of fried bacon and freshly baked biscuits, the noise of conversation, and the sounds of people preparing for work filled the building.

He quickly saw how overdressed he was as he entered the galley. Walls sat at a corner table wearing red-checkered Bermuda shorts, a bold red-and-white-flowered Hawaiian shirt, and reflective pilot shades. Many of the others wore shorts, light shirts, and sandals, a spit-in-the-eye attitude toward the freezing temperatures outside. The station's glycol and water hydronic heating system used waste heat from the generators, keeping those areas not shut down for the winter toasty and warm. A few, mostly those whose duties required them to go outside, wore heavier pants and boots.

Brad grabbed a cup of coffee from the urn and sat down opposite Walls. He eyed Walls' heaping plateful of scrambled eggs, bacon strips, link sausages, pan-fried potatoes, and buttered toast with disgust and decided to stick with his coffee for a while.

"Nothing for you?" Walls asked, shoveling a forkful of eggs into his mouth.

"Too early. I'll have a muffin later. How can you eat all that garbage?"

"I have an enormous breakfast and skip lunch. Besides, I work out."

"You could work out on the ice and not burn that many calories," Brad countered.

Walls frowned and patted his belly. "I've lost eight pounds since I got here. Besides, I use food to replace lack of sex. Speaking of sex ..." He glanced toward the door and whistled softly. "Would you look at that?"

Brad turned in time to see Faith Menendez entering the room clad in a thin white shirt with no bra to contain her melon-sized breasts, which bounced playfully as she walked. She wore a pair of cut-off blue denim shorts that hugged her ass cheeks like cupped hands, drawing more than a few appreciative stares from the men and jealous glares from the women.

"I'd have that for breakfast," Walls remarked, "calories or no."

Brad tried not to stare, but had to admit that Menendez did have an exquisite body, lithe and muscular in spite of her obvious shapely curves. Her pixie-cut blonde hair gave her a forbidden young girl look that she used to its greatest advantage. "After that plate of food, I doubt you'd have room."

Walls stopped a fork laden with a sausage link mid-air and stared at Brad. "For dessert then. She's hot enough to melt ice cream." He continued to stare as Menendez leaned over a table filled with men from the Ice Cube Neutrino Observatory, giggling like a schoolgirl as she displayed her cleavage. "Those guys get on my nerves," he said frowning.

The 'Ice Cube', as most called it, was a cubic square half-mile of sensors embedded in the glacial ice, some as deep as eight-hundred feet below the surface, designed to detect elusive neutrinos from space. Drilling the holes for the sensors with the warm-water drill required the warmer summer months, but the observatory maintained a crew of four throughout the year. Each day they made the long, cold trek from the base to the neutrino observatory. He and Overton had it lucky. They only had to visit the SPT telescope every few days to check on the equipment and could work from the comfort of the base.

"They're okay," Brad replied.

"They think they're jocks, always hogging the basketball court and gym ..."

Walls continued speaking, but Brad ignored him as he focused his attention on Liz as she walked in. She stood for a moment at the door looking around before heading to the food line. Her long blonde hair now hung down to her shoulders. She wasn't wearing glasses. He wondered if she wore contacts or only used the glasses for lab work. She had discarded her lab coat and sweat suit for a light blue skirt and white blouse. Of the entire crowd, she was the only one dressed in a professional manner. Her eyes caught Brad, lingering briefly before smiling at him. To his disappointment, she passed his table and joined Shelia Meyers and Barbara Connelly, one of the lesbian couples.

"You don't think she's, uh …," Walls suggested, raising an eyebrow and grinning.

Brad whirled on Walls. "No way. She's … she's a lady."

Walls held up his hands defensively. "Geez. Okay. Just a thought."

"Don't even think it," Brad warned.

Walls smiled broadly. "I see. Smitten are we?"

Caught like a lovesick teenager, Brad fought to keep his cheeks from turning red. "Just interested."

"Well, good luck."

Walls dug hungrily into his food. Brad slowly sipped his coffee, sneaking an occasional glance at Liz as she conversed with Meyers and Connelly. The way her throat gently fluttered when she laughed, the way she brushed her hair away from her ears, even how she sat with her ankles crossed excited him. *Why then*, he asked himself, *am I so damned afraid of her*? He had never thought himself frightened by women. His studies and his work had demanded most of his attention, but he had found the time for a few girlfriends over the years. Of course, they had been interested mainly in sex, just as he had been. None of the relationships had lasted more than a few months. Maybe he was frightened that Liz presented more than simply a conquest, but a potential mate.

"I'm out of here."

Brad blinked his eyes and realized that Walls had cleaned his plate while he had been musing about Liz. He briefly wondered where the telecommunications expert, not lean and trim but certainly not fat, could put all that food.

"A cigar and then bed," Walls added. "What about you?"

"Oh, I'll read for a while."

"Is it your time to get chilly today?"

"Daryl lost the toss." He had flipped a coin with Daryl the previous night to determine who would make the long, cold trek out to the telescope. He had won.

"Good news on the toss. It's minus sixty-two Fahrenheit out there with thirty-mile-per-hour gusts."

Walls rose from the table, deposited his tray and dirty dishes at the dish pit, gave a final longing glance at Faith, and left. Brad finished his coffee as the galley slowly emptied, waiting for Liz. Finally, she finished her meal and walked by. Brad cleared his throat to attract her attention.

"About last night – I didn't mean to sound so stupid. I just …"

She laughed. "Don't worry. I knew what you meant, at least, I hope an invitation to sleep with you would be presented with more finesse than you displayed last night."

"Oh, it would be," he replied.

She looked into his eyes for a long moment, making him giddy, and then said, "Good. I have to go now. See you later."

"Uh, yeah, later," he stammered, cursing himself for his awkwardness around her. When she was gone, he smacked himself in the forehead with the palm of his hand. "Dunce," he groaned. "How many times are you going to make an ass of yourself?"

At the next table, Charles Lester, one of the engineers working for Raytheon, the company that ran the station, pecked frantically at his laptop keyboard and began cursing. "Son of a bitch, I lost my connection." He turned to Brad. "I was sending an e-mail to my wife," he explained.

Brad shrugged sympathetically. "Mark said the comm system had a few bugs in it. It should be back up soon."

Lester raised an eyebrow. "Yeah, right. Shimoda said something funny's going on."

Matsu Shimoda was a visiting researcher from Japan's Center for Climate Change Action, studying the effects of global warming.

"What do you mean, funny?"

"Pirelli had a long meeting by radio with McMurdo Base this morning before breakfast. Shimoda overheard Pirelli talking about a lockdown at McMurdo."

In the remote wastes of the South Pole, the station rumor mill was usually uncannily accurate. "Lockdown? For what?"

"I don't know, but a lot of people are getting sick there."

A sudden chill passed through Brad. Disease and fire were the two direst threats in an Antarctic base. Of the two, he feared an outbreak most. "Great. A flu epidemic. That's all we need."

He took a sip of his cold coffee and winced. He considered re-heating it, but the coffee didn't seem to be perking him up as much as it usually did. He had only slept four hours and felt sluggish. His conversation with Lester was not improving his mood.

"I've got to go," he told Lester.

He placed his dirty cup on the counter at the dish pit. Like everyone, he had taken his turn in the 'dish pit' washing dirty dishes, up to his elbows in dish suds and greasy pots and pans, a detail he tried to avoid whenever possible, once resorting to bribing a mechanic to take his place with a bottle of rum. With forty-eight personnel available, each person's turn came every six weeks. A quick scan of the duty roster posted above the table showed that his turn was due in six days, and he had nothing left with which to barter.

Outside in the corridor, he tried to decide if he needed more sleep or something to wake him up. He flipped a mental coin and chose entertainment.

"Maybe there's something good on television," he said to no one in particular, but knew from experience that it was unlikely. Because of the base's position so far south of most geosynchronous satellites, they received satellite transmission for only a few hours each day, and the cable from Concordia was far from reliable. After six months, he had seen most recorded movies more than once, even the ones that he had forced himself to sit through the first time.

Entering Pod B headed toward the television lounge, he spotted the Ice Cube crew near the exit donning their outdoor gear for the cold journey to the lab – wool sweaters and fleece-lined pants over their base core layer of warm-up pants and t-shirts, and heavy anoraks, wool pants, and insulated Wellington boots over that. They looked like overstuffed ninjas with their face-covering balaclavas. Only their eyes remained visible. He waved in greeting. One of them, he couldn't tell who, responded by waving an oversized mittened hand.

"You going out to the telescope today?"

He recognized the voice of the waver as belonging to Guy Hughes, a technician against whom he occasionally played pool.

"Not today. It's Overton's turn. Tomorrow."

Hughes grinned. "Too bad. It's going to be a bitchin' day out there today."

Brad watched them file out the door, glad he was remaining inside. He suspected that Hughes got off on the biting cold, even found it embracing, as did many of the overwintering crowd. Though he had grown up in North Dakota where winters often reached double-digits below zero, he had always preferred the milder spring and summer seasons.

Before he reached the television lounge, he saw Walls racing down the corridor toward the communications room. He didn't look happy.

"What's up?" he asked as Walls passed.

Without stopping, Walls replied, "We've lost all the damned satellites and the fiber optic feed from Concordia."

4

August 22, 35 kilometers north of Amundsen-Scott Base

Ravi Chopra urged the snowmobile across the featureless flat plain of ice toward home. His eyes remained glued to the GPS reading. The forty-five-mph wind was kicking up the snow from the ground and driving it into his face. His nose felt frozen beneath the balaclava. He gritted his teeth to keep them from chattering. Ice rimming his goggles made seeing difficult. The blowing snow blotted out the stars, leaving only the dim headlamp of the snowmobile to illuminate his path. He knew well the hazards of checking on his remote weather stations during a blow, but he had postponed the duty for two extra days waiting on the wind to die down. Left unattended, the anemometers for measuring wind speed tended to freeze up. Even his snowmobile was running a bit sluggish in the minus-sixty-degree temperature, when oil became as thick as molasses.

Preoccupied with the GPS, he didn't see the big red Russian thirty-five-ton *Kharkovchanka* blocking his path until the last moment. "*Gandu*," he cursed in his native Hindi as he jerked the handlebars of the snowmobile to the right and just avoided clipping the rear of the thirty-foot-long treaded snow tractor, barely remaining upright. He brought the snowmobile to a stop and stared at the Russian vehicle. The *Kharkovchanka* was a mobile home on treads, with sleeping quarters, a galley, and storage areas. The Russians preferred it to the smaller, more maneuverable American *Sno-Cats*.

"What are the Russians doing nearly eight hundred miles from Vostok?" he said to himself. He had developed the habit of speaking to himself while out on the ice to relieve the isolation.

The vehicle wasn't running, and snow drifted against the treads showed it had not moved in several days. Frost on the windows indicated that the temperature inside was freezing. He approached the door carefully and knocked. There was no reply. He tried the door and found it frozen fast. He kicked at it with his boot until it loosened enough to pry it open. Inside, three frozen bodies stared at him. One sat in the driver's compartment, hands still gripping the steering wheel. Two others lay in the floor. He gingerly stepped over them and checked the rest of the cabin, but found no other passengers. He wiped a layer of frost from the fuel gauge. It read empty.

"Were you headed to Amundsen?" he asked them. "Sorry I can't carry you there on my snowmobile, but I'll send someone out for you. We'll get you back to Vostok with your comrades."

He closed the door to the *Kharkovchanka* and climbed aboard his snow mobile. He glanced over his shoulder as he drove away, just to make certain the big red vehicle was still there and not a mirage dreamed up by his cold-numbed mind. It was real.

"A real mystery," he mumbled.

* * * *

August 22, Amundsen-Scott Base

Liz made a cursory examination of the three Russian bodies while Tony Pirelli watched over her shoulder. His concern showed in his dark eyes and furrowed brow visible over the top edge of the surgical masks they both wore at his insistence.

"No visible wounds that I can see, except a peculiar black patch covering two of the men's chests." She pointed to a series of black lines radiating from just above the sternum of one of the cadavers. "They seem to have frozen to death."

"No disease?" Pirelli asked. He had asked casually, but Liz detected a raised level of trepidation in his voice.

"I'll do cultures if you wish, but there's no way to tell from a visual examination. The black patches concern me. I've never seen anything like it. It could be some kind of vitamin deficiency, I suppose."

"But you don't think so," Pirelli pushed.

She hesitated. "No, it looks more like blood clotting in the surface veins, and the surrounding skin is slightly necrotic." She stared at Pirelli. "It might help if you shared what you thought I might find."

Pirelli shook his head. "I'm not sure. During McMurdo's last communication, they spoke of an outbreak but didn't give me any details. Now, we've lost all communication from everyone."

This last bit of news stunned Liz. "All of them? How could that happen?"

"It could be solar flares."

Liz tried to read the supervisor's worried face. He didn't look convinced by his own suggestion. "You don't believe that," she suggested.

His jaw twitched. "No. Besides, the cable with Concordia is out as well."

She reread Pirelli's face and realized that he was more than simply worried; he was frightened. She covered the body she had been examining with a sheet. "I'll do full autopsies on all three bodies when they thaw. Any idea as to why they were coming here? They've been dead for several days. They had to have left before we lost the satellite feed. Why not simply radio us?"

Pirelli grabbed his forehead with his hand and shook his head. "I have no idea." He peered at Liz. "Don't release the results of the autopsies to anyone but me."

She cocked her head at this. "All right."

"In the meantime, I'll send someone to keep an eye on the bodies."

"They're not going anywhere, Tony."

Pirelli scratched at his chin as he walked out the door. "I don't want anyone near them until we find out what happened to them."

After Pirelli left, she dropped her gloves and mask in the trash, and glanced at her hand-written notes. They revealed surprisingly little about the three corpses. Their ages ran from twenty-eight or twenty-nine to over fifty. All had been healthy individuals before their deaths. One had a recent appendectomy scar. For someone living in the Antarctic where emergency medical help could be days away, this was a common practice. They appeared to have run out of fuel and simply frozen to death. Pirelli's bizarre behavior worried her. Could it be that he knew more than he was telling her?

With the internet down, she couldn't check any medical databases for information on the black rashes. The closest she could come from memory were the black, necrotic lesions of survivors of the bubonic plague, but no one had seen the *Yersimia pestis* bacillus that caused it for decades. The Russians had been drilling into Lake Vostok, some 2.2 miles beneath the ice. She supposed it was possible that they had discovered some new bacteria or virus dormant for millennia, but it was unlikely. Puzzled, she closed the door to the examination room and perused the books of her small medical library for anything she could find.

True to his word, Pirelli sent Trevin Sage, a janitor, to guard the bodies. He didn't seem thrilled with the duty and spent most of his time casting surreptitious glances in Liz's direction. She had been able to ignore him while reading, but now his presence and lecherous gaze irritated her. Frustrated by her lack of progress and Sage's unwanted attention, she abandoned the breached sanctity of her office.

Word of the dead Russians had spread throughout the base quickly, feeding the rumor mill. With the discovery of the bodies and the unexplained loss of communications, the air of the base had become thick with apprehension. People had forsaken their duties and wandered the corridors like furtive onlookers at the scene of an accident. Half were frightened by events beyond their control, and the other half were excited by the variation in the normally dull daily routine. A crowd had gathered outside the communications room waiting for any word from the outside world.

Winter at the pole was a time of physical isolation. The freezing temperatures and six months of darkness prevented any planes from McMurdo from reaching the base. In such extreme cold, engines often failed and stressed metal could snap like wood. Landing skis could not handle the drifting snow. Planes froze to the ice. For the same reasons, snowmobiles and Sno-Cats were useless, and hiking the eight hundred miles to McMurdo was difficult in the summer and impossible in the winter. They were isolated from the real world as effectively as a base on the moon.

She spotted Brad leaning against the wall of the stairway leading to the television lounge. He glanced up at her approach.

"Still no word?" she asked.

"Not a sound since yesterday. What about the Russians?"

She hesitated, unsure of how much she should reveal. "I, uh …"

Brad held up his hand. "Never mind. I'll just bet Pirelli put the kibosh on any information you might reveal. I could see he was frightened." He stared at her. "How about you?"

"All this," she waved her hands in the air, "frightens me. We've lost the signal before but only for a few hours. This time …" She shuddered.

"Yeah, I know. I can't help but wonder what the Russians were doing this far out."

"I wish I knew." She rubbed her hands together to prevent their trembling. "I need a martini."

Brad smiled. "Can't help you there, but I do have most of a bottle of ten-year-old scotch in my room."

Liz returned his smile. She suspected Brad's nervousness was more due to her presence than a fear of the unknown. He didn't strike her as someone easily frightened. "That sounds perfect."

Returning to Pod A, she was dismayed to see that the heavy concrete-filled steel emergency door separating the two pods was sealed. Such an action was usually only taken during a fire drill. Brad swung the door open, ushered her through, and then resealed it behind them. The loud clang as it shut caused her to jump. If Pirelli was trying to prevent a panic, closing the emergency door was not helping.

Brad's room resembled hers, except where her walls contained photos of friends and places from her home state of California and a shelf overcrowded with mementoes of her past, Brad's room was very little different from any of the empty rooms in the cold storage section. A red anorak hung from the wall. A pair of heavy boots sat at the foot of the unmade bed. Several magazines topped a pile of dirty laundry in one corner. She suppressed a smile as he quickly kicked the clothes under the bed and cleared a stack of books from the desk chair for her.

"Sorry," he said. "The maid's day off."

He rummaged through a nylon backpack and withdrew an opened bottle of Dewar's scotch. "No ice, I'm afraid," he said as he poured a liberal amount in each of two glasses. He handed her one.

"Neat is fine," she replied. She eyed the amber liquid hesitantly. Scotch was not her favorite liquor, but having no vodka or gin, it would do nicely. He waited as she took a sip. The flavor was slightly smoky with a hint of vanilla. It was not as strong as she had thought it would be. "Not bad," she said.

He grinned and brought his glass to his mouth. "I brought this from Bottineau seven months ago. I've been hoarding it for an emergency. I guess this qualifies." He took a slow sip, letting the liquor roll around his tongue before swallowing.

"Bottineau? Where's that?"

Removing a folding chair from its hook on the wall, he placed it where the dirty clothes had been and sat down. "North Dakota."

She chucked. "Geez, couldn't you get frostbite there?"

"You can't see the Magellanic Clouds from there." He glanced out the window as if searching for them. The gibbous moon bathed the stark landscape in a ghostly wan light.

"Why not study something you could see?"

"I'm studying dark matter and its relationship with quasars. The Magellanics are close enough for a good view. Besides, Bottineau's a boring place."

"And this isn't?" She caught herself and added, "Usually."

He glanced away and took a long sip of his drink. "I have a bad feeling about all this."

She noticed the way in which he held his glass, tightly, as if the pressure of it in his hand reassured him. When he turned to face her, his face bore a serious expression.

"I was talking with Mark Walls. He's in charge of telecommunications. He said the source of the problem wasn't here or atmospherics. The signals just stopped. The satellite is still there. It's just not relaying anything."

Her heart tried to jump up her throat. "That's … impossible."

"Yeah, that's what he said." He leaned back in his seat, stretching his legs out in front of him. "I can't help thinking that the loss of an outside signal and the appearance of the dead Russians are somehow connected."

She didn't see it. Puzzled by his conclusion, she asked, "How? It would take several days' exposure to the cold to freeze them solid. They must have left Vostok days before that."

He shook his head. "I don't know. I just don't believe in coincidences."

"*A coincidence is a small miracle in which God chooses to remain anonymous*," she replied, remembering a quote from somewhere in her past.

"*Once is happenstance. Twice is coincidence. Three times is enemy action.*"

"Who said that?" she asked.

He grinned. "Auric Goldfinger, an adversary of James Bond. I think this situation is closer to a James Bond film than an act of God."

"Do you think the outbreak has anything to do with all this?" She didn't know how much he knew about the epidemic at McMurdo, but she needed someone to confide in, perhaps to use as a sounding board for ideas.

"There could well be a medical emergency at McMurdo, perhaps one that struck the communications people first, but a worldwide epidemic? I find that difficult to believe, especially one striking so quickly that warnings can't be broadcast."

She recalled the rumors concerning FEMA she had heard whispered by colleagues at a seminar, claiming that political expediency would take precedence over medical effectiveness in an emergency. "Maybe the authorities are trying to keep it under wraps to prevent widespread panic?"

He chuckled nervously. "If so, it isn't working. I'm scared."

Talking to Brad alleviated some of her growing apprehension. He spoke of being afraid, but she doubted that he felt fear in the same way she did. To him, it was an inconvenience, something between him and his work. To her, it conjured images of death and destruction, like the three dead Russians in her examining room. She tipped back her glass and drained its contents.

"Another?" Brad asked.

She held the glass in both hands, rolling it back and forth in her palms; then shook her head. "No. This helped. I need to stay sharp. Besides, it's just mid-afternoon, hardly cocktail hour."

Brad emptied his glass and poured two fingers of scotch into it, but didn't drink it immediately. "Close enough for me."

A thought that had been troubling her worked its way to the forefront of her mind. "What if we lose all communication for good? What if we're cut off from the rest of the world for months?"

Brad answered so quickly that she suspected he had thoughts along the same line. "We have enough supplies to last for three or four months. Someone will come as soon as planes can get here, or they'll drive in. That's two months at most."

Brad's words sounded reassuring, but the thought of total isolation, of not knowing what was happening, of being trapped at the South Pole frightened her. Two months could be a long time.

"What if they don't come – ever?"

A look flashed in Brad's eyes, one of haunting desperation. "Then we walk out," he said. The thought of weeks out on the ice troubled her. She didn't think she was hardy enough for such a journey. "Or we fuel the Russian *Kharkovchanka* and drive out," he added.

"We won't all fit in it," she reminded him.

Brad shifted uncomfortably in his chair, crossing and uncrossing his legs. "Well, someone can go and bring back help."

*From where,* she thought but didn't say it aloud. Instead, she said, "I guess so."

"Everything will be okay. The Russians got lost and ran out of fuel, tragic but not ominous. There's some kind of inverse magnetic field caused by sunspots interfering with communications. Walls will figure it out."

"And this from a man who doesn't believe in coincidence."

He frowned. "I very badly want to believe in coincidence. It's just …"

When his pause continued longer than she hoped, she said, "Just what?"

His eyes sought hers, compelling her to stare into them. In their brown depths, she saw something she hadn't anticipated seeing – fear. He spoke as if reluctant to reveal his past.

"My father was a half-blood Chippewa. That didn't make me very popular in school. Kids called me 'Breed' until I learned to kick ass to shut them up. Somewhere along the line, I guess I got a few medicine man genes or something. Sometimes I can sense when something is about to happen, usually something bad. It's kept me out of trouble a few times, you know – don't go out drinking with some friends, and then they have an auto accident. Stay away from a drag race, and a car goes out of control and kills someone. Don't rise to take a shot at an elk I've been stalking, and a bullet hits the tree beside me just where I would have been standing. I have that feeling now."

She wasn't sure if she believed him, but his voice and manner proved that he believed in what he was saying. "What do your senses tell you?"

His eyes went dark. He threw back his head and downed the remainder of his drink. "Run."

5

August 23, Amundsen-Scott Base, Antarctica

Trevin Sage leafed through a *National Geographic* wishing it had photos of naked, big-breasted Polynesian women, or a topless Riviera Beach, anything more interesting than the life of a Bengal tiger. He checked his watch – one in the morning. Everyone was asleep except for the telecommunications crew trying to sort out the problem. He didn't concern himself with that. Hell, they were in Antarctica. They were supposed to be isolated. Anyway, babysitting three Russian popsicles was better than sweeping and mopping. Even so, he couldn't help but glance into the examination room occasionally to make sure they were still there. The sheets covering them were soaked as they thawed. One's hand draped over the bed, a slow trickle of water pooling on the floor beneath it.

"I ain't mopping up that shit," he muttered aloud.

He rose from his chair and walked to one of the tables. He drew aside the wet sheet to stare at the pale face of the young boy, admiring the boy's penis. "They grow 'em big in Russia," he said. Earlier, the boy had looked so lifelike, as if he would rise from the table and walk away. Now, the black patch on his chest had spread to his face. His open eyes were changing to an angry red. Sage wiped his hand on his shirt. Pirelli had warned him to wear a mask, but it had been too uncomfortable.

"I hope it ain't catching," he said; then he chuckled under his breath. "Pirelli will give me hell if it is."

As he returned to his chair, he glanced into Doctor Strong's office. He wished she were still around. At least she was a looker. He wondered what she would look like undressed. She acted so prim and proper, but he bet she would be a wildcat in bed, maybe wearing black lacey knickers and a garter belt. He sat back and closed his eyes to hold the image he had conjured. A wet, splashing sound dissolved the picture in his mind.

"Damn Russkies," he groaned.

He got up to close the door to the examination room, but stopped with a start when he saw that one of the tables was empty, the sheet lying in a pile on the floor. "What the hell?" he muttered. Wet, naked footprints led away from the table. He followed them with his eyes. One of the Russians, the older man with a beard, stood across the room staring into a mirror, his hand extended as if wanting to touch it. His entire arm and face were a web work of black lines. He turned quickly and saw Sage. His expression turned into one of animal rage. Sage's feet refused to budge as the Russian lumbered toward him.

"Don't," he pleaded as he threw his arm over his face. Teeth sank into his flesh. Pain erupted like fire. He dropped his arm and the Russian's head lunged for his throat. A fetid odor, like death, rose from the Russian's mouth. He tried to scream but no words escaped. More pain, much more intense this time, exploded in his neck. He grabbed the Russian's head and pushed him away, panicking when he saw a chunk of his bloody flesh dangling from the Russian's mouth. He felt blood, warm and wet, running down his chest. Now his fear unfroze his feet. He backpedaled across the room toward the door. From the corner of his eye, he saw the young boy rising from the table, glaring at him hungrily. "Oh, Lord," he cried and began to run.

The corridor was empty and dark. He stumbled against the wall and knocked a photo to the floor. It broke with a loud crash, but no one came to investigate. He held onto the wall to keep from falling. His hands were growing numb and his vision swam. Blurrily, he saw a fire alarm a few paces away. He knew he should summon help. He released his hold on the wall and stumbled forward, but fell on his face. Then they were on him, all three of the Russians. Their mouths tore greedily into his flesh. He struggled to his knees, shoving his fist into one of the Russian's throats to push him away. *They're dead*, he thought. *They have to be dead*. He reached out and grabbed the alarm handle before the weight of the Russians brought him to the floor.

Distantly, he heard the alarm sounding. Help would come but too late for him. The pain was overwhelming, but he no longer had the strength to resist. He remembered the *National Geographic* and the photo of the goat staked out to entice the tiger. *Now, I know how the goat feels* was his last coherent thought.

* * * *

The alarm tore Brad away from an uneasy sleep. His dreams had been full of sinister, shadowy things in dark places, darker than the twenty-four-hour gloom outside his window. He came awake drenched in sweat, his heart pounding. Instinctively, he knew the alarm didn't mean fire. Another danger lurked outside his door. He switched on his lamp and slipped on his pants and boots, and then, after a second's mental debate, pulled his army surplus K-Bar survival knife from the drawer in his desk. Its seven-inch blade gleamed reassuringly. He thrust it through his belt.

Outside in the corridor, others were stirring.

"What's up?" someone called.

"That was the fire alarm," another said, "but I don't smell smoke."

"I don't think it's a fire," Brad said as he walked grimly toward the stairs. His emergency fire equipment was in a locker in Pod B. He didn't think he would need it, but decided to err on the side of caution.

Liz appeared beside him wearing only panties and a t-shirt. He tried not to stare at her breasts. If her flimsy attire embarrassed her, she didn't show it.

"What's wrong?" she asked. "Fire drill?" She frowned at a fierce glance from Brad. "What then?" she demanded.

He shook his head. "I don't know. Go get dressed." She hesitated. "Now," he urged.

She stared at him a moment longer, but returned to her room. He continued to the stairs, taking them slowly, unsure of what he might find waiting at the top. A scream stopped him. Still no odor of smoke tainted the air. He did smell something foul. He tried to recall where he had smelled it before. He pulled his knife from his belt as he remembered. It was the stench of death, an odor familiar to a hunter. He held the knife in front of him as he ascended the stairs. He spotted a body, or what was left of a body, lying in a pool of blood. He couldn't identify who it was. The face and throat were missing. Splotches of blood that might have been bare footprints led toward the galley.

By now, several others had joined him. Charles Lester moaned when he saw the corpse.

"What the hell happened?" he asked. "It looks like a wild animal got inside and tore him apart."

"There are no wild animals here," Brad reminded him. He pointed to the footprints. "Those are human."

"Maybe someone got cabin fever."

Brad nodded, but he doubted a case of cabin fever could drive even an insane person to eat someone. Pirelli hurried down the corridor but stopped when he saw the mess. He had a .9 mm pistol in his hand. As supervisor, he was one of the few personnel allowed access to firearms, a precaution in case of cabin fever or an argument.

"It's Trevor Sage," he said. "I left him to guard the Russian bodies. He's gone and they're gone. I checked."

At first, Pirelli's statement made no sense. Who would steal bodies? Who would kill in such a grisly manner to steal them? Then he remembered the bare footprints.

"My God. Do you mean they're alive? They were frozen solid. How?"

Pirelli shook his head as if trying to clear it. "I don't know, but they're gone."

Brad followed the footprints down the corridor where they disappeared through a door. "I think they're in the galley," he told Pirelli.

Pirelli led the way. He pushed open the door and switched on the lights. An older, naked man with a beard stood in the middle of the room. His face, chest and arms bore a network of tiny black lines. An old tattoo of a Russian naval ship was just barely visible beneath the tracery of black on his arm. The man's eyes were red. Blood dripped from his mouth and hands. *Sage's blood*, Brad realized.

"The old Russian," Pirelli gasped.

As if his voice was a cue, the bearded Russian snarled and attacked Pirelli. Pirelli, to his credit, didn't hesitate. He raised the pistol and fired three quick rounds into the man's chest from just a few feet away. Holes punched through the Russian's flesh, one directly above the heart, but no blood flowed from them, nor did he slow down. He was on top of Pirelli quickly, his heavier weight overpowering the one-hundred-forty-pound, five-feet-eight-inch Pirelli. Pirelli staggered backwards, one hand pushing at his attacker's chest to ward off the man's gnashing teeth, the other beating at his head with the butt of the pistol.

Seeing how ineffective the pistol had been, Brad acted quickly. He ran up and plunged his knife hilt-deep in the man's neck. The tip of the seven-inch blade protruded from the far side of his throat, but the Russian continued his attack on Pirelli, clawing at Pirelli's arms and face with his fingers. Brad grabbed the knife with both hands, placed his foot against the man's side for leverage, and withdrew the blade. This time he brought it down on top of the Russian's skull using both hands. The sharp blade pierced flesh, muscle, and bone. He placed all of his weight behind it and forced the knife deeper into the man's brain. The Russian froze, and then collapsed onto the floor amid a gush of thick, black blood that spewed from his mouth, ripping the knife from Brad's hands. Released from the Russian's grip, Pirelli staggered backwards and fell on his butt, staring uncomprehending at the dead man sprawled on the floor inches away.

"Is he dead?" he asked.

Brad examined the corpse. The flesh beneath the black lines was decaying rapidly. At least one of the bullets had pierced the heart. "He's been dead."

Pirelli broke his stare at the Russian and looked at Brad. "What do you mean?"

Brad placed his foot on the corpse's chest and tugged on the knife handle. After extracting it from the Russian's skull, he wiped it on his pants' leg and replaced it in his belt. "How many people do you know who can freeze solid, thaw out, attack someone, and take a bullet through the heart without blinking an eye?"

"But what …?" Pirelli began.

"He's a zombie."

Both Pirelli and Brad looked at the speaker, Guy Hughes, one of the Ice Cube technicians well known for his practical jokes. This time, however, his face betrayed no hint of humor. "He's one of the walking dead," Hughes continued, "a zombie. How else do you explain the fact that a bullet to the heart didn't faze him?"

"Maybe he was in some sort of catatonic trance," Pirelli suggested.

"He wasn't catatonic," Liz said. She stood in the doorway, her eyes focused on the corpse in disbelief. They mirrored the horror on her face. "He was moving with a purpose. He's not bleeding from any of the wounds. He was dead. I examined him." Her voice broke as she added, "There was no life in him."

"Are you crazy?" Pirelli snapped. "What about all that blood?" He jabbed a finger at the black, viscous blood pooled on the floor.

"It's not his blood. It's Sage's blood, partially digested."

"Well, he's dead now," someone said.

"Yes, but there were three Russians," Liz reminded them. Her face searched Brad's and Pirelli's. "Where are the other two?"

Brad helped Pirelli to his feet. Pirelli scratched at the deep lacerations in his arm inflicted by the Russian and winced.

"Maybe you better have Liz check that arm," he suggested to Pirelli.

Pirelli waved him off. "Later. I'll unlock the arms locker," he said. "We'll split into teams and search the station."

"Aim for the head," Brad said. "I think that's the only way to stop them."

Pirelli stared at him but said nothing.

"I'm coming with you," Liz said to Brad. "I need to go to my lab."

Brad nodded.

Most of the over-winterers remained in the galley gawking at the corpse, but at least fifteen people followed Pirelli to a locker in the corridor outside the galley from which he retrieved two more pistols and two rifles. He handed a rifle to Brad and passed out the other weapons to those who claimed to be able to shoot. Brad checked the .308 Winchester to make sure that it was loaded. He was familiar with the Winchester, similar to the .270 he owned. Intended as a bear rifle, there had been little need for such a weapon in the Antarctic until now. Brad enjoyed the comforting weight of the weapon in his hands. He noticed Guy Hughes was carrying the other rifle.

Pirelli and six others continued down the corridor to Pod B, while two more groups went downstairs with Hughes leading the way. Brad, Liz, and three others entered her office. It was empty. The damp sheets used to cover the bodies were lying on the floor. To be safe, he checked the nooks and crannies and inside the closets. As they left, he said to Liz, "Lock the door. We need to make sure they don't get behind us."

Shots erupted from down the corridor in the direction Pirelli's group had gone. Moving cautiously, they went to check it out. They found Pirelli and the others with him standing over a mangled corpse. Parts of the internal organs were missing, as well as large chunks of flesh from the arms, legs, and face. Fresh blood stained the walls and floor. Fingers of congealing blood ran down the walls. Brad became sick to his stomach as he recognized the blood-soaked Hawaiian shirt worn by Mark Walls.

"It's Walls," he said as he reached down and removed a cellophane-wrapped *Miguel Grau* cigar from Walls' bloody shirt pocket. Remarkably, the cigar was free of blood. Walls would never again have the opportunity to smoke his favorite brand. Brad stuffed the cigar back in Walls' pocket, and then noted the blood drops and splashes in the corridor leading away from the body.

"He was in the communications room with Mike Sampson working on the satellite feed," Pirelli said. "We spotted one of the Russians down the corridor. I fired but I think I missed. I think he went toward the exercise room."

Brad noticed Pirelli's right hand trembling and knew why he had missed. He wondered if the trembling was from fright or from a reaction to the scratches. Though it had been less than fifteen minutes since the incident, the skin around the wounds was livid and puffy from infection. Did the purported outbreak at McMurdo concern whatever was affecting the Russians? If so, was it contagious?

He nudged Liz and drew her attention to Pirelli's arm with his eyes. She gasped when she saw the swollen, discolored flesh around the wounds.

"Tony. You had better let me tend to your arm."

He glared at her. "We have more important things to do now."

"I think it's infected," she said, her voice gentle and calm but insistent.

He stared at her, and then his gaze travelled down to his arm. Surprise showed in his face as he saw the condition of his arm. He held out his hand and noticed the shaking. "It doesn't hurt. In fact, it stopped itching."

"Even so, as base physician, I insist on treating it. The others can continue." She leaned closer to his ear and whispered, "Remember your concern when we brought the bodies in."

Fear dawned in his eyes. He glanced at his arm again and nodded.

To Brad, she said, "I'm taking him to the infirmary."

"Take Tony's pistol. Lock the door behind you."

He watched Liz lead Pirelli away, wishing he could stay with her, but anger at Walls' death surged through his veins. He wanted revenge.

"Come on," he said to the others.

They moved slowly, checking each room carefully by first peering through the glass porthole in the metal door before entering. Satisfied that the room was empty, they locked the door as they left. They spotted Sampson sitting on the floor in the corridor outside the communications room leaning against the wall and holding a piece of torn cloth around his arm. Blood seeped through the makeshift bandage. His face was pale from loss of blood, and his eyes were wild with fright. When he saw them, he tried to push himself to his feet; then recognizing them, collapsed back to the floor.

"He attacked me, bit me." He held out his savaged arm as proof. "The bastard went after Mark. What the hell is happening?" he cried.

"Mark's dead," Brad said and watched disbelief dawn in Sampson's eyes. "Where's the Russian?"

"I heard a noise in the conference room a few minutes ago."

Brad glanced toward the room they had bypassed upon seeing Sampson and nodded. "We'll check there." He pointed to one of the men. "Take Sampson to the infirmary." The man hesitated. Brad grabbed a fire axe from the wall and tossed it to him. "Here. Use this if you have to."

Outside the conference room, he hesitated. Seeing the group bunched together, he called, "Spread out." He entered the room first with the rifle pointed straight ahead. The Russian wasn't there. He looked under the table, but the room was completely empty. Puzzled, he returned to the corridor. Suddenly, the Russian lunged from the adjacent cloakroom containing heavy outdoor gear and fell upon Harry Coombs. Before anyone could help him, the Russian sank his teeth into Coombs' neck and jerked away with a mouthful of flesh. A geyser of blood sprayed the Russian's snarling face. Brad saw the panic in Coombs' eyes slowly fade as he collapsed to the floor, dead. Brad raised his rifle, but at that moment, Barbara Connelly stepped into his line of fire.

"Move!" he shouted, but there was too much confusion as everyone crowded together to avoid the Russian's outstretched arms. Someone stumbled, inadvertently shoving Connelly forward. The Russian attacked her, clawing at her face and chest, biting her lower arm. She pushed him away, but not before he clamped down on her right hand, severing her little finger and ring finger. She screamed in agony. One of the men grabbed her to pull her to safety. Frightened, she fought back, scratching madly at his eyes. It took three men to subdue her and move her from the Russian's vicinity. Seizing the opening that they created, Brad fired. The sound thundered down the corridor. The impact of the heavy .308 bullet in the chest knocked the Russian backwards. His head exploded as Brad's second bullet tore a path through the skull. Thick, black blood and gray brain matter splattered the wall and sprayed the pipes running along the ceiling. He fell to the floor with an audible sigh and Connelly's severed fingers still protruding from his mouth.

The situation had become unreal – walking dead, people eaten, and fingers bitten off. Brad was beginning to believe Hughes' zombie theory. Though he had little regard for cheap fiction, he had watched his share of zombie thrillers as a child. The undead creatures on the screen moved and acted just like the Russians. By what process could the dead return to life – voodoo magic, a rare viral disease? If Pirelli's arm was any indication, now several people were infected.

Brad fought to calm his racing heart. Panic served no purpose. One more of the Russians still roamed the base, the young man. He pointed to a first-aid box on the wall.

"Someone bandage Barbara's fingers to stop the bleeding."

Warren Feinstein, one of the power plant mechanics, took Connelly aside, speaking to her gently in hushed tones to calm her down as he carefully wrapped her maimed hand in gauze. The others in the group stood around, unsure of what to do. Offering words of sympathy to Connelly, something they would normally have done if her injury were from an unavoidable accident or even through carelessness on her part, seemed somehow inappropriate. Brad eyed the group. Most were frightened and well out of their depths. They were equipped to deal with most emergencies around the station or with acts of nature, but facing the walking dead was a situation with which no one had experience. They were simply targets.

"Look, there are too many of us to be effective. Two of you come with me. We'll continue downstairs and work our way back to the other groups. The rest of you take Barbara to the infirmary. Find something to use as a weapon, and then lock yourself in the galley with the others." He glanced at Coombs' body. With no morgue, they would have to move all the bodies, including those of the Russians, outside in the cold soon, Nature's freezer, but that could wait. "Be careful," he added needlessly.

He watched the others as they disappeared down the corridor, hoping that they ran into no trouble. Barbara was so weak from blood loss and shock that it took two of them to support her. Ian Bain, a Brit from northern England overwintering at the Pole on an Oxford grant to study global weather patterns, and Greg Mclean, one of the Ice Cube technicians, elected to accompany Brad downstairs. Bain was slim and wiry, but Brad had seen him working out in the exercise room. He pushed his small frame to its limits lifting weights. Brad doubted he had an ounce of fat on his body. Mclean was tall, rugged, and, though somewhat crude in manner and obnoxious when drunk, was always ready for a bit of heavy lifting or rough work. He had worked during the summer with the drilling crew placing the Ice Cube sensors, manhandling the heavy hot water drills used to bore the holes.

Brad led the way, descending the stairs slowly, stopping often to listen for the remaining Russian. It was difficult to distinguish human noises over the sighing of the ventilators, the soft gurgling of the heating system, and the background noise of the building reacting to the temperature and wind. The television lounge, the first room they came to, was dark. Brad fumbled for the light switch with one hand while holding the rifle steady with the other. The lounge was empty. The arts and crafts room, where personnel could paint, sculpt, or create pottery to pass the time, was equally empty. They entered the gymnasium across the corridor. Their steps echoed in the open two-story room, largest in the station. He looked around the interior, taking in the blue walls and the white Antarctica logo on the wall, remembering Walls playing basketball just that morning, and shook his head. Walls' death was a senseless loss. He would miss him. Like the other two rooms, the gym was empty. The emergency power room took longer to check. The diesel generator, control panels, fuel and water pipes, and stacked supplies, created a maze in which a man could easily hide. They carefully examined each nook and cranny.

Brad started at the sound of glass crashing to the floor in the corridor outside. Rushing out of the room, he saw the third creature that had once been human standing amid a pile of broken glass shards, the remains of a glass display case built into the wall. Sensing or smelling them, the young Russian whirled and snarled at them. It came at them at a slow shuffle, ignoring the glass shards shredding the flesh of its feet as it trod upon them.

"Son of a bitch," Mclean said. He made to take a step forward as if wanting to challenge the dead Russian to a fistfight. Brad held his arm out to stop him.

"Don't get near it," he warned.

Mclean glared at him and clenched his fist. "I can take this bastard," he snarled.

"Whatever infected the Russians may be contagious."

"You mean its bite is dangerous?" Maclean asked.

"And maybe its scratches," he added, remembering Pirelli's arm.

He observed the creature as it approached. It felt no pain. Its feet were bleeding badly from the glass, but it hobbled toward them uncaring. Gazing into its dead eyes was a glance into the depths of hell. Nothing human lingered inside the Russian's fleshy shell. Only animal hunger remained. It stared at Brad as he might stare at a T-bone steak. He could smell its fetid breath, as if its insides were corrupt. He raised his rifle to fire.

Just at that moment, a bullet struck the back of the creature's head, exiting just above its right eye, disintegrating the right portion of the front of its skull and spraying Brad with dark, thick blood. Even so, the creature made one final lunge at him before dropping lifeless to the floor at his feet. The stench became overpowering. Brad's stomach roiled in protest.

"Jesus!" Mclean exclaimed, covering his nose with his hand. "That fucker stinks." He nudged it with his booted foot; then kicked it.

Another group marched down the corridor toward them. Guy Hughes held his rifle casually, but the slight smirk on his face told Brad that he had deliberately timed his shot to test Brad's metal, waiting until the last moment to fire. This angered Brad.

"Got him," Hughes said. Before Brad could express his outrage, Hughes said, "He attacked Adler."

Brad glanced at Bruce Adler's face. A series of parallel scratches marred his right cheek.

"That's the last of them," Hughes pronounced with satisfaction.

"I hope you're right." Brad looked down at the corpse, wondering why his senses told him the worst was yet to come.

6

August 24, Amundsen-Scott Base, Antarctica

The conditions of Tony Pirelli, Mike Sampson, Bruce Adler, and Barbara Connelly worsened steadily. Their injuries refused to heal. Traces of black lines similar to those marking the Russians had appeared around the wounds. Sampson, the first bitten, was coughing steadily and passing in and out of consciousness. His breathing was very ragged, his chest heaving for every gasped breath. His pulse was weak and thready. Liz couldn't understand an infection that spread so rapidly. In addition, four people not wounded or injured were complaining of nausea and headaches. Her examination revealed high temperatures and heavy congestion in their chests. At first, she had attributed it to the high altitude and dry air of the Polar Plateau, but everyone had sufficient time to acclimate over the winter. She prayed that it was a simple case of the flu, but like Brad, found it difficult to believe in coincidence.

With Walls dead and Sampson out of commission, there was no one left to handle communications, though Sampson had informed them that the equipment was working on their end. The problem lay elsewhere. With no way to contact outside help, she was all alone and had to deal with the crisis as best she could. She felt sadly inadequate to the challenge.

Her quick examination of the three Russians before Brad insisted that they move them outside, revealed internal organs consistent with corpses several days old. How then, could they move and, if not think, at least recognize a potential food source? What inhuman hunger drove them, for in her mind, inhuman they had become? Without a more powerful electron microscope, she had no way of determining the source of their infection or a method to combat its spread among them. So far, her cultures had indicated nothing abnormal. If it was an airborne virus, they were all doomed.

She rubbed her eyes and leaned back in her chair. She had gone without sleep for thirty hours and was bone weary. Her muscles ached and she could not think clearly. She struggled to grasp the fact that supposedly dead men, men whom she had proclaimed dead by every medical criterion she knew, had arisen and killed people. Not just killed, had eaten them. Some in the base had panicked and locked themselves in their rooms with several days' supply of food and water. She couldn't blame them. From a medical perspective, she could offer them no words of comfort or reassurance. Their guess was as good as hers, their fears just as valid. She was an overwhelmed nurse on a WWI battlefield, offering only platitudes, placebos, and a change of dressings.

"I prescribe another shot of scotch."

She looked up to see Brad standing in the doorway holding out the bottle of scotch they had shared, *when was it? Oh yeah, two days earlier*. She appreciated his attempt to take her mind off her problems.

She shook her head. "I can't. If I do, I'll fall sleep."

He drew up a chair opposite her, set the scotch on her desk, crossed his arms on the desk and leaned on them. "You need sleep. You look exhausted. Someone else can keep watch."

"A death watch, you mean?"

He arched an eyebrow at her morbid remark. "Don't think like that."

She sighed. "I feel so helpless. I don't know what to do. This is something I've never seen before. I'm frightened."

"So is everyone else. There were only about a dozen people at breakfast this morning." He cocked his head to one side and stared at her. "Speaking of breakfast, when did you last eat?"

"Oh, I had an apple not long ago."

Brad glanced into the garbage can. An apple core, brown and shriveled lay in the bottom. "By the looks of it, it was more than 'not long ago'," he chided. "If you won't leave, at least let me bring you something."

His offer touched her. Perhaps food would relieve the gnawing in her stomach, though she doubted it was hunger. It tasted more like despair. "Thank you. I could use some coffee and perhaps a sweet roll."

He rose from his seat. "Back in a jiff."

She rubbed the bridge of her nose and closed her eyes to think. The key to the problem lay with the Russians. Since she couldn't ask them any questions, the only thing she could do was suggest someone visit the Russian *Kharkovchanka* snow tractor and search for clues. If their destination had been Amundsen-Scott with a warning of some kind, perhaps they had brought some proof of their story. If they were escaping, maybe they could learn from what. She was hesitant to send someone to the tractor, but everyone was probably exposed already.

A series of high-pitched screams roused her from her quasi-sleep. She leaped to her feet and rushed to the infirmary to find Connelly backed up against the wall screaming at Pirelli, who was convulsing in seizures. His body arched to the point of snapping his spine as he bounced on the bed. His face had become a mask of black lines; his open eyes rolled back into their sockets showing only the whites of his eyeballs. His hands clutched at the air. Liz took Connelly's good hand and led her away from her bed. Sampson and Adler were too weak to move. They watched helplessly from their beds as she then went to Pirelli's side. She called his name to no effect. As she prepared a hypo of sedative to calm him, his convulsions suddenly ceased. He lay there staring upward at the ceiling, a soft sigh escaping his lips. Checking his wrist, she found no pulse. He was dead. As she watched, the black lines on his face and chest slowly receded, leaving behind dead, scaly skin.

Connelly's screams had brought several people to investigate, but no one summoned the courage to enter the room. Instead, they stood crowded at the door staring at Pirelli's body as if expecting it to rise and walk. Liz was half expecting it herself.

"Two of you carry him outside," she snapped, angry with herself at her inability to save him. She didn't know Pirelli well enough to call him friend, but she did like him. His loss would severely affect morale. No one moved. "Please," she asked more gently.

"I'll help," Brad said.

She looked up at him. His eyes held so much sympathy that she almost burst into tears. He had returned with a tray of food for her. He set it on her desk. She looked at the plate of food and shuddered. The smell of roast pork, which she had once found so enticing, now nauseated her. She didn't know if she would ever eat again. Her stomach was so queasy that she wondered if the unknown virus had now infected her. She glanced at Pirelli. Suddenly, her legs refused to hold her weight. As she fell forward, Brad grabbed her under her arms and dragged her to her chair.

"I'll be all right," she said, trying to brush him aside. She had no time to collapse. She still had patients to attend to.

"Sit still," he demanded. "You're tired and weak. You need rest."

She saw the others watching her warily and knew that Brad was right. If she fell apart, no one else would dare care for the sick. She grabbed his arm and looked into his eyes.

"You're right. I'll lie down in one of the beds for a while."

"Then you'll eat."

It was not a question. She nodded her assent, though the aroma from the pork was almost more than she could bear.

"Someone help me carry Tony outside," he said.

Liz watched as two men stepped forward, each taking a corner of the sheet beneath Pirelli's feet. Brad took the end by his head. Together, they carried Pirelli's body from the room to place in the freezing cold outside the base, along with the other bodies. Her dizziness passed. She rose and helped Connelly back to her bed. Connelly was in a state of shock, crying for Shelia Meyers, her lover, but Meyers was not present. Meyers, like so many of the others, had locked herself in her room. Liz finally managed to coax Connelly into bed. She gave her the sedative that she had intended for Pirelli. He was beyond pain now.

The crowd slowly broke up. *Now that the show is over*, she thought with disdain for her fellow Antarctic castaways, and then mentally chastised herself for her judgment of them. If she with her store of medical knowledge was frightened, how much more frightened were they? Brad returned a few minutes later, still wearing the heavy, bright red anorak and gloves he had donned to venture outside. He glanced first at the untouched tray of food, and then at Liz.

"Eat or sleep," he said, "one or the other." He removed the gloves and coat, and then placed them on the floor. "I'll keep watch."

The emergency with Pirelli had eroded the last vestiges of her will power. Exhaustion was quickly seeping in. "Okay, but just for a short while."

She couldn't bring herself to lie in the bed so recently vacated by Pirelli. Instead, she chose a folding cot stored in one of the closets. When setting it up proved too much for her to handle, Brad once again came to her aid, setting it up and covering it with a blanket. She lay down, realizing that it felt remarkably good to get off her feet. Brad covered her with a second blanket, whispering, "I'll wake you in two hours."

She nodded and gave herself to the comforting arms of oblivion.

* * * *

Ravi Chopra re-ran the air sample tests for the fourth time, and still he couldn't accept the results. He must have made an error. *Or perhaps*, he thought, *the Russian snow tractor contained radioactive materials and contaminated my samples.* He quickly dismissed that unlikely scenario. The Antarctic Treaty of 1961 banned the possession and testing of nuclear weapons and the disposal of radioactive wastes. Russia was a signatory to the treaty. No one from the party retrieving the bodies from the *Kharkovchanka* had reported finding anything unusual. There had to be a more reasonable explanation for his unexpected results.

Discovering the three dead Russians had brought Chopra few minutes of fame with his fellow scientists, but he had quickly become a pariah when the Russians began their killing spree. He couldn't understand his fellow scientists' attitude. Was it his fault that they attacked people? Did they think he should have just let his discovery of the Russians go unreported? He was equally at a loss as to how supposedly frozen corpses could reanimate. His field was meteorology, not biology.

He recalled from his youth the Hindu myth of the *Vetala*, spirits that could inhabit corpses and haunted charnel yards. It was a tale told to frighten young children and he didn't believe in children's fairy tales. However, the reading of an atmospheric radiation count four times higher than normal was no fairy tale. Had someone, possibly the Russians, ignored the nuclear ban? The obvious conclusion for their reanimation was that Doctor Strong had made an error in declaring the Russians dead. Some small spark of life must have remained in their super-chilled bodies, rekindled as they warmed. He knew that the Antarctic species of Toothfish, also known as Chilean Sea Bass, contained a type of antifreeze protein that prevented their blood from freezing in the sub-zero waters, so such a thing was possible. The cold, and possibly radiation exposure had damaged the men's brains, driving their insane killing rage. What had happened was not his fault.

He grabbed the edge of the worktable to steady himself as a wave of nausea swept over him. His first concern was radiation poisoning, but the Geiger counter resting on the table read within normal limits. He moved it closer to the vial containing the air sample and the meter shot higher. The sample was hot, but should not adversely affect him. He relaxed, but a second, more intense wave of nausea struck him. His stomach writhed like a living creature seeking escape. He leaned over the garbage can and vomited. He had not eaten since the previous night and had very little on his stomach. The bitter taste of bile filled his mouth, as well as a metallic tang. He was startled to see flecks of blood in the clear liquid. He wiped his mouth with the back of his hand, blinking back burning tears to clear his vision. Tiny black lines slowly crawled from the fingertips of his trembling hand toward his wrist. His chest burned as if on fire. He could not inhale deeply enough to fill his aching lungs.

Gasping for breath, he reached for the telephone to call Doctor Strong for help. He knocked the receiver from the base but couldn't force his uncooperative hand to grasp it. He fell to his knees, leaning against the end of the wooden workbench. He began to cough, spraying the lightly stained oak with a foamy black liquid. The viscous fluid seemingly defied gravity by running up the wood toward the top of the bench. He reached out a finger to touch the strange ebony substance. It rose, swaying like a shadow in a shadowy breeze to meet the tip of his finger. It was cold to the touch, yet somehow warm and inviting, as the fluid joined the tracings on his hand. His chest heaved in another spasm of coughing, but this time no more of the marvelous fluid escaped.

His lungs ached as if filled with cement. The lack of air did not worry him. His fading mind connected his condition with that of the Russians. If he was infected, then others in the base were as well. Why, then, was he not alarmed?

He could feel his brain shutting down, neuron by neuron. Memories went first. He no longer remembered who he was, but found that he did not care. Senses were next. His world became as black as the liquid running through his veins, claiming his body as its own. He could no longer see or hear, nor could he feel the roughness of the wood against his face or smell the urine running down his leg. His mind dwindled until only a small kernel remained; then, it too faded.

* * * *

Guy Hughes and Greg Mclean loaded as many cans of food as they could carry into their backpacks and then slung them over their shoulders. Hughes also carried one of the .308 Winchester rifles. He was no coward, but witnessing the insane zombie hunt had shaken his faith in his invulnerability. Pirelli was dead leaving no one was in charge of the forty-something frightened survivors. He was certain chaos would soon ensue. It was human nature. Better to be away from the base when that likelihood occurred. The Ice Cube lab seemed the likeliest location in which to seek refuge. Two people could hold out a long time.

Many of the others still thought the Russians had been in some sort of catatonic state when they had attacked and eaten Walls and Combs. He knew better. He had heard rumors about the *Providence* disaster from one of the Aussie sailors who had helped sink the American nuclear submarine. The sailor, a Boatswain's Mate, had drunk enough booze to loosen his tongue but not enough to erase the constant guilt he felt over the devastating secret he carried. He had hinted at zombies, devoured corpses, and government cover up. At the time, Hughes had written the Boatswain's Mate off as insane, a drunken bum, but seeing the Russian attack Combs had changed his opinion. There had been no life in the Russian's eyes, no hint of recognition. Hughes didn't know how many of his fellow over-winterers might be infected, but he suspected that at least a few were. He didn't want to wait to find out whom.

"Be sure you bring a pair of radios," he told Mclean.

Mclean stared at him apprehensively. "Why?"

Hughes shook his head. Mclean had seen the zombies but still couldn't grasp the significance. "If help doesn't come, we might have to drive out."

"In a Sno-Cat?"

"Had you rather walk?" Hughes challenged.

Mclean turned away and continued donning his cold-weather gear. Mclean was frightened. Hughes didn't hold that against him. He had chosen Mclean for his skill as an Antarctic explorer. Mclean had spent weeks at a time out on the ice and knew how to handle himself in the sub-zero cold. If they had to make the rough journey to McMurdo, he didn't want to be saddled with a novice.

Hughes had deliberately chosen the early morning hours to abandon the base. He didn't want the others to discover what he was doing. He felt badly enough about leaving the others in the lurch, but he could live with his conscience.

"Ready?" he asked.

Mclean threw the hood of his anorak over his head. "As ready as I'll ever be," he snapped at Hughes.

Hughes shot back, "You can stay here; take your chances with the others."

Mclean didn't reply as he headed for the Beer Can, the cylindrical stairwell leading to the underground power plant and the parking garage. He kicked the door open with his booted foot. "I want to survive, too."

The pair said nothing as they walked through the cold tunnels hacked from the ice. They avoided the power plant in case one of the mechanics was working there. As they stepped outside into the bitter cold and darkness, Hughes wondered if he had made the right decision.

7

August 26, Amundsen-Scott Base, Antarctica

Sampson died next. His body joined the others outside. Six more people were ill. When they discovered Chopra's body and brought it to Liz, the condition of his body puzzled her. He had not been bitten or scratched, nor had he complained of any illness. She worried that his early exposure to the Russians' bodies had led to his death. If so, the disease was likely airborne and they were all infected. None of her twenty-four hour or forty-eight hour cultures had turned up anything abnormal. She lamented her lack of equipment. A scanning electron microscope might help her identify the culprit for certain, but she suspected a virus.

Connelly and Adler slowly slipped into comas. Nothing she did seemed to make a difference. She distributed *Tamiflu* to the ill and issued platitudes to the frightened. She could offer no assurances. She was too exhausted to maintain a gracious bedside manner. Brad was her knight in shining armor. He made certain that she ate and offered her encouragement where she felt discouraged. He tended to the sick with the aplomb she lacked. Many of the others, those not locked in their rooms or labs, looked to him for leadership. In spite of this, he didn't see himself as a leader. He was one of those rare human beings blithely unaware of their affect on others. In fact, their veneration frightened and embarrassed him. She and Brad sat at her desk, laden with trays of dirty dishes and half-eaten meals.

"With Chopra, that's six dead," he said, counting on his fingers.

"Barbara and Adler will be next. I can't help them."

He glanced into the next room at the immobile patients. A mask of fine black lines covered large portions of their faces. "How many are sick?"

"Ten have reported symptoms so far. God knows how many are ill behind locked doors." She looked at Brad. "I can't help them either."

"Some might have the flu or a common cold."

She shook her head. "I doubt it. We've been isolated for months. They have whatever affected the Russians."

"Will they ..." He paused. "Will they become like the Russians?"

She shrugged her shoulders. The motion made her neck ache. She massaged it with her hands. "I don't know. I don't know what's wrong with them. If we place the dead outside to freeze, I don't think so. The Russians were immobile until they thawed."

He nodded. "No problems from them, then. I'm more worried about some of the others who've locked themselves away. Some aren't even answering when I yell through the door to check up on them."

"They're frightened." She knew exactly how they felt. She wanted to lock herself behind a door as well, but her oath to heal the sick wouldn't let her. Though she could not help them, her patients needed her.

"I understand their reluctance, but we must all work together to beat this ... this crisis."

"What if ..." She paused.

He looked at her, waiting for her to complete her thought.

"What if we can't beat it?"

"Are you giving up?"

A sigh escaped her lips. She slumped in her chair. "No."

He turned to look at Connelly, and then Adler. "Can we isolate everyone who becomes ill?"

"Not if it's airborne. Besides, would you want to be confined in a room with someone who might turn into a zombie?"

He jerked his attention from Adler to glare at her. "You too?"

"I don't know what else to label it. The dead reviving and eating human flesh – zombie is as close as my medical knowledge comes to describing what I've witnessed."

"I'm sorry. Hughes' label seems to have stuck. I've heard the term more than once over the past couple of days. It just seems so ..." He searched for the right word.

"Bizarre," she suggested.

He smiled at her. "I was going for unnatural, but bizarre will do. It's like a page from some horror novel. Something else that concerns me – no one replaced any of the weapons in the firearms locker. It's not safe having frightened, armed people running loose."

"Do you still have your rifle?"

His sheepish grin spoke for itself. "It's in my room," he admitted.

They both turned at a slight tapping on the open door. It was Ian Bain, the English global weather expert. "Can I come in?"

"Certainly," Liz replied. She noticed that he glanced at her two patients and frowned. "How can we help you?"

Bain cocked his head to one side. "I'm not certain that you can. It's just that … well, I was reading through Ravi's notes and found something quite disturbing."

"I'm sorry about Chopra," she said. "Was he a close friend?"

"A friend? No, he was too reserved for a close friendship, but he was a colleague and I liked him."

Brad brushed aside Liz's attempt at condolences. "What did you find?"

"According to Ravi's last weather readings and air samples, the outside radiation levels have increased almost four-hundred percent."

Brad sat forward in his seat. "Is it dangerous?"

Bain shook his head. "Not yet. Ravi was concerned that entering the Russian snow tractor might have inadvertently contaminated his samples, but I don't think so. To double-check his findings, I went outside today and collected fresh samples."

"And," Brad prompted.

Bain looked at the two of them before replying. "The count is increasing, still not dangerous, but significantly higher than normal."

"And you're certain it's not related to the *Kharkovchanka*? Maybe the Russians …" Brad swore under his breath and slammed his fist on the desk. "Hell, I'm just grasping at straws."

Bain scratched his head. "It looks more like fallout from a nuclear bomb."

Liz clutched her chest as her heart froze. "Here?"

"No, no," Bain said quickly. "But someone somewhere has set one off, maybe more than one."

"That would explain the lack of communication," Brad said. "An EM pulse from a nuclear detonation high in the atmosphere would wipe out satellites." Then he frowned. "But that wouldn't explain the fiber optic cable going out."

"War?" Liz asked, incredulous. She felt suddenly cold and crossed her arms over her chest. "Do you mean we went to war?"

"Maybe not war and maybe not us," Bain pointed out, "but someone has definitely detonated a nuclear weapon. The radiation signature is very specific. It could be above-ground nuclear testing, of course," he added, but he sounded doubtful.

"We can't tell the others," Brad said. Bain and Liz both looked at him. Seeing their quizzical stares, he continued, "This would cause a panic. We have enough problems as it is. If the world's at war, we can't do anything about it from here. Who else knows?" he asked Bain.

"Shimoda, I guess."

"Speak to him. Tell him to keep this under wraps, at least for a while."

Bain looked unconvinced, but Liz had decided that Brad might be right in withholding such dreadful news. "Look, Ian. Everyone is frightened. Stress levels are high. If people become convinced that no one is coming or that people they love might be dead, they might lose hope."

Bain nodded. "I see your point. I'll caution Shimoda to keep quiet, but if the levels get any higher, we might have problems."

"One problem at a time," Brad replied.

After Bain had left, Liz confronted Brad with her fears. "Do you think what happened to the Russians and what Ian just told us are related?"

Brad winced. "Don't you? First, we receive news of a mysterious outbreak at McMurdo; then all communication ceases. Next, we discover dead Russians who revive as zombies and infect some of our people." Liz noted that Brad now had no problem using the term 'zombies'. Like her, his mind had come to grips with the impossible. She also realized that he had carefully avoided suggesting that all of them were infected. "Now, we learn of some kind of nuclear exchange, but we don't know how involved it was, or is," he corrected himself. He closed his eyes and shook his head. "They're all part of the same disaster, whatever that is."

She was out of her league. Her specialty was colds and broken bones. Most of her job consisted in prescribing vitamins and treating frostbite. Epidemiology was not her field. If the disease that had struck the Russians was part of a widespread epidemic, she could well understand the rise in radiation levels. She had once read in some medical journal of a controversial protocol using nuclear weapons as a last resort to sterilize infected cities or populations. At the time, she had dismissed the report as conspiracy theory. She couldn't believe any civilized country would do such a thing to its own people, but many less ethical countries now had nuclear arsenals and would have no qualms about using them on its populace.

She glanced up and noticed Brad staring at her.

"You okay?" he asked.

She nodded. "Just frightened."

He forced a smile to his face. "That makes two of us."

\* \* \* \*

Shelia Meyers sat naked on her bed with her knees drawn up to her chest and her arms clasped tightly around them. Her blue eyes were red and swollen from crying. She hadn't brushed her short brown hair for days, and it stuck out at all angles. She no longer worried about her appearance, just survival. She had lowered the shades on her window because staring outside into the constant darkness only deepened her growing depression and sense of despair. The love of her life was dying, and she couldn't bring herself to visit her. She wanted to hold Barbara in her arms; offer her encouraging words. Instead, she was cowering in her room afraid. Uneaten scraps of food and empty water bottles littered the floor. She hadn't eaten a hot meal in two days, sustaining herself on protein bars, potato chips, and cold cereal. The room stank of perspiration and urine. An uncovered bucket sat against the door containing her waste. She couldn't bring herself to leave her room long enough to go to the bathroom.

Meyers had watched in disbelief, and then in horror as the Russian had attacked Pirelli. She had seen Walls partially eaten corpse, but still she found it difficult to believe in zombies. Barbara had been bitten, losing two of her long, beautiful fingers in the attack, and now she was dying of whatever disease had killed the Russians and Pirelli. The thought of her lover turning into one of those lifeless creatures dismayed her. Was it wrong of her to hope that Barbara died quickly and painlessly?

A disturbance in the corridor drew her from her lethargy for a brief moment. She listened with mounting fear as footsteps approached. She tightened her grip on the ski pole she had taken to use as a weapon, and then relaxed as the footsteps receded. She had ignored repeated attempts to coax her from her room. Now, they no longer bothered her. She didn't know how much longer she could hold out. She was almost out of food. She couldn't face her fellow over-winterers. She couldn't face her lover. She couldn't even face her own image in her mirror afraid of what she might see. At first, she had examined her body every few hours for telltale signs of black lines. Now, she didn't bother. She expected to die.

This was her fifth year at Amundsen-Scott. She had helped to build the base. As an electrician, she had prowled the frozen bowels of the base running wiring and chasing down electrical shorts. She thought of the base as home. She had given up her apartment in Chicago and had made no real plans for a return to a normal life. Finding love with Barbara changed all that. They had discussed moving to Tucson and working for Raytheon. As an engineer, Barbara was well qualified to work anywhere she chose.

More footsteps. This time they stopped outside her door.

"Shelia. Please come out. We need to talk."

She recognized the voice of Brad Niles.

"No. Go away!" she shouted.

Brad paused. "Barbara's dead. I'm sorry."

Her heart pounded in her chest. She clenched her fists until her knuckles ached, but she found she could shed no more tears. She was all cried out.

"Shelia?"

Meyers shook her head. "Go away."

As Nile's footsteps faded, she thought, *why go on?* She eyed the sharp tip of the ski pole. *We're all going to die.* She crawled off the bed and stood in front of the mirror, wincing as her aching muscles sent bolts of pain though her body. As she feared, fine black traces of lines circled her right breast and down to her belly button. They itched but didn't cause her pain. She rubbed them gently with her finger, smiling that the blackness did not rub off on her fingertips. She jabbed her left palm with the tip of the ski pole, wondering why she didn't feel the pain it should have caused. She dipped her right finger into the welling blood, and then wrote 'Barbara' on the mirror, using her blood. She smiled at her handiwork and positioned the tip of the ski pole against her skin just beneath her right breast, above the heart. She lowered the grip end until it rested in the corner formed by the desktop and the wall. Satisfied it wouldn't slip, she leaned forward until the ski pole buried itself in her flesh. Surprisingly, she felt no pain.

"I'm joining you, Barbara," she whispered.

She lunged forward, feeling a brief moment of pain as the sharp tip pierced flesh and muscle, and then slipped between her ribs into her heart. Her blood, strangely dark and viscous, splashed onto the top of the desk and sprayed across the mirror. She raised her hand and placed it against the glass, leaving a bloody handprint. Goosebumps rose on her arms, as if a cold breeze had entered through the unopened window. Her body shuddered as she fell to the floor. It did not move again – for days.

8

August 26, McMurdo Base, Antarctica

Malosi edged carefully around the side of the storage shed that he had made his home. Zombies were everywhere and he didn't wish to become their meal. An unlucky Adelaide penguin made an appearance, distracting the horde of zombies long enough for Malosi to slip beneath the floor and push through the floorboards he had loosened instead of risking using the door. He deposited his armload of food and bottled water on the floor, and warmed his hands over the small propane heater he used for cooking. The constant stream of volcanic smoke and ash from nearby erupting Mt. Erebus disguised the odor of his cooking and made it difficult for the zombies, who he had discovered had an acute sense of smell and hearing, to smell him.

He was the only living soul at McMurdo. He had discovered a brief note in the radio room during one of his earlier explorations explaining what had happened and describing the survivors' exodus via the same C-130 that had brought death to them. He doubted their chances of reaching civilization, if indeed any still remained.

His six-day journey from *Resurrection City* had been an ordeal for one not used to harsh Antarctic conditions, but he had survived. It was during the last leg of his journey that disaster had struck. Exhausted but unwilling to stop so near his destination, he had hit a partially snow-covered rock with one of the snowmobile's front skis. The Yamaha tumbled, dumping him on the ground. The sled he was towing almost doomed him. It flipped, landing on his right leg. The pain had been excruciating before he blacked out. He regained consciousness an hour later, trapped beneath the sled. It had taken an hour of digging to free himself. The leg wasn't broken, but his knee was badly swollen and too painful to support his weight. He packed as much food as he could carry and extra ammunition into a knapsack and, using the broken ski as a walking stick, hobbled the five remaining miles to McMurdo.

The sight of the abandoned base, many buildings fire ravaged and damaged beyond use, with throngs of zombies prowling the deserted streets, was a sad one. He had expected no rescue but had hoped to avoid a repetition of his harrowing experiences in *Resurrection City*. Surviving would be a difficult task, especially for a crippled man.

Even now, his knee still plagued him, aching badly at times. He was certain he had torn some cartilage, perhaps even chipped the patella, but it served him well enough to keep him ahead of the zombies. He opened a can of soup, poured it into his pot, and set it over the stove to heat. While he waited, he sipped the last dregs of cold Rishi green tea. He had found only Lipton tea in his canvass of the base's food stores. It would have to do.

He had fled *Resurrection City* for fear that some military, the US or other, might target the base in an attempt to stem the plague. Now, he considered the opposite tact. It was possible that survivors aware of the base's existence might launch an expedition in search of a cure. His chances of survival were greater at McMurdo than in *Resurrection City*. When an expedition came, they would undoubtedly radio ahead. He would monitor the radio and wait for their call. He need only survive until someone came. He pulled his *Sony* Android from his pocket and frowned at the low battery light. With no electricity, his charger was useless. He would have to find a way to recharge it soon.

9

August 31, Amundsen-Scott Base, Antarctica

Brad scratched at his itchy beard. He was certain it was just his imagination, but it felt as if cooties were running amok in it. He hadn't bothered shaving or bathing in days. There was simply too much to do. Mostly, it seemed as if the effort was for naught. The somber pall of a funeral parlor had descended over the base. Five more had died. Shelia Meyers, distraught over her lover's death, had committed suicide, as had Leland Greene, one of the cooks. Nattie Mullins had found his body in the kitchen lying face down in a pool of blood, his wrists sliced to the bone with a paring knife that he still grasped in one lifeless hand. Adler and Connelly had finally died, having never regained consciousness. Another person complaining of chest pains and dizziness had also died. Their bodies joined the growing display of corpses outside in a neat row beneath the building. The infirmary was full to overflowing. Liz was overworked. He tried to help her as much as possible, but he couldn't stomach long hours of watching people slowly die.

Hughes and Mclean had disappeared. Brad suspected they had retreated to the Ice Cube lab, but he hadn't found the time to go check on them. His own duties at the telescope had taken a backseat to his efforts to keep the disparate collection of tortured souls of the base functioning as a unit. In this, he was failing. Keeping them from closing themselves away entirely took up most of his time. Each day he walked the corridors knocking on doors. Each day, fewer people answered his knocks. He felt impotent. He could offer them no encouraging words. He just knew that if they were to survive, they would all have to work together.

As if the rising radiation levels weren't enough to worry about, the outside temperature had gradually increased. Whereas the normal average temperature for late August was minus fifty-five degrees, the thermometer now stood at minus forty. In most cases, the temperature didn't reach minus forty until November. Whether it was a natural phenomenon or, as Bain postulated, a result of the nuclear blasts, didn't matter. Brad was afraid that a temperature increase would thaw the now safely frozen bodies. He didn't want to see if they became zombies as the Russians had. His repeated attempts to recruit more people to help him burn the bodies had failed, and it was too big a job for him alone. Simply dousing the corpses in diesel and setting them afire without benefit of ceremony or decent burial seemed too cold and unsympathetic.

Twice, the power plant had shut down when the generators ran out of fuel. It seemed that of the three power plant engineers, only Warren Feinstein still bothered to show up for work. Without power, they would have no electricity, and since their only source of heat derived from waste heat from the generators, they would be without heat as well. Mullins, working alone, continued to cook meals for which very few showed up. Brad was afraid that most had given up hope. The loss of Tony Pirelli had been a hard blow to base morale. Pirelli, for all his blustering and pretentiousness, was an efficient administrator. He would have recruited work crews to man the generators and people to see that meals were prepared. He would have been able to berate or cajole enough people to burn the corpses. Brad knew he wasn't the man for the job, but no one else had stepped forward. He was beginning to regret his decision.

As he strode down the corridor toward the communications room to see if there had been any change in their isolation status, he heard someone in the science lab. Peeking inside, he saw Daryl Overton, his astronomer partner, bending over a keyboard. Overton's disheveled appearance shocked him. Overton, normally excessively neat and well groomed, was wearing a dirty, wrinkled tee shirt, equally filthy boxer underwear, and socks. Nothing else. His face bore traces of some past meal and smudges of printer ink marked his hands.

"What are you doing, Daryl?"

Overton leaped from his seat and stared wildly at Brad, brandishing a length of two-inch-diameter pipe that had been resting beside him on the desk. When he saw that it was Brad, he smiled and lowered the pipe.

"Jesus, Brad. You scared the crap out of me."

"Sorry. I was just seeing who was working." He nodded at the laptop. "What are you doing?"

Overton dropped the pipe on the desk, sat back down, patted a loose stack of printer paper, and began typing on the keyboard. "Getting our notes together on 3C-367."

Brad nodded. 3C-367 was a superluminal quasar situated near the center of the Lesser Magellanic Cloud that had been the focus of their observations. He read the screen over Overton's shoulder. The text was a poorly worded, rambling essay about stars and Vincent Van Gogh. Most of what he had written made no sense.

"Why bother?" Brad asked.

Overton looked up at him with a pained expression. "Why? It's why I came. We're leaving in a few weeks. I want to have a paper ready for the fourth-quarter issue of *Astronomical Review*." He smiled. "I hoped you would co-author it with me."

Brad rubbed his temple where a sudden throbbing had started. He worried for his friend. Overton knew that any paper would have to go through numerous peer reviews before publication. Even if he submitted a paper in September and it was accepted, it wouldn't appear before late the following year. As written, his paper would invite only ridicule.

"Maybe it should wait," he suggested. "We have bigger problems to deal with. Why don't you get some rest? We'll discuss it later."

"No," Overton snapped. "I have to finish quickly. They're coming."

"Who's coming?"

Overton pointed outside with one hand, waving it around wildly. He didn't take his eyes from his keyboard. "Them. Can't you hear them?"

"Who do you hear, Daryl?" Brad asked carefully.

Overton stopped typing and stared at him. His eyes were wild and unfocused. "The dead. They want in. They'll be here soon."

"The dead won't hurt you."

Overton laughed and shook his head. "They're not really dead. They're just pretending. They come to me when I sleep, mocking me for being alive, but that's okay; we'll all join them soon. It's the Armageddon."

Brad shuddered with the realization that Overton's mind was slipping away. He wondered how many of the others, unable to cope with the isolation and the threat of death, were following Overton's example.

"Why don't you come with me, Daryl? We'll get something to eat and then get some sleep."

Overton leaped from his seat, grabbed the pipe, and backed away from Brad. He pointed a finger at him. "No. You're one of them. I see that now. That's why you're so calm. The dead have nothing more to fear. Stay away from me!"

Before Brad could stop him, Overton swung the pipe at Brad's head. As Brad ducked, the pipe brushed his hair. Overton raced out of the room and down the corridor. Brad followed, but Overton was too fast. He raced to the Beer Can and through the door.

"You fool!" Brad yelled at him. "You'll freeze to death."

By the time Brad reached the stairs, Overton was gone. He could do nothing more to help his friend and colleague. Overton could have gone anywhere.

Passing back by the galley, he saw several people inside eating. He glanced at his watch and saw that it was almost twelve o'clock, but he didn't know if they were eating lunch or a midnight snack. Time seemed to hold little relevance to him lately. Mullins and one cook stood behind the hot line. He had eaten only twice in the past forty-eight hours, and the aroma of roast chicken, stewed vegetables, and hot rolls made his mouth water. Deciding to take his own advice, he passed through the hot food line and loaded a tray with food. Mullins seemed glad to see another patron in her domain. At least she still had a function. Brad was jealous of her.

He chose a seat beside Charles Lester. Lester nodded politely as Brad glanced around the room. Of the seven people seated at tables, he knew only two by name, Faith Menendez and Lester. The other faces were familiar, but even after nearly six months, he hadn't bothered learning their names. He felt a momentary twinge of guilt at his lack of camaraderie. Menendez, contrary to her usual habit, sat alone, eating quietly. Brad watched her as she finished her potatoes, moved on to her beans, and then her corn, followed by her dinner roll before starting on her chicken. She took small bites, chewing thoroughly before swallowing. Her expression never changed. Her eyes remained focused either on the darkness outside the room, or on her reflection in the glass. The other faces in the room mirrored her cataleptic expression. Only Lester seemed unaffected as he dug into his food with a hearty appetite.

"Doesn't any of this worry you?" Brad asked.

Lester stopped eating and stared at Brad. "Well, I'll tell you. I guess I was scared shitless at first, but then I got to thinking. If whatever is happening is in the air, then either I'll catch it or I won't. If I do, either I'll die, or I won't. Starving or locking myself away isn't going to help. If I survive, I'll be pleasantly surprised." He patted his hip. Brad glanced down and saw that Lester wore one of the .45's. "If any zombies come at me, I'll shoot them in the head. Other than that, I don't know what else to do." He waved his fork at those around him. "You see these people? They're going through the motions, but they're as good as dead. If this plague doesn't get them, they'll end up doing what Meyers or Greene did. Living here during the winter takes its toll on people. It doesn't take much to push them over the edge."

Brad nodded at the engineer's sage wisdom. "Will you help me get the others to come out of their rooms? We need to work together."

"You're beating a dead horse, Niles. Me, you, Doctor Strong, and maybe a few others are plunging through this mess trying to get to the other side. Even a bitch dog knows when she's whelped too many pups and she lets the weakest die. You can't carry everybody, or they'll drag you down with them."

"We can't just let them die," he challenged.

Lester shook his head. "You can't stop them."

Brad stared at his plate, his appetite suddenly fading. Deep down, he suspected that Lester was right. He tossed his fork into his plate with a loud *clink*. Several heads jerked up and looked at him, but then resumed their dispassionate stares. He wanted to shout at them, tell them about the radiation and the bizarre rise in temperature, anything to force some display of emotion to their cold, stoic faces. Instead, he rose from the table with his plate of untouched food and left it in the dish pit, wondering briefly if anyone still bothered checking the duty roster.

Less than a week had passed since normalcy at the base had broken down, yet it seemed as if he had been riding the razor-thin edge of sanity for months. His appetite was shot, his nerves were wound near the snapping point, and like Overton, he looked like a bum and smelled like an offal heap. If he wanted to sway opinions, encourage them to cooperate, the least he could do was to look the part. He decided a shave and a shower was in order.

He ignored the time restrictions on showers and allowed the hot water to stream over his aching body for five minutes before soaping and rinsing. He closed his eyes and leaned against the shower wall for several minutes, relishing the silence and the solitude. A brisk toweling dry revived the nerves in his skin. His hand was too shaky for his Schick razor, so he had borrowed Overton's electric razor. He stood naked in front of the mirror, hardly recognizing himself. He had dropped nearly eighteen pounds from his already lean frame. His heart quickened when he thought he saw a dark line beneath his breast, but it was only a trick of the light, a shadow.

Afterwards, contemplating his freshly shaven face, he noticed the bags under his eyes and a host of new wrinkles on his forehead. He decided to take better care of himself. If he allowed his heath to deteriorate, he would be of no use to anyone.

"That's better."

He spun around. Liz was looking at him and smiling.

"I like the new clean-shaven you."

He grabbed his towel and wrapped it around his waist. "How long have you been standing there?"

She laughed. "I just walked in. Don't worry. I've seen naked men before."

He noticed the towel and a change of clothing in her hand. "It's only fair that I get to see you naked."

"I'll tell you what. If you'll stand watch at the door while I shower, you can let your imagination run wild."

He shrugged. "I guess that will have to do. I'm glad to see you take a break."

She frowned. "I have no more patients."

"What?" he exclaimed in surprise. "Why?"

"My last two patients just died. The others decided to lock themselves in their rooms and hope for the best."

"I'll see to the bodies."

"Don't bother. Trace Wilkie and Evan Deen moved them."

Brad nodded. Wilkie and Deen were heavy equipment operators. Deen had won the last pool tournament. He was glad not everyone had given up. "That's almost a third of us dead."

"I can't stop it," Liz sobbed. "I don't even know what's happening. I'm treating symptoms, but it doesn't do any good. In the end, everyone dies."

He wanted to reach out to her, but suspected that she might resent his sympathy. She was a tough woman momentarily defeated by circumstances beyond her control. His treating her like a frail female might annoy her.

"Go take your shower. Use as much hot water as you want."

As she walked past him, she reached out her hand and stroked his arm. Her self-appointed guardian, he assumed a position just outside the bathroom door, leaning against the wall. As Liz had predicted, his imagination went wild as he listened to the water sluicing over her spectacular naked body. The mental picture that his mind conjured of her rubbing her breasts with a soapy rag excited him. He became so engaged in his visual fantasy that he didn't notice the figure lurking at the edge of the shadows down the corridor until the blast of a pistol roused him. He banged the back of his head against the wall as he dropped to a crouching position. The figure stumbled forward a few steps, and then fell face-first to the floor. Charles Lester appeared from around the corner. He nudged the body with the toe of his boot, and then replaced the .45 in its holster. He walked toward Brad.

"Hope Bradshaw," he said, jerking his thumb over his shoulder at the corpse. "I saw her come out of her room and followed her." He noticed Brad staring at him in shock. "Hell, she was a zombie for God's sake. Did you think I just shot her for the hell of it?"

Brad shook his head. "No. It's just ... When did she turn?"

"Who knows? The real question is how many more are there?"

Brad realized with a sick feeling that Lester was right. He had been knocking on doors, trying to rally everyone to some sort of communal action, but ignoring the possibility that no answer might mean something other than a desire for privacy.

"We need to check every room," he blurted.

Lester raised an eyebrow as he replied, "We? I told you where I stand. If they're locked in their rooms and turn zombie, maybe they can't get out. That's a good thing."

Alarmed by the shot, Liz ran out of the bathroom. She wore a towel wrapped around her body. Her wet blonde hair lay plastered to her shoulders. She glanced at Bradshaw's corpse and then at Brad.

"He's right," she said. "Leave them where they are."

Liz's sudden shift in sympathies confused him. "You were the one trying so desperately to help them."

"I was wrong," she snapped; then paused and shook her head. "I can't help them. No one can."

Brad stared at her. She turned away to avoid his gaze, but he could sense that she was trying to hold something back, something she didn't want to tell him.

"What's going on, Liz?"

She hesitated before answering. "I still don't know what's killing everyone, but I did determine that we are all infected."

Brad backed up against the wall for support before his quivering legs folded. "All of us?"

She nodded. "I haven't checked everyone, of course, but the infectious agent is in the air. I can't culture it, so I haven't been able to identify it, but I have determined that it's very small. People who have been isolated for days have come down with symptoms."

"Why don't I have it, or you, or Charles?"

"Some of us are more resistant than others."

Lester chuckled. Brad glared at him. "Don't you see?" Lester explained. "I was right. You can't help them. You can't even help yourself." He slapped his knee and laughed again. "What a great, glorious, God-damned joke's been played on us."

Lester's callous attitude irritated Brad. Why was the engineer so cavalier when he was so sick-to-his-stomach afraid? "Glad to see you're taking it so well."

"Oh hell, I'm scared, believe me, but what can I do about it? We don't even know what the hell is happening." He pointed to

Bradshaw's zombie corpse. She lay naked in a pool of dark blood, her skull shattered by his bullet. His face became cold and hard. "The moment I feel myself turning into one of those creatures, I'm putting a bullet in my head."

Part of Lester's statement jolted Brad's memory. What was happening? Maybe he knew where to look for an answer. "The Russians were coming here for a reason," he blurted. "They could have as easily headed to the coast. Did they come to warn us, or were they just blindly running from this disease?"

Lester shrugged. "We'll never know."

"I'm going back to the Russian tractor. Maybe they knew what was happening. Maybe there's something in the tractor that might shed some light on this mystery." He looked at Lester. "Will you come?"

Lester glanced away for a moment staring at Bradshaw's body. Brad thought he had lost him, but when Lester turned back to face him, he nodded. "Why not? It beats prowling this tomb."

"I'm coming with you," Liz said. "I'm not staying here."

Brad smiled at her. He did not intend to leave her alone. "Glad for the company. I'll see if I can talk Bain into joining us."

10

August 31, Amundsen-Scott Base, Antarctica

They located Bain in the lab working on his remote weather station data feeds. The feeds were supplied by simple radio telemetry and not dependent on the defunct satellite feed. When Brad explained the reason for the trip, he was eager for the opportunity to get outside for more radiation readings, but less eager to visit the Russian tractor. However, upon hearing Liz's depressing news, he agreed that the Russians might have left clues as to the cause of their demise. The four encountered no one on their way to the changing room to don their winter gear. The base seemed deserted. Even with the smaller-sized overwintering crew, there were always sounds of machinery and lab equipment in operation, or the drone of televisions and conversation. The silence was unnatural and unnerving.

Descending the stairs in the Beer Can, Brad heard noises down one of the ice tunnels, like the banging of metal on metal. He wondered if it could have been Overton, but he allowed the others to talk him out of investigating. They found John DeSousa and Taylor Reed, two of the electricians, barricaded inside one of the Sno-Cats in the underground garage, where the pair had been hiding out for the last four days. At first, DeSousa greeted them with a .45 in his hand, but quickly put it away when he saw that they were not zombies. Empty cans of food and water bottles littered the ground around the Sno-Cat, and Brad thought he recognized piles of frozen human excrement in a corner. Both men looked tired and on edge. The heater in the Sno-Cat would keep the temperatures above freezing, but just barely, forcing the men to live and sleep in their heavy winter coats. DeSousa, a forty-year-old New Zealander, had fifteen years of ice experience and was used to living rough, but Reed, at twenty-three, was a newbie. This was the native New Yorker's first winter in Antarctica and Brad judged by his expression that he was less than thrilled by his adventure so far.

Brad wasted no time with idle chitchat. "We're going to the Russian Kharkovchanka."

The pair exchanged glances. DeSousa assumed role as spokesman. "There's nothing there," he said.

"Maybe the Russians were bringing something to us, something explaining what's going on."

DeSousa crossed his arms over his chest. "We're comfortable here."

Brad doubted that, but didn't want to argue with the burly DeSousa. He was glad when Liz stepped in.

"We're all infected with whatever is killing people."

Reed's face paled. DeSousa frowned.

"I just shot Hope Bradshaw," Lester said. "She turned into whatever the Russians had become, a zombie, I guess."

Upon hearing this, Reed stumbled backwards and sat down on the bumper of the Sno-Cat.

"A zombie?" DeSousa asked unconvinced.

"She was cold to the touch and wanted to eat people. Zombie or ghoul – It doesn't really matter does it, if we can become just like her."

DeSousa didn't reply for almost a minute. Finally, he looked at Reed and said, "Fuel up the snowmobiles." He grinned at Brad. "The Sno-Cat smells kind of rank."

Reed's nervousness showed in his young face as he began fueling the three snowmobiles they would need for the journey. "If we don't find anything at the Russian tractor, can't we just ... you know, keep going?" he asked.

DeSousa was busy checking the batteries and ignition systems on the snowmobiles. He reached out and smacked Reed on the arm. "Kid, it's over eight hundred miles to McMurdo. You don't just whistle up a taxi."

Reed didn't give up. "Can't we refuel the Russian vehicle?"

Brad tried not to let his expression give him away. Refueling the Kharkovchanka and driving it to McMurdo had crossed his mind as well in one of his moments of desperation. His determination not to abandon the others was all that prevented him from agreeing with Reed.

"It's too early to start running," Brad said. "First, we need to find out what's happening. Crossing the Polar Plateau and the Transantarctic Ridge in mid-winter is dangerous."

"More dangerous than what's happening here?" Reed asked.

DeSousa shook his head. "You don't want to be out in the open if a *katabatic* wind starts blowing down off the mountains."

Bain interrupted. "I hate to bring this up, but the temperature is hovering at thirty-four below zero." In his hand, he held a digital thermometer as if it were a holy relic, tapping it with his finger. "That's an increase of twenty-five degrees in four days." He glanced up at the sky. "It could be connected to the radiation – some sort of ionization in the ozone layer."

DeSousa and Reed looked at each other. "What radiation?" DeSousa asked.

As Bain explained Chopra's discovery to the pair, Brad walked over to Liz, who stood quietly staring out the open door into the frozen waste.

"Thinking about how cold it is?" he asked.

She shook her head. "No. I was thinking how desolate it is." She turned to face him. "Why do people come here?"

"Why are you here?" he asked.

Her answer was quick but delivered with no conviction, as if she had repeated it often to herself and others. "I'm a doctor. I came here to help people."

"That's no answer."

Her sigh came from deep inside, the sound of a lifetime of misery escaping. "I needed to get away for a while." She looked into his eyes, searching for a reason to explain further. "I was married for two years. My husband lost his job as a broker. He resented that I had become the sole breadwinner. He started drinking heavily and became abusive. I let him hit me once without calling the cops. Later, he said he was sorry and begged me to forgive him. I did. The second time he hit me, I hit him in the head with a sauté pan, packed my bags, and walked out. I left him lying on the floor bleeding." She said this as if leaving an injured person, even a man who had struck her, was beyond her moral sensibilities.

"We divorced a few months later. I came here to re-evaluate my life. I've been here two years. I don't know where he is, and I don't really care."

He was sorry for broaching the subject. It obviously hurt her to dwell on it. Her story explained her presence in Antarctica, but not her reason for remaining. He decided not to press further.

"Hell of a place for a vacation isn't it?" he said.

This brought a smile to her lips. "It's better than North Dakota."

"I won't argue that." He glanced back at the others. "I think we're ready."

In all, six people would make the journey to the Russian Kharkovchanka – Brad, Liz, Lester, Bain, DeSousa, and Reed. They took three snowmobiles, Ski Doo Alpine 640-ER's. Rugged and adapted for the extreme cold weather, the Alpines were the mainstay snowmobiles for the Americans. Each was painted bright yellow for high visibility and had remote-control systems that allowed the operator to dismount and safely traverse the vehicle over ice crevasses. This came in especially handy when the snowmobile hauled a loaded sledge. Brad had driven snowmobiles in North Dakota and felt at home on one. Liz rode behind him. Lester rode behind Bain and Reed behind DeSousa. Bain knew the exact GPS position of the *Kharkovchanka* and led the small expedition. The open cockpit provided no relief from the cold, but Brad had experienced colder temperatures than thirty-four below in North Dakota. Bundled up in three layers of clothing, including a balaclava, snow goggles, and heavy gloves, he felt more invigorated than cold. Gunning the Ski Doo's 640-cc engine, he burned off his frustration by racing over the ice. The wide, open space, even though shrouded in darkness, provided more freedom than the confines of the base. Liz held on with her arms wrapped tightly around his waist, pressing the rifle strapped to his back uncomfortably into his spine.

The Antarctic Plateau was a mysterious, starkly beautiful plain of snow and ice over 16,000 square-miles in area, the size of Massachusetts and Connecticut combined. At 9800 feet above sea level, the air was thin, cold, and dry, made even colder by the two miles of ice beneath the Plateau. The ice moved constantly, slowly flowing to the sea under the immense pressure of the heavy mantle of millennia of accumulated ice. The Plateau was a vast, frozen desert. Little snow fell, but the perpetual wind eroded the snowdrifts into patterns resembling a beach at low tide. Closer to the mountains, dune-like *sastrugi* made travel more difficult. If it had been daylight, the horizon would have been almost invisible as snow and sky collided. At night with only the stars to illuminate it, the Plateau seemed to continue forever.

As the lights of the station and outlying buildings dwindled in the distance, swallowed by the darkness, the urge to keep driving, to run away, threatened to overwhelm Brad. He knew it would be a foolhardy attempt, even with extra fuel and supplies, but the thought of returning to the zombie-infested station seemed ludicrous. There was no moon, but the headlight revealed no obstacles in his path. He could have closed his eyes and ridden without fear of hitting anything.

After an hour, Bain's headlights picked out the snow tractor in the distance. Its massive red hulk loomed surreal and ghostly in the darkness. Bain pulled up almost to the door. Brad and Liz parked beside him. DeSousa and Reed stopped some distance away. Bain, Brad, and Liz entered the tractor, while Lester hung back, reluctant to go inside the dead-man vehicle.

"It's larger than I expected," Liz commented as she stepped through the door into the driver's cabin and removed the hood of her parka. She brushed her hand on the wall, dislodging a shower of sparkling ice crystals. Frost covered everything. An empty vodka bottle rattled across the floor as she accidently kicked it with her foot. Everyone froze at the unexpected sound. Brad pushed open the hermetically sealed door to the rear cabin.

"It has beds," he said, surprised at the comfort the vehicle provided.

"It's designed for long term ventures on the ice," Bain explained. "It can accommodate six to eight people for weeks."

Brad played his flashlight over the cabin. An uneaten bowl of soup sat on the table. The bowl's contents were frozen and unrecognizable, but the strong odor of brine and the licorice-smell of tarragon still lingered in the air. Brad picked up the bowl by the spoon frozen in its contents and banged the bowl on the table.

"*Rassolnik*," Bain answered Brad's questioning look. "It's a briny, cucumber-based soup with vegetables, potatoes, and kidneys. It's too salty and sour for me, but the Russians love it. Hmm. It looks as if they weren't very hungry."

"They were dying," Liz said, reminding them of the reason for their journey.

The bunk beds were unmade. Brad eyed the Russian AK-47 lying atop one of the beds, an extra clip of ammunition beside it. "Looks like they expected trouble."

Liz was rummaging through a pile of papers littering the floor. "Here's something," she said, holding aloft a sheet of paper. I can't read Russian, but I recognize the caduceus on the logo. It's a medical bulletin."

"I read some Russian," Bain said. Liz handed him the paper. Brad looked over Bain's shoulder as he read. He recognized the caduceus as the snake wrapped around a staff, but the Cyrillic lettering was like a coded message. "Hmm," Bain said, rubbing his chin with his mittened hand. "It's from the Russian science council to the commandant of Vostok Base, a Vasily Dubcek. It advises him that a plague is spreading through Moscow, and he is to lock down the base. Fighting has broken out in the Middle East and parts of the Ukraine and Uzbekistan." He looked up at Brad and Liz. "He is ordered to avoid contact with any outsiders." Bain dropped the paper and stared at Liz. "It seems they were trying to get close enough to relay the message by radio to us but couldn't. They were too ill. The Russian commandant didn't suspect the disease was airborne and that his warning would contaminate us."

Brad considered another reason. "It's more likely that they were simply fleeing Vostok and figured here would be safer."

The three rummaged through more stacks of papers and magazines but found nothing relevant to their search.

"We've learned all we're going to," Brad said. His frustration at the lack of information had blackened his mood. He had hoped for something more definite and useful.

"I agree," Bain said. He looked at the Kharkovchanka. "Maybe we should return later with extra fuel. We might need this tractor."

Brad was amused that Bain was arriving at the same conclusions that he was – no one was going to come for them. They were on their own. Lester stuck his head in the door.

"Are you guys about finished? The wind's picking up. It's kind of spooky out here."

"We're through," Brad replied. He walked back to the bunk, picked up the AK-47 and extra ammo, and handed it to Bain. "We might need this," he said. Bain accepted the weapon without comment.

As he stepped outside, Brad heard a strange susurration riding the rising wind. It reminded him of the ululations of Arab women greeting their men. *No wonder Lester is worried,* he thought.

The three snowmobiles strung out across the ice on the return trip. Brad didn't worry as long as he could see the lights of the other vehicles. He didn't want to separate from the others and wind up lost. As they neared the base, the light shining through the windows was a comforting sight. Despite the horrors within, it was an oasis in the frozen desert.

Brad brought the snowmobile to a sudden halt as he saw two figures moving toward the garage in the darkness. He unslung his rifle and called out. "Who's there?"

After a few seconds, a voice called out, "It's me, Hughes. I'm with Mclean."

"Hughes. Are you all right?" Brad yelled.

"Is that you, Niles? We're headed in for more supplies. Where have you been?"

Brad waited until Hughes drew nearer before answering. "We went to the Russian tractor looking for answers."

"Did you find any?"

"None that you'll like."

Hughes leaned on his rifle and eyed the six people on the snowmobiles. "Is this it?"

"We don't know. Some have locked themselves in their rooms. We've lost fifteen that I know of."

"Jesus Christ!" Mclean shouted. "What a fucking disaster."

"It's worse than that."

"How?" Hughes asked.

"No one's coming to help us. The Russians came to warn us but wound up bringing the disease here. Somebody dropped a few nukes somewhere. The radiation level is rising. So is the temperature."

"Any more bad news?"

"Yeah," Lester added, "I shot Bradshaw. She turned into a zombie." He glanced at Liz. "According to the Doctor here, we all might."

Brad thought Mclean might become hysterical at the news. He began pacing the snow in a circle, moaning loudly. They all stared at him until he stopped suddenly and pointed toward the base.

"Who's that?"

Four figures were coming toward them, but it was too dark to recognize them. Hughes lit a flare and tossed it in front of them. To their horror, they recognized the faces of Greene, Adler, Pirelli, and Chopra.

"Jesus, it's Pirelli!" McLean yelled, pointing as Pirelli made a beeline for Mclean.

Staring at the group of walking dead, Brad saw no hint of recognition in the cold, dead eyes of his former companions. They moved purposefully, a demonic hunger written on their faces. It was a scene from some horror movie.

"Jesus!" Mclean exclaimed again and began running. He ran directly into the outstretched arms of Barbara Connelly who had come up behind him. They both fell. Mclean screamed as she bit into his neck. Blood from McLean's severed artery spurted across her face and stained the snow crimson beneath their struggling bodies.

Hughes reacted quickly. He shot Connelly in the head with his rifle. Brad watched in horror as Connelly's head exploded and she collapsed to the ground, her arms flailing for a few seconds. Lester fired from the seat of the snowmobile, hitting Pirelli in the face. Pirelli spun in a circle, stumbled toward Brad, and collapsed to his knees, his arms outstretched beside him. His head jerked once as Lester fired again.

Brad brought his rifle to bear on Greene. The sight of Greene with his bloodstained wrists from his suicide, more than anything else, convinced Brad that his friends really were dead. There was no possibility of a coma-like condition or some explainable malady for Greene's condition. He squeezed the trigger with the same lack of emotion that he felt while taking aim at a moose or an elk. Greene was dead. He was looking at a creature, an animal. The only difference was that he would not be eating Greene as he might an elk, though he was certain the former cook would have no such qualms about eating him.

"Back on the snowmobiles!" Brad yelled as soon as Greene dropped. When Liz didn't respond quickly enough, he shoved her. She stumbled, stared at him for a moment, and then nodded. She climbed on the back of the snowmobile, as he leaped across the seat and cranked the engine.

Behind him, he saw that Bain and Lester were moving as well. However, DeSousa's vehicle was still stationary. Brad watched with mounting curiosity as DeSousa and Reed picked up Mclean's corpse from the ground and draped it over the seat of his snowmobile. He realized DeSousa's intentions when, using the remote control, DeSousa began maneuvering the snowmobile closer to the remaining zombies, taunting them. As DeSousa had hoped, they chased after it. He led them away from the base and out onto the ice, keeping the snowmobile just ahead of them. He, Reed, and Hughes remained motionless until the zombies had disappeared into the darkness; then followed the others into the garage.

Brad remained on the seat after Hughes closed the door of the garage with Liz leaning against him in shock. Reed fell to his hands and knees and vomited. Mclean's sudden death had taken them all by surprise.

"I thought they were frozen solid," Hughes said.

"There must be some chill factor below zero temperature where they can't function," Bain replied. "The temperature is less than thirty below. I suppose it is above their threshold."

"You suppose?" Hughes snapped. "Mclean could have used a head's up on that little bit of news."

Hughes' mocking tone offended Bain. "What do you want me to do – apologize? How was I to know what they are capable of?"

The two men stared at one another across the garage. Brad decided it was time to intervene. "Look, you two. We have enough problems without a pissing match. I suggest we put our heads together and come up with a plan."

Hughes broke eye contact first. He turned to Brad. "As I see it, we can either hold up somewhere like Mclean and I were doing, or we can get the hell out of Dodge."

To Brad, the first option had its own set of risks. "If we stay here, we'll have to clear the place of zombies and make certain that everyone left is healthy and alive. Of course," he added, "that doesn't mean one of us might not turn."

"I say we leave," Reed offered.

"For where?" Bain posed. "McMurdo was hit before us. We won't find help there."

"We don't know that for certain," Reed said. His voice bore a tone of desperation the others didn't miss. "We might find a ship."

"The coast is iced in for the winter. There are no ships."

"There might be a plane," Liz suggested.

"Can you fly?" Bain asked her.

"No, but maybe someone here can."

"I can."

Everyone turned to stare at Lester. He grinned back. "Shocked? I'm no expert, of course, but I have soloed in a small Cessna. I think I can get a plane off the ground, but landing it somewhere in the dark ... that's a different story."

"I'll take my chances," Reed said.

Brad felt he had to point out one small pertinent detail. "If we went to McMurdo, where do we go from there?"

No one had an answer to that.

He continued. "If this ... disease, this zombie plague, has hit everywhere, we can't just go to a heavily populated area. It would be crawling with zombies. And what if our destination has been nuked or is radioactive?"

Hughes sighed. "You're just full of good news, aren't you?"

Brad shrugged. "I just think we need a plan before we dig a hole and crawl inside to wait, or march off to destinations unknown."

"He's right," Liz said.

He smiled at her, appreciative of her defending him. "First, we have to clear the base and gather everyone together. Some might choose to take their chances here and I'm not going to force anyone to take part in what might be a foolhardy expedition. We'll clear Pod A; then seal it off from Pod B. It's too dangerous to try to reach McMurdo at night. We have to wait until sunrise. That's three weeks away."

"Three weeks," Deen cried. "That's ridiculous! What if more of us turn into zombies? What do we do then?"

"Had you rather be in a Sno-Cat when someone turns?" Brad posed. He looked around at the others. "If someone turns zombie, we shoot them. Who has weapons?"

Brad and Hughes had their .308 Winchesters, Lester had one of the .45s, and Bain had the Russian AK-47 retrieved from the Russian tractor.

"We need more ammunition," Hughes said.

"There should be more ammo for the rifles and the .45s in the weapons locker. An extra clip is all we have for the AK. We'll split up, two weapons per group. Liz, Lester and I will take the second floor. Hughes, you, Reed, Bain, and DeSousa take the ground floor. We have to check each room. Announce yourselves first, but kick in the door if you have to. Explain what we're doing. If they want to remain where they are, let them, but if they shows any signs of illness, board up the door so they can't escape once they turn zombie."

"That's pretty heartless, isn't it?" Bain said. "Some of them may recover."

"If they recover, they can break down the door or call us to release them. If they die and turn into zombies, they'll be safely contained."

Bain held out the AK-47 to Brad. "Can you show me how to fire this thing?"

Brad set it for short bursts, and then made certain it was ready to fire by snapping off the safety. "Point and shoot, like a camera."

Bain looked down at the AK. "Some camera – point, click, kill."

Brad started to reply that if he needed to use the weapon, he wouldn't be killing anything alive, but thought better of it and let the matter drop.

11

They had almost reached the power plant when the lights flickered a few times before extinguishing completely, plunging them into pitch-black darkness so complete that Brad couldn't see his hand in front of his face. He heard Reed whimpering nearby, frightened and invisible in the gloom. The darkness receded as Hughes and DeSousa switched on their flashlights.

"What happened?" Reed asked. He huddled trembling in the small pool of light cast by DeSousa's flashlight, as if the light was shielding him from whatever lurked in the shadows.

"The generators are down," Brad observed. "Must be out of fuel."

"All three at the same time?" Bain questioned.

"I'll admit that it seems unlikely."

Hughes located a storage locker, retrieved three more flashlights, and passed them around. Brad handed his to Reed, who seemed a little more comfortable once he had a light in his hand. They quietly entered the power plant through a side door, inspecting each inky pool of shadows in the long Quonset hut-style building for lurking zombies. They found Warren Feinstein lying on the floor in a pool of fresh, steaming blood, a kitchen knife protruding from his chest.

"No zombie did that," Hughes pointed out, "somebody stabbed him."

"Overton," Brad said, cursing himself at his lack of foresight. "He went off the deep end earlier today. He came down this direction. I never thought he would kill someone."

Hughes shook his head. "Maybe you should have warned everyone a crazy man was running loose."

Brad turned on Hughes, jabbing his finger into Hughes' chest. Hughes' remark cut too close to an accusation. Brad had enough of Hughes' macho-man tirades. "Maybe if you had hung around to help instead of running away, Feinstein wouldn't be here alone."

Hughes scowled and shifted his weight. Brad expected him to throw a punch, but something held him back. *Maybe he's as frightened as I am*, Brad thought. He backed away from Hughes and knelt by Feinstein's body. He took a rag from a workbench and laid it over Feinstein's face. It was the best he could do.

"The power panels are wrecked," DeSousa announced as he played his light over a tangle of shredded wires and broken switches.

Brad rose and stared at the damage. "Can you repair it?"

DeSousa arched an eyebrow. "Possibly, if you give me a week and more spare parts than we have. Overton might be crazy, but he knew exactly what to destroy to cut off power." He went to a smaller panel and opened it. "Damn, here too." DeSousa reached inside the panel and twisted two wires together. Sparks flew, but the emergency lights began to glow dimly. "Best I can do for now. It'll be just the emergency lights in Pod A. Pod B circuit is fried." He angrily slammed the panel door shut and examined the generators. He sniffed at the stench of JP-8 jet fuel contaminating the air. "Son of a bitch also smashed the fuel pumps on the generators. We have no power or heat."

"Let's kill the bastard," Hughes said.

"No, if we find him, we subdue him. He's crazy, not sick. It's not like he was under stress or anything," Brad added with a touch of sarcasm.

Hughes pointed to Feinstein's body. "I think *he's* a little stressed now."

Brad understood Hughes' anger, but he was adamant. Overton, crazed or not, was still his friend. With proper treatment, he might recover. At least he deserved the chance. "No killing unless we have to." He hoped he didn't come to regret his words.

* * * *

Liz had witnessed the exchange between Hughes and Brad with growing concern. Both men were Alpha males, but while Brad felt uncomfortable exerting authority, Hughes' disdain for authority forced him to target anyone whom he felt threatened him. If the two men didn't come to terms with their differences soon, disaster loomed. She watched with interest Brad's treatment of Feinstein's body. His reverent gesture of covering the dead man's face revealed a side of him that she hoped prevailed during the present crisis. The disparate group of survivors needed a mobilizing force, a leader to mold them into a cohesive group that could pull together to survive. Brad's kind heart would serve him in good stead as such a leader, even though he instinctively fought the responsibility that he naturally assumed.

She tried to shrug off the persistent cold fingers of depression that had begun to plague her since reading the medical memo in the Russian snow tractor. Before, her problems were localized, confined to friends and acquaintances. Now, the entire world and everyone she ever knew could be gone. She followed Brad, one hand pressed against his back for support. His strength nourished hers as a small spark can be encouraged into a flame.

The two groups split up in the Beer Can stairwell. Liz, Brad, and Bain continued up the stairs, while Hughes' group, consisting of DeSousa, Lester and Reed, entered the lower level through the closed double doors. The dim emergency lights cast the stairwell in shadows that seemed to whirl around her as she climbed. The echo of their booted footsteps on the metal treads rang loudly announcing their presence. She felt exposed and vulnerable.

Almost immediately upon entering the building, they spotted two zombies in the galley kneeling over the grisly remains of some unidentifiable hapless victim. Their blood-smeared faces turned to stare up at her as she entered the room. She recognized Sid Barrett, one of the botanists. She remembered him as a thin, smiling young man quick with the joke and always willing to help. He led the small ensemble of musicians that played in the gymnasium each week. Now, he snarled at her like a rabid animal, a piece of human liver in his hand. The other man's name was Wolenski, but she didn't know his first name. He had been one of those she had been treating for a high fever and congestion.

She jumped as Bain's AK-47 exploded, stitching both zombies with a line of bullet holes, none of which stopped them. Most of his bullets went wild and ripped through the windows, allowing in a rush of cold air.

"Bastards!" Bain yelled and raised his rifle again.

"Aim for the heads," Brad suggested. The barrel of Brad's Winchester didn't seem to move at all, as he fired from his hip and shot Barrett in the forehead. The back of Barrett's head flew off and splattered gore over a table and the floor. He toppled across the half-eaten corpse. Bain heeded Brad's advice. He took a wider stance to brace himself and pulled the trigger again. This time, several bullets from his short burst blew apart the second zombies' head. Bain looked pleased with himself, but then, after a few seconds, he lowered his AK-47 and began sobbing quietly.

"What's wrong?" Brad asked.

"They were people once. I knew both of them. I shot them."

Brad tried to offer words of comfort. "The people you knew are dead."

Bain glared at him. "How do you know? Maybe they're trapped inside, seeing what's happening but unable to stop it."

"It doesn't matter. If either of them had tried to kill you yesterday and you had that gun in your hands, would you have not fired?"

Bain didn't reply. Instead, he walked over to the small bar at one end of the galley and grabbed a bottle of liquor from behind the counter. He didn't bother looking at the label. He simply unscrewed the lid, turned up the bottle, and took a long swig. Liz stared at the bodies on the floor. It seemed wrong to leave them lying there. She took three red-and-white-checkered tablecloths from a stack and spread one over each body. To her horror, each tablecloth immediately turned dark from the bloody corpses.

"Let's check the dorm," Brad said.

The emergency lighting in the corridor, intended to guide people to exits in case of fire, provided just enough light to discern the walls and floor around the lights. Deep pools of shadow dotted the corridor between the widely spaced lights. She hugged herself and shivered. Without heat, the interior of the base was already growing chilly. Soon it would become as cold as the air outside and they would freeze.

The winter dorm was a separate wing, one of two that gave Pod A its U-shaped appearance. Several of the doors lining the corridor were open. These disturbed her more than the closed ones. Moving carefully, she followed Brad into the dorm. They inspected each open room and knocked on each closed door they came to. Brad suggested that Liz act as their spokesperson as most of the crew would recognize her voice. Several times, guttural sounds accompanied by pounding or scratching at the door, met their inquiries – people turned zombie. In these instances, Brad made sure the locks were secure, drew an 'X' on the door with a felt marker, and left them as they were.

At one door, a voice answered Liz's summons, but the occupant refused to open the door. She explained the situation and their intentions, and still he refused to cooperate. She could see Brad's frustration mounting. They didn't have time to play games.

She tried again. "There's no power. The building will freeze soon. Zombies are loose. If you remain here, you'll die."

"Go away!" the person inside shouted.

Finally, pushed beyond his limit, Brad pushed Liz away from the door, shot out the lock, and kicked the door open. Inside, they found two people, Faith Menendez and Leon Grissom, the Ice Cube crewman who was Menendez's latest folly. Grissom backed against the wall brandishing a fire ax. Liz held her breath, but after a few seconds, he lowered it. He glanced at Menendez lying in bed, no longer the beautiful heartbreaker she had been just a few days earlier. She was deathly pale with dark lines streaking her right cheek and circling her right eye like smudged mascara, but Liz's heart sank as she realized the lines were not from running makeup. The sheet above Menendez's breasts was heaving as she fought for each shallow breath. She could see in Grissom's eyes that he knew that she was dying.

"Can you help her?" he asked her, his voice pleading.

She went to Menendez's side, checked her pulse, and discovered that it was very weak. She pushed up the lid of one of Menendez's eyes and noticed dark specks swimming in the iris. The fully dilated pupil did not blink. The white of her eye was mostly red. She threw back the sheet to reveal Menendez's naked breasts covered with scaly, dead black skin. She suppressed a gasp at the sight.

She shook her head slowly. "She's dying," she whispered.

Grissom nodded. "I know, but I can't leave her."

"No one's coming to help us," Brad told him. "We're gathering everyone to head for the coast. We're leaving as soon as we can make preparations." He glanced at Menendez. Liz followed his eyes. Once, a glimpse of her magnificent naked breasts would have aroused any male on the base. Now, she saw only sympathy in his eyes. "If she ... passes before then, join us."

"Leave me a Ski Doo. I'll follow later."

Liz covered Menendez with the sheet. Menendez's eyes opened for just a second and stared at her before closing again. It was merely a reflex, but Liz imagined that she was pleading for help, help she could not offer. She looked at Grissom. He appeared exhausted by his death vigil. She doubted that he would leave the base, or that he could make the long trek to the coast alone, but she smiled and nodded.

"Keep the door locked," Brad advised.

Once out of the room, she began to cry. She wasn't sure why. Was she shedding tears for Menendez or for Grissom? *Or maybe she was crying for herself, her disconnect from the reality of what was happening around her.* Brad placed his arm around her shoulder, tentatively at first, to comfort her, but when she accepted his offer of solace and buried her face in his chest, he wrapped his arms around her and pulled her closer.

"Don't give up," he whispered in her ear. "We'll make it."

She looked up at him. He had misinterpreted her display of emotion as surrender. "Give up? I'll never give up. I'm crying because I'm a physician, and I can do nothing to help her, to help anyone. Leon is staying here with her. It should be me, but I want to live. I'm crying because I'm glad it's not me lying there. I gave up on Ted and my marriage. He was in pain, angry and lashing out, but instead of being there for him, trying to work it out, I walked away. Maybe I resented being the breadwinner. I don't know. I realize now that I should have attempted to understand. Instead, I ran away from him, from my job, and my life. I'm running now, but for a different reason. Ted is gone. That part of my life is gone."

She pulled away, but her hand remained pressed against Brad's chest, reluctant to break contact with him. "Thanks, Brad. I understand what you meant, but you've got me all wrong. I'm no longer a doctor; I'm simply a survivor. Later, I hope I can be a doctor again."

The core of her hardness surprised her. Maybe she was getting stronger. It seemed as if each death strengthened her. Like some kind of ghoulish vampire, she took the negative energy of death and wrapped herself in it, creating a cloak of invulnerability. She lived because she was afraid of dying.

"Everyone *can't* be dead," she said, basing her reasoning on hope rather than logic. "Somewhere out there, someone is working on a solution. We'll find them."

Brad glanced around the dark corridor. "I hope you're right, but now, we need to search for survivors."

* * * *

Sept. 2, Amundsen-Scott Base, Antarctica

Time mattered very little to the perpetual darkness outside or to the oppressive gloom inside the base. Each interminable hour morphed slowly into the next, little changed except for its passing. By two a.m. of the second day after their journey to the Russian tractor, Brad had been awake for nearly fifty-six hours and was on his last legs. They had spent hours checking each room. The physical exertion of breaking down so many doors to see what lay behind them had exhausted him. The mental torture of arguing with recalcitrant, frightened people had drained him emotionally. They had discovered at least two possible zombies behind locked doors and one person turned zombie ambling down the corridor. He had shot it to end its misery. They had also found four more people in the last stages of infection who would not survive long. For these few, like Faith Menendez, they could offer no comfort or solace. They could only seal the doors, mark it with an 'X', and hope for a miracle.

Between the two search groups, they had located and brought six people to the galley. Ten or eleven people were still missing somewhere inside the base. With no way of knowing if they were hiding or if they had already turned zombie, searching for them in Pod B or the outlying buildings would be too dangerous. Many of the survivors were too weak to travel, deliberately choosing to starve themselves rather than risk leaving the security of their rooms to find food. They would never survive the long journey to McMurdo. They would have to be nursed back to health. The plan to vacate the base as soon as possible had quickly become an impossible goal.

Heat became the first priority. Without the generators, the temperature inside the base dropped quickly, hovering just above freezing. Sous chef Mullins solved the heating problem by lighting all the propane burners in the kitchen and sealing off the galley from the rest of the base. They boarded up the window shattered by Bain's wild shooting spree, creating a safe and cozy refuge. Food was plentiful and candles helped augment the emergency lighting. They shoved the tables to the edges of the room to provide space on the floor for blankets and makeshift beds.

Hughes and Lester returned to the Kharkovchanka in a snowmobile pulling sledges loaded with diesel to refuel the tractor and bring it to the base. Brad watched them leave from the upper rear deck of the dormitory. All of the people they had placed outside who had died of infection or from zombie bites had now turned into zombies. They patrolled the grounds around the base like silent sentinels. He regretted his decision not to burn the bodies as he had first intended. Several zombies followed the snowmobile as it left. He kept his rifle handy, but Hughes threaded a safe path through the zombies. Some of the creatures who had chased after the remotely controlled snowmobile bearing Mclean's dead body had since returned. He tried not to dwell on what had happened to McLean's corpse. He tried to bury any sympathy for the creatures prowling the darkness that had once been friends and acquaintances. Those people were dead, replaced by soulless beasts eager to kill him.

He kept his cold vigil until Hughes and Lester returned two hours later. The sight of the massive red vehicle lumbering out of the darkness with Hughes driving brought a lump of relief to his throat. It represented hope. He spotted one zombie edging too close to Lester's snowmobile and dropped it with a single shot to the head. At the sound, several of the creatures turned away from the tractor and toward him, gathering at the foot of the stairs. He suppressed the urge to kill every zombie he saw, hating them for what they had become, but hating them more for what they represented. He tried to multiply their number by tens of millions, maybe hundreds of millions, and became sick to the stomach at the idea. Ammunition was too dear to waste unnecessarily in a blind rage. He allowed them to mass around the foot of the stairs. A few began slowly climbing. By the time the Russian tractor and the snowmobile were safely inside the garage, several of the creatures had managed to reach the first level. He retreated inside and secured the door behind him.

Moving down the dark corridor, he heard stirrings inside several of the locked rooms. More of the sick had died and turned into zombies. In some instances, the entire conversion process seemed to take only hours after death. He could well imagine the scenes of horror in heavily populated cities as hundreds or thousands of the recently deceased suddenly wakened with a craving for human flesh. The panic as people sought to flee the cities would have quickly become a stampede as overcrowded streets and freeways turned into bottlenecks.

Their own position was just as tentative. With heat and power, they could have secured the base against the creatures outside, but how could they protect themselves from themselves. If Liz was correct and everyone was infected, each person was a potential zombie.

Brad was grateful that Liz became more like her old self, tirelessly tending to the weak. She never rested. She moved among the survivors with words of comfort, bowls of food, and a ready smile. How much was merely an act, a façade of reassurance she presented for the others, he didn't know, but the effect on them was remarkable. She was the base doctor, a physician, and as long as she projected an aura of hope to which they could cling, they rallied. He understood what it was costing her. He wished he could do a better job of masking his own doubts, but they leaked onto his features whenever he thought of what might become of them all. He found it easier to find other things to do rather than face their questioning eyes.

Lester provided him an excuse to avoid the other survivors.

"The emergency batteries will fail soon. If we crank up the emergency generator, we can at least have some lights."

He realized that Lester was right. Searching for any other survivors would be much easier if they had lights. DeSousa, Reed and Hughes were busy readying the Kharkovchanka and the Sno-Cats for the journey to McMurdo. He recruited Lester, Bain, and Eugene Houseman, a computer programmer, to go with him to the emergency generator room. Once away from the warmth of the galley, the cold quickly closed in on them, as did the darkness. The lower level was even colder as the cold air settled. In the greenhouse, once the source of all their fresh vegetables, the plants had withered from the cold. One of the hydroponics lines had frozen and ruptured. Water seeping beneath the door into the corridor had frozen into a pool of ice.

"Did someone leave a door open somewhere?" Lester asked, pulling his parka's hood over his head.

"We sealed all the outside doors as we searched," Brad replied.

"Well I feel a draft," Lester insisted. "It's damn cold down here."

"It's just air moving from the colder part of the station," Bain said.

Lester glanced at the weatherman and arched his eyebrows. "And just how is it doing that?"

Bain sighed and began lecturing Lester as if he were a first-year graduate student. "Look, it's simple enough. Cold air is heavier than warm air. The cold air on level two is moving downward, forcing the warmer air on level one to move upward. It's cyclical, the same way storm fronts operate."

Lester grimaced. Bain's condescending tone might have offended him, but that wasn't what was bothering him. "No, I meant, where is the air coming from. We secured the fire doors on both levels." He glanced down the corridor. His light reflected from the slightly ajar fire door. "Someone's opened them."

The hairs on the back of Brad's neck began standing at attention. Only one person would do that – Overton.

The emergency lighting was not functioning in Pod B. It was dark and cold, but it was not silent. Eerie noises drifted down the dark corridors. Sounds that might have been muffled footsteps and moans emanated from deep within the darkness. They could have come from frightened residents or from zombies. Brad swallowed to force down the growing lump in his throat and tightened his grip on the rifle. They reached the generator room without incident. To Brad, the maze of pipes and cables was as puzzling as a 3-D Rorschach inkblot test and as hopeless as a tangle of jungle vines. He half-expected to see a monkey clinging to the pipes, chattering at them. One wall sprouted panels and switches as if a mad sculptor had been busy with a torch and a screwdriver. He stood there dumbfounded, staring at them, and then turned to Lester.

"I hope you know what you're doing."

Lester didn't look or sound too convincing as he scratched his head and replied, "Looks simple enough. Bain, can you check the fuel tank?"

Brad motioned for Houseman to follow him. "Grab Bain's AK-47. We'll stand guard while he and Lester work." They took up positions just outside the door. Brad stared down the corridor as he listened to the two men talking.

"It's full of fuel," Bain announced.

"Good. I'll start her up," Lester said.

The whine of the generator as the starter spun filled the room. The noise continued for a full minute before stopping. The silence that followed was disheartening.

"Damn thing won't start," Lester snapped. Brad heard a thud, as if Lester had resorted to kicking the generator. "What's wrong with it?"

Lester tried again with the same lack of results.

"I smell fuel," Bain said. "There must be a leak somewhere."

Laughter rang out from the corner of the room. Brad recognized the short barking laugh of Daryl Overton. He rushed back into the room.

"Daryl," he yelled. "Come on out. We're leaving for McMurdo."

"No one's leaving," Overton replied.

"What do you mean?" Brad shook his head as he noticed Lester's hand reaching for the pistol on his belt. "No," he whispered. "Maybe I can talk him into coming out."

"He killed Feinstein," Lester reminded him.

Overton overheard Lester. "He tried to prevent me from destroying the generators," he shouted. "We have to keep the base cold, like a tomb. It's the only way to stop them. That's why I sabotaged the generators and why I opened the doors."

"Son of a bitch," Lester muttered. "He's letting the damn things inside."

"It's warming up outside, Daryl. The zombies are thawing out."

Overton's voice became frantic. "I'm too late, too late."

"It's not too late. Come with us."

Overton's laughter was sepulchral, deep and dark. A sobering chill began nibbling at Brad's spine. His anxiety increased as the astronomer continued. He realized he was listening to the voice of madness.

"There's nothing out there, Brad," Overton said. "Don't you see? It's the end of the world at the ends of the Earth – the Apocalypse." He laughed at his joke. "This place is *Sheol,* a dark, deep place where lost souls go. We're in an ice cold Hell."

Brad wondered why Overton, a non-practicing Jew, would now cling to the religion he professed to despise. He tried to sway his friend. "The sun will return in a few weeks. It'll be light again soon. We're going to McMurdo and try for home. There have to be survivors somewhere."

Overton's voice went quiet and cold. "Not here," he intoned. "Here, we're all dead already." A flare ignited in the corner of the room, illuminating Overton in brightness. Somehow, he had lost or removed his shirt. He was naked except for a pair of ragged underwear hanging loosely from his narrow hips. His eyes were as cold as his voice. His jaw twitched in spasms of either despair or ecstasy; Brad couldn't tell which. He was relieved to see none of the black patches on Overton's chest that had marked the other infected people. Overton lifted the flare above his head, an avenging angel with a flaming sword, ignoring the bits of burning material that dropped onto his bare arm and shoulder. "If cold won't stop them, maybe fire will." He cocked his arm to throw the flare.

Brad, realizing Overton's intent, yelled out, "No!"

It was too late. Overton tossed the flare toward the JP-8 jet fuel pooling behind the generator.

"Run!" Lester screamed as the flare tumbled end-over-end through the air. He and Bain scrambled out of the way.

Brad remained frozen for a few seconds in disbelief that his friend and colleague could ever do such an insane thing.

"Move it!" Lester yelled, slamming into Brad and shoving him toward the open door.

Finally, fear dissolved his doubt and his legs began pumping furiously, conveying him away from the generator. Behind him, the flare landed, bounced twice, and then ignited the fuel. The explosion he had expected did not come. Instead, the fuel simply caught fire and began to burn. A wave of flame swept across the room and crept beneath the generator. Brad paused outside the room, staring back into the trying to decide if he should rescue Overton. Lester grabbed him by the shoulder and yanked him aside just as the room exploded. The concussion shook the entire building, shattering windows in the managers' offices. A rush of hot air roared from the room, propelling him like an autumn leaf in the wind. He rolled head-over-heels down the corridor, his ears ringing from the concussion. Flames licked the corridor wall opposite the doorway and ignited furniture and curtains inside the offices.

"I thought jet fuel didn't explode," he moaned to Lester, who lay across his chest.

"There were barrels of cleaning solvents in there. The flames ignited them."

He heaved Lester off him and climbed to his feet. He peered into the generator room from a safe distance. The room was awash in flames. Overton could not have survived the explosion and resulting fire. As Brad watched, the ceiling began to cave in, and flames leaped upward through the gap into the Ice Cube lounge upstairs. The library and its hundreds of books would ignite quickly. The entire station was at risk. Brad yanked a fire extinguisher from the wall and began spraying foam on the walls.

Lester grabbed him by the shoulder and spun him around, yelling to be heard over the roar of the flames. "It's no use. We'll have to secure the fire doors on both levels or we'll lose the entire base."

The heavy concrete-filled steel fire doors' functions were to separate the two pods in just such an emergency. The four men made it through the door and dogged the hatches just as a second explosion, larger than the first, jarred the entire building. The floor of the building became a rolling ship's deck, sending Brad reeling like a drunken sailor. The emergency lights flicked several times, and then failed completely. Tiny fingers of flames began to dance along the edges of the warped fire door.

"It's not going to hold long," Lester warned.

As they raced for the stairs, Brad noticed something odd and stopped to look. The door was pulsing, bulging outwards from its frame, and then receding, as if it were breathing. The tendrils of fire grew longer, groping the surrounding wall and licking the bubbling paint from the door. With the sound of wrenching metal, one hinge snapped and flames shot down the corridor and along the wall. Brad took the stairs two at a time with the flames nipping at his heels.

He reached the top of the stairs to see Houseman, outlined by Bain's flashlight, struggling with the heavy second-level fire door. Before anyone could assist him, three zombies pushed through the door of the adjacent summer dormitory wing, allowed into the building by Overton's senseless act of opening all the outer doors. Two of the creatures fell upon Houseman. In his haste to close the door, he had carelessly leaned the AK-47 against the wall of the corridor several feet away. The zombies were between him and his weapon. Lester saw the creatures and drew his pistol, but didn't fire for fear of hitting Houseman. His hesitation allowed the third zombie to lunge at him. He ducked beneath its outstretched arms, raised his pistol, and placed a bullet through the creature's chin and into its brain. The top of its head exploded in a geyser of thick black blood.

Brad, still reeling from his push up the stairs, didn't stop to think. He rushed in, grabbed one of the zombies attacking Houseman by the arm and yanked it away. The creature bounced off the wall and fell to the floor. As it struggled to rise, Lester shot it in the head. Brad then turned his attention to the remaining zombie. He was too late. The zombie had his face buried in Houseman's shoulder. Houseman screamed in pain and lunged backwards, slamming the zombie into the metal door in a frantic attempt to dislodge it. Finally, the creature released him, its face glistening with Houseman's blood. Houseman staggered out of the zombie's reach. Brad didn't have time to unsling the Winchester strapped to his back. He grabbed the AK-47 leaning against the wall while on the run and placed a quick burst into the zombie's head and chest. It slid down the wall, leaving a smear of dark blood.

Houseman, illuminated by Bain's light, leaned against the wall holding his left hand to his savaged right shoulder. Blood seeped between his fingers and down the front of his coat. The pain of the wound was intense, but the wretched look of fear on his face came from the realization that he was now infected. He had seen what had become of Pirelli and the others once bitten. He looked at Brad, his eyes pleading with him to do something, but Brad could do nothing. Brad still held the AK-47 in his hands, but he couldn't bring himself to pull the trigger on a living human being, even to end his pain.

Beyond the fire door, flames now billowed into the corridor from the library and the Ice Cube lounge. Smoke poured up the stairwell from the fire below. The building shuddered once more. Pictures fell from the walls, their glass shattering on the floor. Lockers toppled like a row of dominos. Pipes running the length of the ceiling twisted from their brackets and tumbled down. The overloaded steel supports designed to raise the building as snow accumulated beneath it groaned from the stress, a building in pain. The elevated building trembled as Pod B tilted by fifteen degrees. The entire base was quickly losing its structural integrity.

More zombies appeared in the Pod B corridor through the smoke beyond the fire door. Houseman glanced in their direction, and then back at Brad. His face so recently filled with fear and dismay suddenly calmed. Brad guessed his intentions as Houseman pushed away from the wall and stepped through the fire door. Brad stepped forward to stop the injured man; then stopped. Houseman was a dead man and he knew it. He had the right to choose in what manner he wished to end his own life. He had made his decision.

His eyes held Brad's for a moment as he leaned into the heavy door to close it from the other side. A sad smile played on his lips in the final few seconds before the door shut. Brad's last glimpse through the door was of a wall of flame rushing down the corridor like a rampaging beast, immolating the zombies in its path, and Houseman.

He turned away from the door. Bain and Lester were staring at him in astonishment. The flashlight in Bain's shaking hand cast the corridor in a strobe-like effect. Brad noticed Liz in the corridor outside the galley, washed in candlelight.

"We have to leave now," he said. "We don't have much time."

## 12

Liz felt the building vibrate seconds before she heard the explosion. She immediately knew something had gone terribly wrong. In the kitchen, Mullins and the cook dodged heavy pots falling from their racks, clattering to the tile floor. Stacks of dishes toppled and crashed. Mullions rushed to shut off the gas to the stoves. In the cafeteria, windows cracked. Tables and chairs danced around the room. The emergency lights went out, leaving them in candlelight. A single scream pierced the gloom. Loud moans and groans reminded her that others were as frightened as she was.

"Stay calm," she urged, though her own lack of composure provided no example. Her hands shook so badly that she reached down to clutch her thighs to hide their trembling, glad for the dim lighting. However, she couldn't hide her apprehension. She suspected that Brad and the others were near the source of the explosion and feared for his safety. Moments later, a second shudder rippled through the building. Glass exploded from the cracked windows peppering people with shards of glass. A water pipe burst, extinguishing most of the candles in a shower of water. One of the one-inch-diameter gas pipes on the ceiling snapped in half and fell, impaling a dim figure against the wall. His agonized scream ended abruptly as the floor canted several degrees. Gas hissed from the ruptured pipe. It was becoming too dangerous to remain where they were. Liz reversed her original decision.

"We must leave," she called out. "Grab your coats and food and water. Hurry!"

"Where are we going?" someone asked.

She turned on them. "It doesn't matter. We can't stay here."

She stepped into the corridor just as rifle shots rang out. She pressed against the wall to avoid being accidently shot. Flames rushing down the corridor from the opposite end of the base silhouetted several figures. They suddenly disappeared as the emergency door slammed shut, closed by someone from the far side. Relief flooded over her when she saw Brad illuminated by the beam of a flashlight. She ran up to him and hugged him.

"What's happening?"

He pushed her away and laid his hands on her shoulders. "The building's on fire. It's collapsing. We have to get everyone out."

She nodded. "They're getting ready now."

He smiled at her. This simple act calmed her more than any words could have. "Good job. We have to get to the garage. It's our only chance."

She rushed back to the galley. The confusion and panic had settled into a kind of quiet stampede. People gathered winter gear and grabbed cases of water and food. She slipped her arm around one man still too weak to manage on his own. Acting as part den mother-part subway conductor, she urged her wards to move more quickly. The scream of grinding metal grew in volume as girders twisted by the heat collapsed under the weight of the building. Each weakened leg placed more stress on the remaining supports. They could give way at any time, bringing the entire structure down around them.

Their only was through the Beer Can. She led the way. With so many windows shattered by the death contortions of the base, the hollow structure had become a chimney, funneling smoke from the lower level. She raced down the stairs through an acrid haze of blinding smoke that bit her throat. She covered her mouth and nose with one hand in a futile effort to keep out the smoke as she supported the weak man with the other. As they reached the first level, waves of scorching heat swept down the corridor. Flames had already reached the greenhouse. The sizzle of the hydroponic liquid reminded her of the sound of grease in a hot skillet. The laundry room was ablaze. Water gushed from freshly thawed broken pipes and sprayed the walls, but had no effect on the spreading flames. She panicked when she lost sight of Brad in the smoke, but then she caught a glimpse of him ducking back into the building and entering the emergency supply room. She choked on the thickening smoke, waiting breathlessly for him to reappear. The man she was helping down the stairs grew restless, pulled away from her, and began hobbling down the stairs in his haste to escape the flames. She breathed a sigh of relief when Brad re-emerged a minute later loaded down with blankets.

"Go on," Brad urged, as he pushed her ahead of him, glancing over his shoulder to make certain no one was left behind. She caught up with her ward, grabbed him around the waist, and propelled him down the stairs ahead of her, hoping he didn't stumble.

Flames engulfed the entire building on both levels. Walls exploded and collapsed inward. The ceiling crumbled into the corridor, dumping blazing piles of furniture and equipment from the upper level, blocking the corridor and preventing the exit of anyone left trapped inside. The Beer Can swayed like a tree in a hurricane as the rest of the building began to pull away from the structure with the sound of paper tearing. The stairs bucked beneath her feet as they sheered away from their steel supports with a popping sound. She paused to look back, shocked that a building could burn so quickly. *Not just any building*, she reminded herself. It had been her home for two years. Her few mementos were lost, her clothes, her hairbrush. She thought it petty and silly that she could think of such things amid such tragedy.

They reached the ice tunnels beneath the building. Water, freed from its frozen state for the first time in millennia, poured in steady torrents from the sculpted ceiling. Liz groped her way blindly with her right hand outstretched to touch the wet wall to keep her bearings. The ground shuddered as explosions rocked the base, sending blasts of hot air down the tunnel. She felt a moment of claustrophobia, fearing that the ceiling would collapse and trap her beneath tons of ice and snow. Finally, a rectangle of light ahead allowed her to get her bearings. Figures silhouetted by the light disappeared as they burst out of the tunnel into the garage. Hughes and DeSousa met them there, waving flashlights.

"Is this everyone?" Hughes asked.

Liz nodded mutely as she helped her ward sit on the floor. She looked into his face expecting to see pain but saw only mute horror. "No one alive behind me," she intoned with numbness in her voice that was rapidly overtaking her body.

Hughes closed the door, cutting off the smoke pouring down the ice tunnel. "We should be safe here. The tunnels will collapse and provide a firebreak. How bad is it?"

"The entire building's on fire and collapsing," Brad answered. "The fire door didn't hold."

"What happened?"

"Overton, that's what happened," Lester said, glaring at Brad. "The crazy bastard opened all the doors and let the zombies in, and then he started a fire in the emergency generator room." He rubbed his scorched arms. "I feel like a piece of toast."

Liz could see in Brad's eyes that he felt responsible for the disaster. He had been the one who prevented them from hunting for Overton. He marched away from Lester and Hughes to one of the snowmobiles where he leaned. Liz shot Lester a deprecatory look and followed Brad.

"It's not your fault, Brad," she said. "Overton was insane."

He raised his head and looked at her. His face was awash with pain and regret. "No, it is my fault. I should have gone after him the first time, tried to help him. Now, Houseman's dead and the base is gone."

His gaze wandered the garage. Her eyes followed his. In the poorly lit interior, she saw very little other than the vehicles and drums of oil, antifreeze, and diesel fuel stacked along one wall. A winch dangled long chains from a ceiling beam overhead. A long workbench, scattered with tools, and a storage locker took up most of a second wall. The remaining wall was bare. She made a quick mental inventory and noted very little to sustain them – no food, no water, not even a warm place to sleep. The base, containing all their supplies, was a blazing inferno.

As if reading her mind, Brad said, "We have no power, no heat, and very little food. We can't stay here."

His statement surprised her. "I thought you said it would be too dangerous trying to reach McMurdo in the dark."

He held out his hands, and then made fists and shook them, as if he were searching for a target on which to take out his frustration. His jaw tightened. "We have no choice," he forced out through clenched teeth. He dropped his arms to his side and sighed. "We can either eat up all our food waiting for help that might never arrive, or we can try for McMurdo."

She glanced at the people around her. They were frightened and unsure of what was happening. Some huddled for warmth around the two kerosene heaters someone had lit. Most, too dazed by events even to notice the heaters, milled aimlessly around the garage. She realized with a heavy heart that Brad was right, but it didn't ease her apprehension. "Some of these people are still too weak. It took all their energy just to manage this far."

Another long sigh noted his frustration. "Then we have to wait, but not too long. We don't know what we'll find at McMurdo."

He had touched upon another of her fears. They were a long way from McMurdo, and McMurdo was a long way from anywhere else. They were isolated and most of the zombies were dead, consumed by the fire that had also consumed their supplies. Their biggest threat now was starvation or freezing. How could they cope with hundreds or even tens of thousands of zombies?

Hughes walked over shaking his head. "I guess you realize that we're screwed." He waited for Brad to challenge him. When Brad said nothing, Hughes continued, "I've been taking inventory. We have enough food to last maybe three weeks if we stretch it. Water we can get from snow and ice, but every drop of fuel we burn for heat means just that much less for the vehicles."

Brad considered their options, which were few. "Check the Kharkovchanka. Maybe there's food in it. We'll sift the ashes of the base for anything edible if we have to. These people are our responsibility."

"Any ideas?"

"McMurdo," Brad replied.

Liz expected Hughes to object and was surprised when he nodded.

"It won't be easy," Hughes said, "but Deen and Wilkie drove a convoy up the snow road. They can help. I'll prep the vehicles."

"We can't leave yet."

Hughes frowned. "Why not?"

Brad glanced at Liz. "In Liz's opinion these people are too weak to make the journey. They need time to recuperate."

Hughes' scowl betrayed what he thought of Liz's judgment. "Let 'em rest up along the way. Time's ticking away."

Liz took umbrage at Hughes' dismissal of her medical advice. Health matters were her responsibility. "They need food and rest. If we leave now, some might die."

"We might all die," Hughes snapped.

"If you're so frightened, take a Sno-Cat and leave." She waved her hand at one of the vehicles in the garage. "It's my job to keep these people alive."

"I'm staying with her," Brad said.

Hughes half turned away, and then spun back around. She tensed, expecting him to lash out at her. Instead, he smiled. "Damn, you're stubborn." He looked at Brad. "Both of you. Well, I guess I'm in. I never expected to live forever."

As Hughes walked away, Brad reached out and grasped her hand. She surprised both him and herself by kissing him. His enthusiastic response roused a stirring within her breast that she hadn't felt in a long time, not since the early days of her failed marriage. She let the kiss go on for what seemed like an eternity, but was probably only a few seconds, and then broke away with reluctance.

"Thank you, Brad," she said.

"Mmm. Thank you."

She wanted to stay with him, wrap herself in his arms, but she was a doctor. She couldn't prevent them dying from the zombie plague, but she could make certain they didn't die from complications of starvation. "I have to see to my patients."

13

Sept. 6, the ruins of Amundsen-Scott Base, Antarctica

On the fourth day after the fire, Brad, Hughes, Bain, and Wilkie ventured outside to explore the ruins. Brad's heart sank when he saw what was left of Amundsen-Scott Base. The ashes had grown cold, but wisps of smoke still rose from lingering hotspots in the ruins as fires smoldered deep beneath piles of twisted metal and charred equipment. Melted snow and ice had refrozen into beautiful, exotic crystalline shapes that might have been beautiful elsewhere if they did not serve as markers for so many graves. Pod B, the source of the fire, was completely gone, reduced to rubble. Pod A had fared better, but the flames had gutted the interior. A few zombies driven away by the fire wandered the outlying edges of the base among the drums of fuel and storage containers, but they didn't come near the sad remnants of the former technological marvel of Amundsen-Scott Base.

"The good news is that radiation levels haven't increased," Bain announced. "The bad news is that the temperature is near freezing."

"I can live with that," Brad replied.

"Well, actually, that's very bad news. We have to traverse ice bridges, glaciers and an ice shelf to reach McMurdo. We're on a sea of ice, constantly moving. It wouldn't do to fall into a thousand-meter-deep crevasse."

Brad hadn't considered that possibility. Had they delayed too long already? During the Antarctic winter, one didn't normally think about the ice thawing.

Digging through the ashes, they had found nothing useful – no food, no blankets, and no weapons. The fire had consumed everything. Brad eyed the storage trailers among the heavy equipment.

"What's in those?"

"Spare parts for generators, spare scientific equipment, camping gear for summer expeditions – no food," Hughes said. "That was all there." He pointed to the ruins.

"Anything in the Ice Cube labs? I know there's nothing at the telescope," Brad paused before continuing, "except maybe a bag of chips and a cherry soda or two." He winced inwardly as he thought of Overton, whose love of cherry colas and salt and vinegar potato chips had almost caused a rift between them when an empty potato chip bag had jammed the telescope's delicate gears, ruining a full night's work. Overton and Walls had been his closest friends. Now, both were dead.

Hughes' voice was bitter as he replied, "If there were, Mclean and I would still be there."

Hughes' mention of Mclean reminded Brad that everyone among them had lost friends. It was a shared loss. He noticed two zombies coming toward them. "We had better go back before we draw too much attention."

Liz met him as he entered the garage. The broad smile she lavished upon him warmed his heart. The smile vanished as she noticed they had brought back nothing with them.

"No supplies?" she asked.

"Not a crumb," Hughes answered. He went directly to the huge Russian tractor, where he had been spending most of this time. Wilkie joined him.

"There's nothing left of the base, just ashes," Brad told her.

He could tell that his news jolted her, but she recovered quickly. "We'll make do with what we have."

"I'm going to go warm up," Bain said, rubbing his hands together.

To provide sufficient space for all the survivors, they had sealed off a small corner of the garage with plastic sheeting as a living area, reducing the need to heat the entire garage. The two kerosene heaters kept the space toasty and warm. Bain pushed through the plastic barrier and disappeared inside. The space was tight and confining, but not as confining as the snow tractors would be on the trip. Piles of blankets on the floor, sleeping bags, and a few cots provided places to sleep. Meals were as lavish as they could make them to help replenish the strength of the weak. To conserve the bottled water for the trip, they melted ice and snow for drinking and washing. Melted ice didn't taste as good as the water supplied by the base's water plant, but without power, the plant was useless, and without waste heat from the generators, the well was froze solid. An unheated, makeshift portable latrine provided for their sanitary needs – uncomfortable but functional.

The health and overall condition of most of the survivors had improved steadily with an improved diet and a sense of security. They were consuming precious food and fuel at an alarming rate, but the half-starved survivors needed calories to replace lost muscle mass during their confinement. The human body burns more calories in cold climates, up to four-thousand per day just to stay warm. Every pound of food, every gallon of fuel used for heating improved their health, but reduced their chances of reaching McMurdo alive.

"We can't delay any longer," Brad said. "We have to try for McMurdo." He nodded his head toward the people inside the shelter. "Can they make it?"

Her hesitation concerned him. He trusted her medical opinion but hoped that she didn't err on the side of too much concern for her patients. She delivered her assessment cautiously.

"Most of them can. A few … I'm not sure. Must we leave so soon? A few more days …"

Brad cut her off. He understood her reluctance, but they had to consider the welfare of the entire group, not just a few. "We don't have a few more days. Each day depletes our supplies just that much more. We don't know what we'll find at McMurdo. I don't want to resort to eating seals like Shackleton's *Endurance* crew on Elephant Island to stay alive. Start getting them ready to leave."

She nodded and left. He hated to be harsh with her. He loved her. He knew that now. Their relationship had turned a corner in the last few days, not sexually consummated in the crowded shelter, but a mental and spiritual joining of their two kindred souls. They needed each other. She relied on his strength, and he relied on her humanity. Now was the time for strength.

He joined Hughes and Wilkie as they worked on the Kharkovchanka. The big Russian tractor could hold all of them, but by using both Sno-Cats, they would reduce crowding. It was an unspoken thought among them that by dividing the survivors among the three vehicles on the journey, they tripled the chances that at least some would get through. The trek would be treacherous, especially at night. With no functioning GPS, the stars and landmarks would be their only means of navigation just as the early sailing ships had reached Antarctica in the early 1800's.

"Will it make it?" he asked Hughes.

Hughes emerged from beneath the tractor with grease smearing his face. He dropped a large wrench into a toolbox and wiped his face and hands with a rag.

"It's a twenty-five-year-old piece of shit, but it'll make it." He reached out and patted the Kharkovchanka's side. "The Russian's made these babies to last. It drinks diesel like a sponge and drives like a barge, but it can handle anything thrown at it."

"What about the Sno-Cats?"

"They're ready to go, but only four of us have any real experience driving – DeSousa, Wilkie, Deen, and myself."

"I can handle a snowmobile."

Hughes smiled. "That's like the difference between a canoe and an aircraft carrier."

"You can give me lessons along the way."

Hughes nodded. "If you're game." He looked at Brad, noticed the hardness in his face, and smiled. "So, when are we leaving?"

"Soon. We can't waste any more time."

"We're going to need more fuel for the journey." He waved a hand at the drums along the wall. "Most of these are oil or hydraulic fluid."

"Where's the diesel?"

Hughes pointed outside. "Out there. With the zombies."

* * * *

An hour later, Brad and Hughes left on one of the snowmobiles pulling a sledge. A second vehicle carried Leonard Morgan and Lars Hendrickson, who had agreed to join them, while Wilkie and Lester loaded supplies onto the Russian tractor and the Sno-Cats. Morgan, at sixty-one, was older than most of the over-winterers, but as an avid hiker and a legendary health-food guru, his age was no hindrance. He had come to the Antarctic to test his pet theories on caloric content. Hendrickson, a botanist, was out of his element on the ice but he had grown weary of the confines of the garage shelter. Only Hughes and Brad carried weapons, as neither of the others professed any competency with firearms.

They located the storage container containing fuel drums, broke the lock and shoveled away three feet of blown snow that blocked the doors. The drums of JP-8 diesel were marked clearly. They managed to load eight drums onto the sledge before the first zombie appeared. Hughes shot it, but the sound drew more of the creatures.

"We need to secure these drum s on the sledge," Brad told them.

Morgan grabbed a strap and began to wrap it around the drums. Hendrickson helped, but he focused most of his attention on searching the area for zombies.

"Hurry," Brad urged.

Reluctantly, Hendrickson took one end of the strap and held it in place as Brad began to tighten it. At the sound of a second shot from Hughes, Hendrickson dropped the strap and backed quickly away from the sledge, staring back toward the base.

"Come back, you fool!" Morgan called out. "We need you."

Hughes appeared from around the side of the container. "You'd better hurry. There are six more of them."

This was all Hendrickson needed to hear. He made a guttural sound deep in his throat and ran toward the second snowmobile. Hughes took up the slack of the strap as Brad secured the drums. The sound of the snowmobile cranking surprised them all. Hendrickson wasn't waiting on anyone. He was saving himself first. Hughes and Morgan jumped on the vehicle pulling the sledge, while Brad grabbed his rifle and hopped onto the sledge on top of the fuel drums. The six zombies were getting too close. He dropped one with a shot to the head, but missed the second as the sledge jerked when Hughes gunned the engine. Laden with the heavy drums, the zombies were catching up to them quickly.

Hendrickson, ahead of them but unfamiliar with the snowmobile, turned too sharply and flipped it. He tumbled away from it and lay there stunned. Hughes pulled alongside the wrecked snowmobile and yelled at Hendrickson.

"Get on!"

Hendrickson, either ashamed of his actions or frightened by the rifle in Brad's hands, rose to his feet and began limping away from them. As Brad climbed down from the drums to go help Hendrickson, the sledge began moving.

"Wait!" he yelled to Hughes.

"No," Hughes answered and continued toward the base.

Brad felt pity for the frightened and confused Hendrickson, but he had abandoned them. Now they had to abandon him. When

Hendrickson noticed he was going in the wrong direction, he turned and began to retrace his steps, but with his injuries, he was too slow. The zombies caught him before he reached the snowmobile. The creatures dragged him to the snow and began tearing at his body with teeth and hands. Hendrickson's screams lasted almost a full minute before thankfully, the wind and the roar of the snowmobile muffled them.

Back in the safety of the garage, Brad leaped off the sledge to confront Hughes. "You could have waited."

"We all risked our lives for that diesel. We need it to reach McMurdo. Hendrickson made a poor decision. In the Antarctic, poor decisions kill."

As Hughes turned to walk away, Brad, not satisfied with Hughes' explanation, grabbed him by the elbow and spun him around. "We could have shot the zombies."

Hughes's expression took a darker side. His lips tightened and his nostrils flared. He slapped away Brad's hand and growled, "Leaving was your decision. Do you want to risk everyone's lives for one stupid, frightened man?"

"So you think leaving for McMurdo is my poor decision."

"I would go. Bringing everyone is your decision. We'll have to wait and see if it was a poor one." The anger left Hughes' face. "I have to fuel the tractors."

This time, Brad let him go. His argument wasn't with Hughes; it was with himself. Hughes was a survivor and he might be right. Brad knew enough about battlefield triage to know that sometimes you had to ignore those who couldn't make it to concentrate on those who could. Hendrickson had panicked and it had cost him his life. In his gut, Brad knew that before they reached safety, more would die. It didn't make things any easier to stomach. To vent his anger, he kicked an empty can. It flew through the air and bounced off the wall, rattling across the floor to a spinning stop. He felt no better.

14

Sept. 7, Amundsen-Scott Base, Antarctica

Liz ignored the noisy arguments around her as she helped Vince Singleterry, the man she had helped escape from the fire, into the rear of one of the Sno-Cats. Singleterry was still pale and weak. She suspected that he suffered from more than simple malnourishment, perhaps a weak heart, but she had no equipment with which to verify her diagnosis. Even her stethoscope had been lost in the fire. She should have ridden with Singleterry, but as she waited for Brad, someone pushed in ahead of her. She was disappointed to see Brad climb into a Sno-Cat beside Hughes without coming to her before leaving. He had been unnaturally quiet since his return with the diesel fuel, but she attributed his disposition to the loss of Hendrickson. He had confided that he and Hughes had words but didn't elaborate.

She brushed her hair away from her eyes, dismayed by its condition. It was filthy, hung limply and lifeless, and clung to her scalp. The heat of the fire had singed a few stray strands of hair. They had no water to spare for washing. Looking at the dirty faces of those around her, she imagined her face looked no better. She picked up a handful of snow, rubbed it in her face, and then wiped it away with her sleeve. It might not improve her looks, but the cold snow invigorated her. She walked dejectedly to the Kharkovchanka alone.

The interior of the Russian vehicle was toasty and warm, a stark contrast to the chilly garage with the doors flung wide open. The wind had picked up and whipped into the building relentlessly, as if it wished to scour the remaining traces of mankind from the ice. She removed her heavy parka and sat back on one of the bunks to catch her breath after the mad dash to load everyone. The tractor jerked as it moved forward. DeSousa was wasting no time leaving.

Through the round, ice-rimmed window of the tractor, she gazed at the ruins that had been her home for two years. Barely visible through the blowing snow, the remnants of Pod B had collapsed into a depression in the ice gouged by the intense heat. Only its roof protruded from its icy grave. Pod A, her office, her home, sloped some thirty degrees toward its gutted twin. Flames, rekindled by the wind, licked the canted roof through broken windows. The aptly named Beer Can lay on its side like a discarded, crushed beverage container. Flames reached skyward through cracks in the ice from the underground power plant, washing the death scene with a macabre orange-crimson glow that reminded her of a portrait of hell. She watched the flickering inferno until it disappeared behind the tractor as DeSousa nosed the chunky, thirty-foot-Kharkovchanka north toward McMurdo and safety.

The storm grew in fury as the small caravan of snow tractors slowly trekked north across the frozen wastes of Watson Escarpment toward McMurdo. It seemed odd to describe their direction as north, since they were moving almost perpendicular to their intended destination, but at the South Pole, all compasses pointed north. Winds off the ice sheet unhampered by any obstacle in its path reached speeds of sixty miles per hour, reducing visibility to near zero. The *katabatic* winds were a savage, hungry, howling beast seeking to obliterate them from its domain. Later, as they neared the coast, the winds would increase in strength as they fell from the two-mile-high frozen escarpment to sea level.

The snow tractors crawled along the wind-swept remnants of the snow road without stop for almost twenty hours carrying the remaining fourteen survivors of the forty-eight who had inhabited Amundsen-Scott Base, all of them weary, worried and disheartened. They approached the edge of the Transantarctic Range, a 2100-mile-long mountain range bisecting Antarctica with concern. Ahead, lay Leverett Glacier, a fifty-mile-long river of ice, four miles wide, their route down to the Ross Ice Shelf. The terrain became rougher with ten-foot-high *sastrugi* running like rows of sand dunes across their path. Rocky *nunataks* protruded through the ice and snow, the tips of solitary mountain peaks thousands of feet high, their roots buried in the bedrock of the continent. In such low visibility, any mistake could plunge the tractors into an ice crevasse or send them crashing into a wall of solid granite. Finally, exhausted and half-blinded by the near-whiteout conditions, DeSousa called a halt. He radioed the other two tractors to declare his intention.

The trio of vehicles parked close together in a triangle, providing a barrier against the raging wind through which the weary occupants could move safely from one vehicle to another, redistributing the uneven loads entailed by their hasty departure. Liz had slept fitfully in a series of short naps during the journey, jostled by the bouncing of the heavy tracked vehicle. Meals had been cold – bread, cheese, and canned fruit, served with hot tea brewed in a Russian electric percolator – and consumed in silence. No one spoke of the recent ordeal or of their expectations. A dark lethargy had settled upon the reticent riders, a combination of elation at escaping the destruction of the base and of guilt for being one of the few survivors. They had each left behind too many friends and colleagues. No one knew how many had succumbed to the zombie virus, or how many had found a secure place to hide only to perish in the fire or in its freezing aftermath. The Angel of Death hovered above all of them on silent wings. Each cough, each nervous twitch, produced a wave of unconscious recoil flowing through the crowd, subsiding only when the hapless offender proved he or she was not falling prey to the zombie virus.

Liz was overjoyed when Brad entered the Kharkovchanka. She was less enthused by the blast of frigid wind that accompanied him through the hermetically sealed door that separated the cab from the rest of the vehicle. His smile when he saw her thrilled her far more than she expected. She ran up to him and hugged him, surprising him at first, but he quickly responded by wrapping his arms around her. For that few seconds, she felt safe.

"I'm beat," he said, as he pulled away.

She walked him to one of the bunks. "Sleep here for a while. How long are we stopping?"

"A few hours anyway. We need to refuel."

"What then?"

"Hughes, Deen, and I are going ahead a ways to check the road."

She didn't know Brad as well as she wished, but she could tell that he was lying. "How far ahead?"

He grinned and scratched his head. "Well, we want to see what's happening at McMurdo before traipsing in as a group."

She sensed an underlying current of doubt in his voice. "You're afraid everyone's dead, aren't you?"

Brad threw back his hood and sat on the edge of the bed. "There were a couple of hundred people at McMurdo. If they started turning zombie ..."

He didn't have to explain further. They had been unable to control thirty of the creatures. If a significant portion of the winter crew at McMurdo had become zombies running rampant, it would have been a massacre. She tried to curb her imagination, as her mind began to fill in the gory details. She could almost hear the screams of anguish and the pleas for help as friend attacked friend in a bloody, one-sided fight for survival. The survivors would have done as they had done – huddled alone or in small groups awaiting rescue or maybe they suspected that no rescue was coming and attempted to leave.

As she sat down beside Brad, her hand sought his. "I don't want to die, not here in this frozen wasteland." She looked into his tired face, her face own pleading with him. "Don't go."

His grip on her hand tightened. "I have to go. I started this whole thing."

She looked away, not letting him see the tears she blinked away. Then she nodded. She knew she couldn't hold him back. "You're right. Get some sleep now."

She released his hand reluctantly. He removed his parka, wadded it into a pillow, and stretched out on the bed. Within minutes, he was snoring softly.

Ten minutes later, the door of the Kharkovchanka flew open again. This time she paid no attention to the cold air. A man stuck his head in and yelled, "Doctor Strong! Someone is turning zombie."

\* \* \* \*

113

It was a false alarm. In their fright, the people in the Sno-Cat had mistaken the coughing and choking of Singleterry as symptoms of the zombie disease. It was a heart attack. Weakened by his self-imposed starvation and by the trials of the evacuation, his heart had simply given out. As he lay across the rear seat, pale and gasping for breath, his eyes never left her face, as if he was fixing her features as an anchor to keep the last wisps of his soul from breaking the bonds of his fragile flesh. As she tried in vain to massage life back into his failing heart, the other passengers stood around outside in the freezing cold of the storm rather than risk being in the same space with him. She found she could bear them no ill will. They were simply frightened. When his heart finally succumbed, she sat back and wept, even though she hardly knew him. His death was just one more stain on her too-bloody hands. Even if she dismissed the other deaths as inevitable, unavoidable, she should have been able to save him. She had saved others before under similar circumstances. What she feared most was that in some dark recess in the back of her mind, she had asked herself, "*Why bother?*" What sort of future did he have, did any of them have? If no rescue awaited them at McMurdo, they had no way off the ice-bound continent, and it was unlikely that anyone would come to rescue them even when the seas thawed. Eventually, their supplies would run out – their food, their fuel. They would face being marooned on the most inhospitable place on Earth. Without rescue, their chances of survival were dismally small.

After she had sobbed out her grief, she cajoled two men into removing Singleterry's body from the tractor. They hacked out a shallow depression in the ice with ice picks, and then without ceremony, placed him in the ice and covered him with snow. It was a pitiful end for any human being. She consoled herself with the fact that in ten thousand years, his perfectly preserved body would wind its way to the sea to feed the fish. She couldn't shake off the depressing feeling that perhaps his fate was better than theirs was.

* * * *

With just a few words of departure to Liz and with pangs of regret at leaving her, Brad joined Hughes and Deen in the Sno-Cat. The storm was still raging. Travelling in the dark during a storm would have been a prelude to disaster at any other time, but they had no choice. Singleterry's death had rattled people badly. One more such alarm, false or not, would drive them beyond the limit of their nerves. He didn't want people wandering alone on the ice. It would mean a sentence of certain death.

Brad had noticed the depth of Liz's anguish but could do nothing about it. The needs of the group came before her need or his. Hughes had been right about that. She was strong enough to snap out of the depression into which she had fallen. They all faced difficult choices. As a physician, she was used to making such calls. The others looked to her for guidance. He was certain her instincts for helping others would take over eventually. He had to fight off the fog of doubt that threatened his mind. All his senses tingled, but he could pinpoint no specific danger, just a vague sense of dread.

Because of his intimate knowledge of the snow road, Deen drove the Sno-Cat, but Brad noticed the unease with which he stared into the blinding snow and darkness.

"Any problem?" he asked.

Deen's grin didn't alleviate Brad's apprehension. "It's just a lot harder than it was this summer. I can't see as far as I could piss."

Brad glanced at the speedometer – twenty miles per hour. "Then maybe you had better slow down."

Deen waved his hand toward the windscreen. "There's nothing out there for miles. It's when we reach the edge of the glacier that I'll need to take it easy."

On his flight to Amundsen-Scott, Leverett Glacier had looked like a highway made of ice, spilling the contents of the Antarctic Plateau into the Ross Ice Shelf. He knew that close up it would be broken pressure ridges of ice thrusting like daggers into the air, crevasse that might reach hundreds of feet deep into the surrounding ice, and snow bridges that could collapse beneath them. Moving at five miles per hour in the twenty-four-hour daylight, the supply convoy had encountered no such difficulties, but they would be driving in total darkness, trying to find what few flags still marked the road. Without a functioning GPS satellite feed, they would depend upon Deen's ability to locate a few familiar landmarks. Brad hoped Deen was up to the challenge.

Hughes showed no concern. He reclined in the rear seat softly humming to himself. Brad listened closely and recognized the song – *Don't Fear the Reaper* by Blue Oyster Cult. His eyes locked onto Brad's, and he smiled.

"You're loving this, aren't you," Brad shot at him, annoyed by his composure.

"I'm resigned to the journey. There's a difference. If a problem arises that we can deal with, we will. If we can't …" He shrugged.

"You sound like Charles Lester."

"Lester has the right attitude. Worrying solves nothing. The worst that can happen is that we fall into an ice chasm. The next worst is that we get lost. If so, we just head for Mt. Erebus. We'll find McMurdo."

"I wish I could be as calm."

"Sometimes it helps others just to look calm."

Brad didn't know if he should take Hughes' remark as a slight or an admission that Hughes was more worried than he appeared. Their earlier row after Hendrickson's death had increased the tension between them, but it had not yet arisen to the level of open confrontation. In spite of Hughes' cold demeanor, Brad respected his knowledge and experience. They would depend on Hughes over the coming weeks. Deen continued driving for several more hours before asking Hughes to take over, but Deen swapped seats with Brad, alert and carefully observing the landscape through the snow. Finally, the peaks of the Harold Byrd Mountains and Tapley Mountains through which the Everett Glacier flowed showed their peaks in the distance. At times, Hughes reduced their speed to less than ten miles per hour as he picked a safe path between jagged pressure ridges, any of which could have ripped a hole in the Sno-Cat's oil pan, stranding them in the frozen waste.

The dark and light banding of the glacier, a result of rocks relentlessly ground from the surrounding mountains and picked up and carried by the ice, was less visible from close up. Each separate river of ice flowed at a different speed. The boundaries where they met became tortured zones of fractured ice. At times, deep crevasses yawned just feet from the rubber treads of the Sno-Cat. Near the lower end of the glacier, where it spilled into the frozen sea, the banding became wider and the fractures more numerous.

On the third day of their journey, as Brad regarded with trepidation one chasm that he considered a trifle too close, the vehicle suddenly lurched and began to tilt toward the crevasse. He grabbed the edge of the seat and hung on as Hughes cursed from the driver's seat of the vehicle.

"What's wrong?" he asked.

"Ice quake. A piece of the wall broke away beneath us."

At first, Brad thought that Hughes was rocking the Sno-Cat forward and backwards in an attempt to dislodge it. He quickly realized the tractor was not the only thing in motion. Rills of ice shattered and toppled. The ground rose and fell in graceful waves. The crevasse upon which they were perched split wider as the far edge broke away with the sound of dried twigs snapping and tumbled into the Stygian depths. Brad closed his eyes and waited for the final lurch that would send them plunging over the edge to their deaths. After several breathless seconds, the trembling stopped. They were still alive, but still trapped.

Hughes gunned the engine. Three of the treads tossed plumes of ice and snow into the air as the fourth spun uselessly. The Sno-Cat didn't budge from its precarious perch. In fact, the tractor tilted even farther toward the precipice.

Deen began donning his anorak and heavy mittens, and then looked at Brad. "I'll need some help. We'll have to shove something under the right rear tread to gain some traction."

Brad didn't hesitate. Without the tractor, they would die. He began dressing for outside. "What can we use?"

"There should be some aluminum ladders secured to the back of the tractor. They might be enough. If we lay them across the crevasse, the Sno-Cat might be able to crawl along one to solid ground."

"If they aren't?" he asked, knowing he would not like the answer.

"If we keep rocking it, it's going to slide in. We'll be on foot."

Brad understood the consequences of that. They could never make it to McMurdo on foot and might never find the other vehicles if they tried to backtrack. Outside, staring into the depths of the crevasse, he was glad it hadn't suddenly opened up beneath them. The seemingly bottomless split in the ice was thirty feet long and eleven feet wide, easily large enough to swallow the Sno-Cat. Working carefully along the brittle edge of the yawning chasm, they placed the ladders just at the front edge of the right rear tread. The two extension ladders were each just twelve feet in length. Their legs barely clung to the edges of the chasm. If they slipped into the crevasse, they would have nothing with which to free the vehicle.

Satisfied that the ladder placement was correct, Deen opened the cab door. "Don't gun it," he cautioned Hughes. "Just move forward onto the ladders."

The Sno-Cat inched forward. One of the ladders slipped slightly.

"Stop!" Deen yelled.

He jumped down from the tractor and began rummaging through a storage bin, where he found a bag of pitons used for ice climbing. Using a hammer, he carefully drove several of the metal pitons into the ice behind the ladders. Then, to Brad's amazement, he secured a nylon climbing rope to one of the ladders, and then tied the rope around his waist.

Seeing Brad's consternation, he said, "If we lose the ladders, we die."

Deen lay on the ice, his head just inches from the tractor tread as he said, "Okay, try it again." If the tractor slewed sideways, it would crush him.

Brad stood well back and watched as Hughes inched the Sno-Cat onto the aluminum ladder. He glanced through the open door at Hughes. From the slight smile on Hughes' face, he was certain that Hughes was enjoying himself. Brad felt like throwing up. He admired Hughes' guts, but wondered at the temperament of a man who faced death with such glee. He had always hoped that he could face death without fear, but had never considered tempting death for a thrill. During his years hunting in the frigid North Dakota winters, he had always travelled prepared for emergencies. The closest he had come was when a bear had wrecked his camp and had eaten his food. Even days away from his vehicle, he had not felt as much concern as he did now. Then, he had broken the ice on a river and caught fish to survive the long trek back to his jeep. Here, the danger was much more intimate.

The ladder shuddered and bowed as it accepted the weight of the tractor. The pitons bent as the movement of the tread pressed the ladder against them, but the right rear tread clambered atop the first ladder. With the additional support, the tractor moved forward but still dangled precariously over the precipice. Brad held his breath as the tread edged toward solid ice. Now, both ladders supported it. Suddenly, two of the pitons popped free of the ice. The first ladder slipped, plunging into the chasm. The second, roped ladder shifted, sliding toward the edge. Deen leaped backwards, dug his heels into the ice, and pulled on the rope with all his strength. For a few seconds, it appeared that Deen was supporting the entire weight of the tractor. Then, the errant tread was on solid ice and the tractor shot forward. Brad relaxed the fist he had kept clenched throughout the entire ordeal and exhaled.

As Deen lay sprawled on the ice, breathing hard from his exertions, Brad walked over to help him to his feet. To his horror, the second ladder broke free and tumbled into the crevasse. The rope snapped taut around Deen's waist. Deen grasped the rope with both hands and held on, but the momentum of the heavy ladder yanked him forward across the slippery ice. His upper body disappeared from view. Brad had no time to think. He leaped into the air and grabbed Deen's feet just as they slid over the edge. Now, he was holding the full weight of both Deen and the ladder. His arms felt as if being pulled from his shoulder sockets, but he couldn't let go. If he did, Deen would die. His body began to slide forward. He tried to dig the toes of his boots into the ice for purchase, but he was inching inexorably forward to his death.

Hands gripped his ankles.

"Got you," Hughes yelled.

He crawled over Brad's body until he could reach Deen's feet. Together, they tried to pull Deen up, but the ladder was too heavy, weighting him down.

"Cut the ladder free," Hughes called.

"We can't lose the ladder," Deen replied. "We might need it."

"Lose the ladder!" Hughes snapped.

Brad felt Deen wriggling beneath him. Suddenly, the great weight lessened. The ladder rattled as it banged against the side of the crevasse on its plunge into the depth of the chasm. They pulled Deen back onto the ice.

As the three of them lay there fighting for breath in the dry, thin air, Deen gasped, "Don't ever let me do something that stupid again."

15

Sept. 14, Ross Ice Shelf, Antarctica

Once safely off the glacier and onto the relatively flat surface of the Ross Ice Shelf, travelling became easier. The wind didn't let up, but visibility improved. While the others took turns driving, Brad handled the cooking of food on a small stove and made sure there was plenty of hot chocolate and coffee available. During the descent of the glacier, neither of his companions offered him the opportunity to drive, for which he was extremely grateful. His skill at driving the Sno-Cat was limited, and he had no great desire to drive it over an ice cliff or into another crevasse. He was satisfied being a passenger.

In spite of the tedium of the long hours in the vehicle and the lack of conversation as each man kept his private thoughts of what they might find to himself, the number of miles behind them slowly grew larger than the miles ahead of them. Even so, the journey took seven weary days. Finally, they neared their destination.

Jutting above the horizon of frozen ice, the twelve-thousand-foot cone of volcanic Mt. Erebus was visible even in the darkness. A thick, black column of smoke billowed from the mouth of the volcano like a chimney spewing from lakes of fire in the bowels of hell. Streaks of lightning from static discharge highlighted the ash cloud. The volcano's ominous rumbling was audible above the roar of the diesel engine. In the daylight, it would have been an awesome spectacle. At night, it was spectacularly frightening. McMurdo Base shared Ross Island with Mt. Erebus. At a distance of less than seventy miles from the raging volcano, Brad wondered what the personnel at the base were experiencing as the earth erupted and the ground trembled. *If any were still alive,* he reminded himself.

They tried the radio, but got no reply. The radio had been useless for the last five days. They couldn't reach any of the other vehicles. Several miles from the base, Hughes brought the Sno-Cat to a halt and killed the engine. The sudden silence and lack of motion after so many days with the diesel engine roaring in the background was unsettling. The low rumble of the volcano quickly filtered through the silence reminding them of the dangers they faced.

"We should walk in from here," he announced.

"No closer?" Brad asked. The thought of leaving the Sno-Cat behind concerned him. In spite of the claustrophobic confines of the vehicle, it had become a womb protecting him from the realities of the world outside. Facing them might be more than he could bear.

"The noise might attract unwelcome visitors," Hughes explained, "and any one left alive might be trigger happy."

Realizing that Hughes was right, Brad sighed and began donning his anorak and mittens. He shoved his heavy gloves in his pockets. He couldn't pull the trigger of the rifle wearing them, and he wanted to be ready if they confronted any zombies. Carrying only their weapons – the two .308 Winchesters and the Russian AK-47 – they began their hike across the ice. Brad felt exposed on the open ice after so many days inside the Sno-Cat. He trod carefully, despite the fact that the ice beneath his feet was nearly eight-hundred-feet thick. It didn't allay his fear of the two-thousand feet of ice-cold water beneath it. The darkness could hold a thousand zombies. He strained his eyes to pierce the surrounding gloom.

They approached the base with caution. No lights were showing, but that didn't mean that there were no survivors. However, it was not a good sign. With no generators running, the base had no source of heat other than wood-burning stoves. The wind blew toward them bringing a cloud of choking ash from the volcano. The astringent smell was strong enough to mask but not completely conceal the stale odor of burnt wood. Any fires at the base were long dead.

"It looks dead," Deen said, voicing Brad's thoughts.

"Not everything dead is harmless," Hughes warned. "Keep an eye out."

It was immediately obvious that no ships were in port, but Brad knew there would not be. The winter ice was too thick for even the mightiest icebreaker. Any rescue for survivors would have been by air.

Trying to keep his nervousness from his voice, he asked Hughes, "Do you see any planes?"

"McMurdo has three runways – Pegasus, Williams Field, and Sea Ice. Pegasus is near Black Island – too far away to see. Williams Field is on the other side of the island. If there are any planes, they would be there."

The dark, volcanic rock and dirt of the island jutting from the surrounding ice with the volcanic plume of Mt. Erebus reminded Brad of a whale breaching in the surf, only this whale was not friendly, and the three of them were not on a pleasant whale watch in peaceful San Diego Bay. They climbed the low rise of the rocky beach toward the scattered collection of almost a hundred buildings that comprised McMurdo Base. Observation Hill towered over the small city. The row of summer dorms would be empty, as would many of the buildings. Capable of accommodating twenty-five hundred or more summer visitors, only about two hundred maintenance staff remained in McMurdo during the winter months. Brad had spent many hours in the Albert P. Crary Science and Engineering Center, named for the first man to set foot on both the North and South Poles. He tried to remember the name of the astronomer from Harvard who had briefed him on the facilities at Amundsen-Scott – *Hendricks; yeah that's it, a short, terse man with a rotund belly and an insufferable braying laugh. And there was Andrea Coleman, the woman who had given the winter survival lecture.* He wondered if either was still alive.

"I see something," Deen hissed between clenched teeth.

Brad looked in the direction Deen was pointing and saw two figures moving, barely visible in the moonlight. "Are they human?" he whispered.

"Can't tell."

"Do we shoot or say hello?" he asked Hughes.

Instead of answering, Hughes clicked on his flashlight and played it over the two figures – zombies. One had suffered horrible burns on its upper body, its facial features unrecognizable. The other was a naked older woman, her breasts crisscrossed by black lines. The creatures focused on the light and began moving toward them. Brad raised his rifle to fire.

"No, don't," Hughes said. "A shot will bring others." He pointed toward a row of buildings – the summer dorms. "Let's head there. Maybe we can lose them inside."

They began to trot toward the dorms and reached the first one well ahead of the zombies. The first door they tried was bolted. As Hughes pushed at the door with his shoulder, Brad glanced back over his. The zombies moved slowly but remained eagerly intent upon their prey. Hughes, too, noticed their approach. He backed up two paces and lunged into the door. With a loud crash, the doorjamb shattered and the door flew open. The room was dark, cold, and empty. No one had been inside since the last visitors left in March. They passed through the dorm to the opposite door and exited quietly, leaving the pursuing zombies behind them, still searching for their lost prey.

The odor of burnt wood permeating the base had not come from fires built for warmth. Many of the buildings were now blackened skeletons. McMurdo had suffered the worst calamity a polar base could endure other than zombies – a fire. Whether started accidently in an effort to keep warm, or as protection against zombies, the wind had whipped the fire into an uncontrollable inferno, sweeping through the base, leaping from building to building like a living creature seeking to quench its hunger on ash and misery. The destruction of Amundsen-Scott paled in comparison. More than half the buildings showed some signs of damage.

"There's nothing here." Deen's quivering voice betrayed his bitter disappointment. He collapsed on an overturned oil drum, sitting and staring at the wreckage. "We came all this way for nothing. Nothing."

"Any C-130's would come in from Christchurch," Hughes said. "They wouldn't be here. They would be on the runway out on the ice."

Deen raised his voice until he was shouting. "It means they're gone, or dead. No one's coming."

Brad fought to keep his own disappointment under control. He wasn't ready to give up so easily. "Maybe the radio's working. Maybe we can contact someone."

Deen glared at him. "Contact who – the Navy? No ships are coming. The National Science Foundation – they're dead. Everyone's dead. We're stuck here in this frozen white hell. We're going to die here." Hughes placed a hand on Deen's shoulder but Deen shrugged it off. "Leave me alone," he snapped. "Both of you leave me the hell alone."

Hughes walked over to Brad. Speaking softly, he said, "We have to check out the buildings. The others will be here in a day or so. We have to find a secure place to hold up, gather supplies. We have to try to survive."

Brad nodded. Hughes was right. They couldn't give up hope. Doing something, anything, would keep them focused. Liz was coming. When she arrived, things would be better. Together, they could manage.

"Okay." He glanced at Deen, quietly muttering to himself and kicking at the volcanic ash with the toe of his boot. "We can't leave him here."

"He'll be all right. He has to get this out of his system. He's a survivor. He'll come around."

Brad hoped that Hughes was right. They needed everyone if they had any chance of surviving until either help arrived or they discovered a means of leaving Antarctica.

"The science building looked intact. Maybe … maybe Liz can figure something out, a cure or a vaccine."

"Maybe." Hughes' narrowed eyes and tightly set jaw contradicted his words, but Brad saw no advantage in confronting him over it.

His own conviction was largely due to hope rather than faith. He had never been a man of faith, deriving his order of the universe in the stars he observed through his telescope more willingly than in a deity he could not. Science was not a catch-all, could not provide all the answers, but it did allow a more thorough questioning of the questions that mattered. If man's science had created the zombie virus, then science could defeat it. However, if it was due to an act of nature, all bets were off. By some cosmic spin of the dice, mankind had rolled snake eyes and was anteing up to the gods of chance.

Rather than leave Deen alone in his misery and at the mercy of a possible zombie attack, the two explored the nearby buildings to keep an eye on him. An intact garage held several snowmobiles, three vans, and a snow tractor, but nothing with more range than their own vehicle. They quickly discovered the fates of many of the crew at McMurdo. Eight partially consumed bodies and dozens of bullet-riddled zombies lay scattered around the outside of a supply building. Moving carefully in case any survivors mistook them for zombies and shot first, the entered the building. Inside, they found only carnage, but not one inflicted by zombies. Five bodies, three men and two women, lay on the floor. Three of them looked as if they had simply lain down to die. They rested in a solemn row, hands folded over their chests, their wrists slit. Pools of blood surrounded them and stained their clothing. The last two had been shot, a murder-suicide, or a double suicide. There was no way of determining which. The sight dismayed Brad more than Shelia Meyer's suicide had. There, a distraught lover had ended her life. Here, five people had agreed to a group suicide. They had lost all hope and had given in to their darkest urges.

Hughes walked around the room examining the bodies, and then the revolver beside one of the bodies. He shoved it into his coat pocket and left the building without saying a word. His stony face betrayed no emotion. Brad followed him outside and confronted him.

"Say it," he demanded.

Hughes shook his head while staring at the ground. "They were weak. I'm not." He looked up at Brad. "You're not."

Brad's anger drove his words. "Maybe they were surrounded, out of ammunition, out of food. Maybe they were weak, but that's no reason to dismiss them so easily."

"If zombies were around, they would be nothing but bones." He slapped the pocket with the revolver. "There were two bullets left in the pistol. They could have killed four zombies. Instead, they gave up hope, not just of rescue, but also of surviving. I have to dismiss them. They're dead."

"They're still people."

Hughes kicked one of the zombie corpses outside the building, a man wearing green coveralls and a cap that read Bell, one of the helicopter pilots. "They're corpses just like this poor sod." He swung on Brad. Brad, thinking Hughes was going to strike out, backed up two paces and held out a hand, but Hughes only continued. "We have to concentrate on the living. Anyone who gives up and wants to die should die, or they'll drag down the others. This is no time for weakness, Niles. Intelligence or physical strength isn't much use now. Strength of character will determine who survives and who doesn't."

Brad wanted to argue, to refute Hughes' words, but deep down inside, he knew Hughes was right. Instead, he said, "It doesn't matter. We need everyone."

Hughes nodded. "For now. Later ..." He shrugged his shoulders.

The next building was empty, but a dismembered corpse lay blocking the rear door, which swung ajar in the wind, producing a loud squeaking noise. A five-gallon fuel can lay inches from the man's outstretched hand. Brad picked up the fuel can.

"It's full," he said to Hughes.

Glancing out the rear of the building, he spotted a red twin-engine DeHavilland Otter tied down and covered by a tarp against the volcanic ash. Boxes of supplies covered by a fine layer of ash sat on the ground beside the open cargo hatch. At the sight of the undamaged plane, Brad's hopes inched upward.

Elated, he yelled, "It's an Otter," to Hughes and ran to check out the plane. The DeHavilland was in good condition. The tires were inflated, and a quick check of the cockpit showed that the battery was charged. A pistol lay in the pilot's seat. It looked as though the dead man had been loading and refueling the Otter when zombies attacked him. *So close*, Brad thought as he pocketed the pistol, a Smith and Wesson .38 caliber revolver. With a range of only about five-hundred miles, he wasn't sure where the man thought the plane could carry him so that he could escape in the small aircraft, but Brad admired his gumption.

Hughes dashed his hopes. "Even if we had somewhere to go, it wouldn't seat all of us. It holds eight people at most. Besides, why is it up here behind a garage instead of at one of the runways? It probably won't fly."

"It might. If so, it might get some of us to another base where we could find help for the others."

"And if there's no help there, or fuel for a return trip?"

"I don't know. It's … it's an option."

Hughes said nothing for a few seconds as he stared at the plane. The Kharkovchanka and the Sno-Cats were more valuable than the Otter, but Brad didn't want to dismiss the plane as readily as Hughes had. Finally, Hughes nodded.

"Okay, it's an option, but let's stay quiet about it for a while."

"Why?"

Hughes shrugged. "Someone else might want to climb in and take their chances as much as I do."

Brad stared at Hughes in wonder. Hughes' stolid demeanor was just a façade. He was just as frightened as everyone else was. Brad's respect for Hughes raised a couple of notches. He could trust a man who was as scared as he was but kept the fear from his face.

"Maybe it's a good thing neither of us can fly," he replied.

A grin broke across Hughes' face. "Come on. Let's find Deen and check out the science building."

Deen was waiting for them at the edge of the road. He held the AK-47 in his hands.

"I heard a noise," he said, jabbing the AK-47 toward the building in question. He began edging in that direction.

"Leave it," Brad said. "Don't look for trouble."

Deen's nervous smile worried Brad. "No trouble," Deen replied. "Maybe we should thin the herd a bit."

Deen's reference to the zombie 'herd' struck close to home. It had been too easy at Amundsen-Scott to forget that the creature's they had been killing were once friends and colleagues. Here, where most were strangers, it would take no effort to think of the walking dead as animals, dismissing their prior humanity. He wanted to chide Deen for his callousness. Instead, he said, "Any shots will only draw a crowd of them."

The trio carefully avoided any groups of zombies, threading an indirect path between buildings and through stacks of fuels drums and crates of supplies. Zombies haunted the base like ghosts in the night, mute and spectral, wandering the dirt streets. A few stood and stared toward the erupting volcano, as if the light show and the sound evoked some spark of memory. Others fought over scraps of flesh on frozen skeletons. Brad shuddered realizing that these bits of flesh might have belonged to acquaintances.

The A.P. Crary Science and Engineering Building was actually three separate units on different levels of a hillside connected by a covered walkway. Several different branches of science shared the labs – glaciology, climatology, meteorology, and marine biology. Brad had attended three lectures there while training for his over-winter at Amundsen-Scott. They entered from the lowest level, the Aquarium Pod, but first had to force the door open. The giant seawater tank was smashed and empty. A pool of ice filled with the frozen corpses of sea creatures formerly inhabiting the tank spread across the floor, partially blocking the entrance. The ice glittered diamond-like in their flashlight beams. The scene reminded Brad of a frozen fish market. Continuing upward, they reached the second level containing the Earth Sciences Pod and the Atmospheric Sciences Pod. The Earth Sciences Pod had suffered fire damage from an unattended boiler. A six-foot-wide gash in a section of outside wall had allowed volcanic ash and wind-blown snow to accumulate several inches deep. The Atmospherics Science Pod, which Brad thought would be of special interest to Bain and Shimoda, had fared better and was relatively intact.

In the uppermost level, the two-story Biology Pod and the Core Pod, which contained equipment rooms, stockrooms, offices, and the boiler room on the first floor and a library and a lounge on the second floor loft, were equally intact, but cold and dark. Entering the Core Pod first, the three checked each room carefully before closing them off. Upstairs, they found no bodies, but streaks of blood marked the floor. Not everyone had escaped unharmed. In the small lounge, a pot of coffee sat frozen on the table, surrounded by three partially filled coffee mugs. A sheaf of papers, a pair of dark-rimmed glasses, and half-eaten doughnut lay on the table beside one of the cups.

"They left in a hurry," Brad noted aloud.

Hughes picked up the doughnut and squeezed it between thumb and forefinger. It crumbled into a fine powder. "It's stale. This happened weeks ago."

That placed the time of the abandoned meal sometime after they had lost contact with McMurdo. "Then people were still alive after the outbreak. It happened slowly."

"Some were alive," Hughes agreed, "but it doesn't mean they are now."

Brad wouldn't give up. "Maybe they're still here somewhere hiding," he insisted. "We have to search for survivors."

"Our first priority is to secure a safe place for the others. Any survivors that have managed this long, will manage another day."

Brad's hopes shrank when they found the first bodies in the Biology Pod. Several zombies lay in a pile in front of the smashed door of the chemical storage room. All had been shot in the head.

"Somebody figured it out," Deen said with obvious admiration for the shooter or shooters in his voice.

Inside, frozen blood glittering like dark rubies covered the floor and two of the four walls. Chemicals, some frozen solid, lay in pools of shattered glass. More zombies, one whose face was half-eaten away by acid, lay on the floor amid bits and pieces of flesh, internal organs, and a few gnawed bones. Brad grimaced as he recognized a human femur. There were no whole corpses, but judging by the degree of carnage inside the room, he doubted anyone had made it out alive.

"They trapped themselves here," Deen said.

Brad detected a trace of condescension in Deen's voice, as if he had contempt for anyone so stupid as to seek refuge in a place with no windows or other exits. Brad didn't know the circumstances of their deaths, but decided to speak up in their behalf. "Maybe they had no choice. They certainly didn't go quietly."

"Someone made it out alive," Hughes said.

"How do you know?" Deen challenged.

Hughes smiled and replied, "No gun. Who shot them?" and then walked away.

They encountered the first zombies in Loading Dock A, the staging area for freight destined for expeditions out onto the ice or to the Dry Valleys. Brad almost walked into one of the creatures as he rounded a corner. Three more stood in the open loading door across the room. Upon seeing Brad, the first zombie growled and lunged at him. Brad dropped his flashlight and fended the creature off with the butt of his rifle as he backed down the hallway. Neither Deen nor Hughes could get a clean shot at it in the close confines of the hallway. As they stumbled backwards, their flashlights played across the zombie like spotlights at a movie premier. The creature's red eyes never left Brad, solely intent on its next meal. The zombie was surprisingly strong, pushing him backwards into a glass display case. The glass shattered and cascaded over Brad. If not for the thick anorak he wore and the coat underneath it, the sharp falling shards of glass would have sliced him to ribbons. Even so, a small piece cut his right cheek. The smell of blood enraged the zombie, doubling its efforts to get at him. Finally, Brad managed to shove hard enough to throw the zombie off balance. He quickly reversed his rifle, placed the barrel against the creature's head, and pulled the trigger. The head exploded like an over-ripe melon, splattering the wall with thick, black blood and bits of dead flesh. Blood drenched his gloves and sprayed his face. The stench was overpowering, the smell of a disinterred body.

"My God," Deen said, choking on the smell. "He stinks worse than a cesspool."

Hughes was more matter of fact. "We had better take care of the others."

Alerted by the shot, the remaining three zombies made a beeline across the dock for them. Brad followed Hughes and Deen while fighting down the bile rising in this throat. He removed his blood-spattered gloves and tossed them to the floor, and then fell to his knees to vomit. He wiped his face with his hands. They came away covered with black blood. For a few seconds, his mind slipped into a zone away from his body. He saw himself kneeling, the headless zombie a few paces away. He wanted to leave, to escape the insanity surrounding him; wander the universe opening before him. He heard three shots and fought to regain his feet, but they refused to support him. Another wave of nausea swept over him. He dry heaved the contents of his empty stomach. The sound of the roll-down door closing brought him back around. He rose slowly, ashamed at his reaction to the dead zombie, and joined his comrades.

Deen strutted around the three corpses like a game rooster. He stood over one of the zombies, smiling, and nudging it with the toe of his boot. Brad half-expected Deen to reach down and scalp the dead creature, a trophy for his belt. Brad suddenly realized that he disliked Deen very much. Hughes had dismissed the three corpses and was examining a generator he had spotted in a corner of the dock.

"Maybe we should stay here," Hughes said, finally agreeing with Brad's original idea. "We can power the equipment with the generator, you know, for Doctor Strong's research."

Brad nodded, not trusting his voice. Hughes stared at him, cocking his head slightly to one side.

"Are you okay?" Hughes asked. He thankfully didn't mention Brad losing his lunch.

"I think so," Brad answered. "Just shaken. Yes, I think this place will do. Liz can use the lab here to find out just what we're fighting."

"I think I can enlighten you gentlemen."

All three turned at the sound of the strange voice. Deen pointed his AK-47 at the man standing in the door. The man held a revolver in his hand, but he casually shoved it into his coat pocket. A long piece of steel fashioned into a machete with a duct tape handle dangled from his waist.

"You won't need that, sir," he said, smiling at Deen. Ignoring the threat of the rifle, he continued into the room. "My name is Doctor Gregory Malosi. I'm glad to see you gentlemen. It's been a rather lonely couple of weeks."

Brad studied Malosi's face. Malosi appeared to be about forty years old. He was very thin but not emaciated, as if he had always been a thin man. He sported several weeks' growth of beard and walked with a slight limp. Noticing Brad's scrutiny, he said, "I took a spill on the snowmobile some miles out and injured my knee. It has not healed properly."

"You're not from McMurdo?" Brad asked.

"No. I was … elsewhere when the Demise struck."

"The Demise?" Hughes asked.

Malosi took a few more steps into the room. Hughes played his flashlight across the newcomer's face. Malosi warded his face from the light, frowned, and shot Hughes a scathing look. "Well, the Australians called it that. The rest of the world had various names.

The Apocalypse would fit nicely, I suppose, the end of the world as we know it."

"Do you know what happened here?" Brad's heart began to race. He was eager for answers and any news from the outside world. Malosi's enigmatic smile shook him. What could the man find humorous about the end of the world?

"Not all of it. I arrived to find the place crawling with zombies. Everyone living was gone. I found a hastily scrawled note in the radio room dated August 12. The writer didn't know very much. A C-130 had landed a week earlier to bring in some supplies in a rare night landing. Soon afterwards, several people became ill, died, and came back to life as these creatures. They soon learned that it was happening all over the world. They gathered the survivors and evacuated the base in the C-130, the fools."

Malosi's condescension mystified Brad. "Fools?"

"The disease came here from Christchurch aboard the very plane in which they were escaping. What did they expect to find there? They probably never made it. We're all infected to some degree or the other, you know." Malosi paused to judge the effect his words had on them, grinning when he saw that they already knew. "How many frightened people do you think concealed their symptoms in order to escape? Can you imagine zombies on a plane?" He shook his head. "Better that they had stayed here."

"Where were you if not here?" Hughes asked.

"Out on the ice."

When he saw that Malosi was not going to expand on his statement, Hughes pushed.

"Where on the ice?"

Malosi sighed. "Does it matter? I'm a biologist. I was out collecting samples. I prefer solitude. Most people bore me." He turned to face Brad. "You knew that we're all infected. How?"

"I'm more curious as to how you knew?" Brad asked.

"It was obvious. People became infected and died who had not been bitten."

"What about natural immunity to the disease?"

Malosi's grin seemed darker this time, as if he had a secret that only he knew and savored the power it gave him. "Do you truly believe this is a natural disease?"

"How have you survived here alone for over a month," Deen asked.

"I move about quietly. I have my revolver and this." He touched the makeshift machete with his hand. "I have a safe cubbyhole in which to hide, enough propane to provide heat for cooking, and sufficient food to last for some time."

"There are no other survivors?" Brad asked.

"No one. Where did you come from?"

"Amundsen-Scott."

"Ah, Polies. I have never been to the South Pole. I hear it is a very stark and barren abode."

"It is now," Hughes answered.

"Are you all that remain?"

Brad answered. "No. More are coming soon. We came ahead to scout around."

Malosi walked over and examined the generator that Hughes had been examining, running his gloved hand along its surface. "Alone, I could not hope to secure this building. A group could do so."

"We have a doctor with us," Brad said. "I want to get the labs running. We have to determine what this infection is and find a cure."

"Oh, I can tell you what it is – microscopic nanites."

Deen scowled. "What the hell are nanites, some kind of ice termite?"

Brad had heard of nanites, but wasn't certain if he believed Malosi's claim.

"Nanites are tiny, man-made self-replicating robots that can move through the human blood stream. They are neither virus nor bacteria, so antibiotics will not work on them. Gentlemen, there is no cure."

16

Sept. 10, Port Augusta, Australia

Val Marino stood by the fresh grave, dirty Stetson hat in hand, weeping openly, not caring what the others present might think. His tears ran warm down his cheeks, mingling with the beads of sweat elicited by the unnaturally hot day. Elliot Anson had been his friend and colleague. If not for the gruff Australian, Marino had no doubt that he would still be stuck in Antarctica or more likely, dead. He would miss Anson, and the small mound of earth and building rubble didn't seem monument enough for all Anson had done.

Alex Nelson from Coober Pedy offered him a few words of comfort. He slapped Marino on the back and said, "It seems to me that Anson died in the way he lived – by his own rules."

Marino nodded. He had known Alex only a few days, but the opal miner – he called himself a *fossiker,* another Australian *stine* term Marino didn't understand – had made a quick impression on him. Like Anson, Alex was hard enough to cut diamond but easy going and friendly.

"I shouldn't have left him."

"The flash drive is important," Alex reminded him. "It allowed Jeffries to fine tune the devices. It will save lives."

Marino nodded. "Maybe, but it didn't save Anson's."

When the two had landed in Adelaide just five days earlier – *Has it only been five days?* Marino thought. *It seems like a lifetime* ago – searching for Anson's sister and brother, they had set out north for the Flinders Range after them, only to find them murdered by a highwayman. Their chance encounter with Nelson had prompted Marino's return to Woomera with him to deliver John Gilford's flash drive that they had brought from Resurrection City. He knew he shouldn't have left Anson alone, but Anson had insisted. Anson's thirst for revenge on the murderer of his siblings had driven him to take chances. They had found Anson, or rather, Anson had found them, in Port Augusta as Marino, Alex, and the scientists from Woomera used Electro-Magnetic Pulse devices to clear the city of zombies.

The properly tuned EM waves rendered the nanites inoperable, killing their zombie hosts, but at a safe distance, they were harmless to humans. In fact, the EMP provided temporary relief from nanite infection, a rudimentary cure. However, Anson's injuries, a bullet wound to the stomach, were so severe that only the nanites infecting him kept him alive. Using the new device would only kill him.

"He took his own life to save you from having to do it for him."

Marino turned on Alex angrily, his fists clenched; then relaxed as he realized that Alex was right. "It doesn't make it any easier."

"It doesn't get any easier, mate. It never will." With those parting words, Alex left Marino alone by the grave.

Marino shoved his hat back on his head. Alex was right. They still had work to do. Australia was Anson's home. He wouldn't want anyone slacking off because of him.

Port Augusta was clear. So far, almost a hundred survivors had staggered out of their hiding places, starving, filthy and numb, but now free of the zombie threat that had lingered over them. It was a small number for a city of thirteen-thousand souls, but more might come out. They had finally contacted the military. Remnants of the ADF station near Melbourne had been killing zombies from helicopter gunships in Port Augusta for sport, inadvertently forcing the humans scavenging the city for food into hiding. Their commander, General Aubrey Hayes, had pledged his small surviving force to the task of cleansing the cities of zombies.

Marino looked down at the grave with its wooden marker. "It's time to go now, Elliot. We're headed to Adelaide. I'll see if Tabitha is still around."

Tabitha Jewels had been the slightly insane woman they had met at the Adelaide airport where Anson had landed the Hercules C-130. She had tried to imprison them for their services as pilots to help evacuate the city. They had left her to her delusions with the promise to bring more pilots to her. In a way, they would be keeping their promise.

As Marino trudged through the rows of barracks tents set up for the survivors, trying not to stare at their gaunt, vacant faces, he wondered how his friends and acquaintances in Tucson were doing. Was there still a Tucson for him to return to? He spotted Nicole Blalock standing with Doctor Winston Jeffries and Alex. Nicole had her arms around Nelson's waist, leaning against him. Marino envied him and his relationship with her. According to Alex, she had turned him into a human being. Human beings were a rare commodity now days.

He faced the three and smiled. "I've said my goodbyes. I guess it's time to move on and move out. It's time to go to Adelaide."

This time, he would be returning to Adelaide in a fleet of helicopters equipped with loudspeakers announcing what they were going to do, and two hundred soldiers to secure a safe refuge for the survivors while they detonated the EMP devices. In this manner, they intended to retake all of Australia. He owed Anson that much.

## 17

Sept. 10, Leverett Glacier, Antarctic Plateau

Liz stared out the window at the unchanging landscape. Darkness prevailed. Stars studded a black moonless sky. The wind created a ground haze of blowing snow that made picking a safe path among the crevasses and ice ridges difficult. Somewhere along the way, they had lost the Sno-Cat bearing Trace Wilkie, Matsu Shimoda, and Mattie Mullins. Wilkie, with his superior knowledge of ice road conditions, had insisted on leading the two-vehicle caravan. For two days, the slower Kharkovchanka had trudged along behind the Sno-Cat, following its tracks like a hound after the fox. By the third day, Wilkie, frustrated with the Russian tractor's slower pace, had increased the distance between the two vehicles. DeSousa pushed the Kharkovchanka to its limits to keep up, but abruptly, the Sno-Cat tracks disappeared, vanished with the wind. They searched blindly for several hours but found no trace of the vehicle. Now, they had to decide on a course of action.

Liz knew what she wanted. She was eager to continue, to reunite with Brad, but felt they couldn't abandon anyone. "We must wait for them," she suggested. "Once they notice we aren't following, they'll backtrack and find us."

DeSousa disagreed. "There are hundreds of paths they could have taken off the glacier. I haven't seen a marker flag or any sign of a road all day. I don't know exactly where we are. The chances of them finding us are infinitesimal. Besides," he pointed to the radio, "I haven't been able to raise them on the radio."

"You told me it had a very limited range. That's why we can't reach Brad."

He nodded. "That's true. That means Wilkie is way ahead of us. We're too slow for him. He's left us behind."

Deep down, she worried that DeSousa's assessment of Wilkie might be true, but she could not allow herself to dwell on it. "He wouldn't do that. We can't leave them."

"We're not leaving them; he left us."

DeSousa's reasoning didn't move her. "The sky is clearing. We can shine a light upwards or start a fire with lots of smoke. Maybe they'll see it."

Bain, the third member of the small group in the Kharkovchanka's driver's cabin, had sat quietly listening to them argue. Finally, he ventured his opinion. "She may have a point, although the wind is blowing much too hard for smoke to rise very high. Waiting a few more hours won't hurt."

DeSousa shook his head. "Look, Wilkie has a better chance of reaching McMurdo than we do. The longer we wait, the more fuel and food we use. If the weather turns nasty, we'll regret the time we lose waiting."

"Just a few more hours," Liz pleaded.

At first, she thought DeSousa was going to ignore her request and continue, but finally he relented. "Okay. I'm tired. I'll sleep a few hours, but then we leave. I'll hook a spotlight to the battery and shine it upward, but I don't think it will help. Wilkie would have to be right on top of us to see it and knowing him, he just kept going toward McMurdo."

Liz relaxed. Her shoulders ached from the prolonged tension. She prayed that DeSousa was wrong about Wilkie, but if he had indeed gone ahead without them, she also hoped nothing had happened to them. She had seen the yawning crevasses and the razor-sharp ice rills around which DeSousa had so deftly maneuvered the ungainly Russian Kharkovchanka. The smaller, more agile Sno-Cat should have had no difficulty choosing a safe path.

She and Bain left DeSousa up front. He had seldom left his seat during the entire journey. She worried that DeSousa's dogged determination to do all the driving was exhausting him. Tired men made bad decisions. She was tired as well. She hoped her insistence to wait for Wilkie didn't come back to haunt her.

In the rear cabin, Lester, Reed, Maurice Jernigan, one of the heavy equipment operators, and Lillian Kopenski, a botanist, were all asleep. She eyed the small group with a sense of sorrow and loss. With Wilkie, Mullins and Shimoda missing, and Hughes, Deen and Brad out of communication, they were all that remained of the original forty-eight over-winterers at Amundsen-Scott. She tried to recall the names of the dead – Pirelli, Walls, Menendez, Meyers, Connelly, Singleterry. The litany of the dead went on, but the names and the faces became jumbled, morphing from the faces she remembered to the masks of horror of their zombie counterparts.

Guessing her thoughts but misreading the emotion showing on her face, Bain offered, "None of the dead were your fault. This … disease is beyond anyone's medical acumen. To be honest, I'm surprised that this many are still alive. Why us? Are we few immune?"

She had often pondered that very question in the weary minutes before forcing her body to sleep and in the hazy, nightmare-ridden moments upon awakening. "I don't know what's causing the transformation, so I can't be certain that we're immune. The disease has an unusual incubation period. Some people died quickly, but others didn't fall ill for several days. It's in the air that we all breathed." She shook her head. "I don't know what makes some of us different. I don't know anything."

"Perhaps we'll learn the truth at McMurdo."

"Yes, McMurdo."

She poured a cup of hot coffee, clasping the mug tightly with both hands to absorb the heat. The interior of the tractor was not cold. The heater kept it warm enough to shed her heavy coat and gloves, but a chill not being birthed by the freezing temperatures outside or the relatively comfortable interior was steadily growing in her core, as if her doubts and fears were sucking the heat from her body, from her soul. Nightmares plagued her sleep. Her stomach rumbled from hunger. They had begun rationing the food to make it last. She had reduced her caloric intake so that the others who needed it more could eat. For two days, she had been living on coffee, peanut butter sandwiches, and bad dreams.

Sitting at the table across from Bain, she watched as he sipped his tea. He nibbled on a piece of stale Russian black bread they had found in the tractor's pantry in lieu of scones or biscuits, dunking it in the tea to soften its chewy texture. He looked so prim and proper, so British, that she could almost ignore his disheveled appearance and five day's growth of beard. He caught her staring at him and smiled.

"It's not the tea; it's the idea that counts."

She smiled back at him while shaking her head. Bain had used his last remaining tea bag for the third time. The tea must have been weak and flavorless, but he drank it with gusto, more for the solace the ceremony provided than for the actual taste.

"You look as if you're taking tea at the Savoy."

"I'm certain they would frown upon my present attire. Have you been to London?"

"My ex-husband and I visited London a few years ago, before we were married. They had just redecorated the Savoy. It was lovely." It saddened her that thoughts of her ex were not as painful as they had once been. There had been good times as well as bad times. She was tired of dwelling only on the bad times. It was time to move on with her life.

He looked pensive for a moment before replying, "Ah, yes, they redecorated in 2010. Alas, I haven't been in years. I do miss London."

"You'll go back."

He frowned and raised an eyebrow. "Indeed."

Charles Lester moaned in his sleep, fighting the blanket covering him for a few moments before rolling over and settling down.

"Someone else is having nightmares," Bain said.

She set her cup on the table. "You too?" she asked.

"I can't help thinking that I'm destined never to see England again."

"Don't say that."

"Even if I survive, it's doubtful that long distance travel will be possible. Oh, we might reach Christchurch or Australia, so my accent will be the norm, but reaching America or England will be very difficult." Seeing her dismay, he quickly said, "But of course there are American Naval vessels in Australia. Perhaps we might hitch a ride." He smiled again, "Or stowaway."

"What do you think we'll find at McMurdo?"

He peered over the rim of his teacup. "I think we'll find more death." He noticed her look of consternation. "Don't pay attention to my prattling. I'm depressed because I haven't had a decent cuppa in days. No matter what we find, we'll be eight-hundred miles closer to home. Come summer, we can build a boat and sail to Australia."

She appreciated his attempt to humor her, but she had read the stories of early polar expeditions disasters and she knew why their reaching Australia by boat was unlikely.

The Antarctic Circumpolar Current encircled Antarctica like a spinning Hula Hoop. Flowing perpetually west to east, unbroken by any continental coastline, the ACC and the upwelling of nutrients from the deep cold currents it caused were the source of the phytoplankton that fed the abundant sea life of the Southern Ocean. This plethora of fish, seals and whales first drew early explorers to the bottom of the world. The ACC could also brew horrendous storms that drove icebergs to penetrate the hulls of wooden ships, or crush unwary ships in a sea of ice, such as Shackleton's ill-fated *Endurance*. Large modern fishing vessels and cruise ships weren't immune to its fury. She doubted a small ship could safely reach Australia. Freezing to death where they were or drowning in the sea were poor choices.

Liz noticed the ripples in her coffee before feeling the almost imperceptible shaking of the Kharkovchanka. She wondered what could move a thirty-ton vehicle. She glanced at Bain and saw that he, too, had felt the trembling. He looked at her questioningly. His look of bewilderment turned to one of horror as the heavy tractor suddenly slewed sideways and began bucking like a wild mustang.

"Ice quake," he shouted. "Everyone outside!"

People tumbled from bunks, half-asleep and confused, tripping over one another in their eagerness to escape the dancing tractor. Liz grabbed her heavy coat and joined them in their mad rush for the door. Outside, she spotted DeSousa lying in the snow. Thinking he was injured, she ran to help him, but he climbed to his hands and knees and scuttled away from the tractor. The spotlight he had set up to signal Wilkie lay on its side, shattered. She quickly counted heads and saw that everyone was out of the tractor. The ground continued to shake, but the convulsions were subsiding. After another minute, they ceased.

"What happened?" she asked Bain.

"The rapid temperature rise has weakened the ice. It shifted. We were damned lucky a crevasse didn't open up directly beneath us."

"Can it happen again?"

Bain hesitated. "I don't know ice as well as I know the weather, but I would say yes. The air temperature has almost reached the freezing point. That's unprecedented for this time of year this far inland. That places an inordinate amount of stress on the glacier."

DeSousa walked up, brushing snow from his anorak and pants. "Glacier, hell. I'm more worried about the ice shelf."

"What do you mean?" she asked.

"In '56, a chunk of ice the size of Belgium broke away. A few years ago, a piece twice the size of Dallas floated out to sea. Recently, a slab three-hundred square miles in diameter broke off the Pine Island Glacier. I'm no glaciologist. I'm more into ice cubes in a tumbler of gin and tonic, but a quake this size means big trouble. We have to cross the Ross Ice Shelf to reach McMurdo." He looked from her to Bain. "What if we can't?"

Liz's heart went cold in her chest at the possibility of not seeing Brad again. "We have to. We just have to."

18

Sept. 14, McMurdo Base, Antarctica

"I knew it," Hughes said as his eyes bored holes in Malosi. "When I heard about the *Providence*, I knew that somebody, somewhere, had let the genie out of the bottle." He slammed his fist into his thigh. "Son of a bitch!"

Malosi raised an eyebrow. "Indeed. Very few people knew of the *Providence* incident. The government tried very hard to keep it quiet."

"How do you know about nanites and the *Providence*?" Brad asked.

"Gentlemen, I'm afraid I have not been completely truthful with you." Malosi moved his hand toward his coat pocket. Remembering that Malosi had a pistol in his pocket, Brad raised his rifle and pointed it at him. "Be very careful."

Malosi reached into his pocket very slowly and withdrew a piece of paper. "This is my military security card. I worked on Project *Resurrection* at *Resurrection City.* I'm afraid I'm one of the people who doomed us all."

Deen took two quick steps toward Malosi, yanked the identity card from his hand, and read it aloud. "Bastard's right. Albert Gregory Malosi, 42, biologist. DOD security clearance Level 3." Deen tossed the card on the floor and stepped on it. "Won't be needing this again, will you?"

Malosi watched the card flutter to the floor, and then scowled at Deen. Deen pushed his face closer to Malosi's. "We ought to kill you."

"Back off, Deen," Brad called out.

Deen glared at Brad. "This bastard caused all this shit."

"Maybe, but there's nothing we can do about it now. We might need him."

Hughes added his opinion. "I say shoot the bastard."

Deen smiled. "Two to one, Niles. We shoot him."

"Do you know anything about nanites, Deen? Do you, Hughes?" Brad challenged. "If you do, go ahead and pull the trigger. Murder him. If not, shut the hell up and back off. We need him alive."

Malosi looked at Brad. "I appreciate your intervention, but at the risk of losing my life, I must reiterate my first assessment. There is no cure."

Deen danced around waving his AK-47. "See! See! He admits it. We're all screwed and it's his fault." He pointed the rifle at Malosi.

Brad leveled his rifle at Deen. "Deen, if you pull that trigger, I'll kill you."

Deen looked from Brad to Hughes, who made no move to interfere. "You're bluffing, Niles. You won't shoot me."

Brad put as much strength into his words as he could muster. He fought to keep his hands steady. "We need this man. If you murder him in cold blood, I'll shoot you where you stand. If you're capable of murdering one person, you're capable of murdering another and we can't trust you."

Deen chewed on his lower lip as he tried to decide if Brad would really pull the trigger. Brad was afraid Deen would call his bluff, if indeed he were bluffing. Allowing Deen to get away with murder would destroy the integrity of the small group of survivors as surely as the plague. He didn't want to pull the trigger, but suddenly decided that he could if Deen forced his hand. To his immense relief, Deen lowered his rifle and backed away from Malosi. It was only then that he saw that the barrel of Hughes rifle pointed at Deen. Hughes had decided to back him. That surprised him.

"Calm down, Deen," Brad said in an attempt to relieve the tension in the room. "You might have your chance to shoot Malosi later." He turned to stare at Malosi, "If he doesn't cooperate."

Malosi dipped his head slightly in a polite bow of thanks for saving his life.

Brad continued his interrogation of Malosi. "Where the hell is *Resurrection City*? I've never heard of it and why the lie about where you're from."

"I didn't know how much you knew about the plague. I wished to know more about you. As for *Resurrection City*, few are even aware of its existence. It's a small government facility in Oakes Land leased from the Australian government. It has no true name, simply a DOD designation number. We call it *Resurrection City* as a kind of joke. Doctors Willis Cromby, John Gilford, and I were working with nanites to reconstruct human flesh, especially nerves, in military amputees. Our benefactor, General Terrence Scott, put pressure on Cromby to test an unstable serum, AR-10, derived from a sailor aboard the *Providence,* on a second patient. Unfortunately, Scott's biohazard suit developed a pinhole leak, contaminating all of us. He spread the infection to Washington. From there ... well, you understand how quickly it could travel the globe."

"So you contaminated McMurdo," Deen challenged.

Malosi shot him a look of disdain. "No, as I said before, an airplane from Christchurch did that. The same happened to all the bases eventually – Vostok, Mawson, Casey, Scott, and your own Amundsen-Scott. They're all gone. Oh, there might be a few survivors in very remote locations, but they will die as soon as their fuel and food is exhausted."

"We should kill all you bastards," Deen snarled.

"I'm afraid you're too late. Cromby committed suicide. Gilford was still alive when I, uh, departed. In fact, Gilford was busy killing people to assure his own survival. I think he went a little mad."

"If there's no cure, why did this Gilford fight so hard to survive?" Brad asked.

Malosi shrugged. "Why didn't I simply lie down in the snow and go to sleep when I crashed my snowmobile and injured myself? I suppose it is human nature to postpone death for as long as possible."

Brad listened to Malosi's glib answer and understood that he was revealing just enough of the truth to allay their suspicions, but he felt he couldn't help the nagging thought that the biologist was withholding something vital. He decided to probe further.

"You mentioned biohazard suits. Just how did your decontamination system work?"

"No help there, I'm afraid. We degaussed with high frequency Electro-Magnetic waves, UV light, and an antimicrobial fog, but we designed them to eliminate external contamination on our suits and from the air. The frequencies needed to inactivate the nanites inside the human body would turn your organs to mush."

"Just what did you do for this little group of mad doctors?"

"As I said, I am a biologist."

"What's your specialty?"

"Endocrinology."

"Endocrine ... What's that?" Deen asked.

Malosi favored Deen with a condescending look. "I study the human endocrine system, the organs that secrete hormones – the pituitary, thyroid, and adrenal glands, the pancreas, ovaries, and testes, balls to you."

Deen growled and took a step toward Malosi. Brad raised his voice to focus Deen's attention on him instead. "Is that how these creatures function?"

Malosi smiled. "Very good! Yes, the nanites act upon certain glands, which allow the body to repair itself. Nanites are essentially microscopic robots repairing flesh. Somehow, the mutated serum allowed the nanites to attack healthy flesh rather than repair damaged tissue. They destroy the brain, but leave the *truncus encephala*, the brainstem, intact. A zombie reanimates, breathes, moves, functions on an animal level, and craves human blood for energy. They are unstoppable, mindless, killing machines."

"Unstoppable?" Hughes said. "A bullet to the head does a good job."

"Yes. Severing the brainstem or stopping the flow of spinal fluid will kill the creatures, but their bite, their saliva, or their body fluids will contaminate a healthy individual. The nanites act much more rapidly this way than when introduced through the lungs. The zombies spread their infection as a means of nanite survival and reproduction. That is what I meant by unstoppable. Eventually, zombies will rule the world."

As he spoke, Malosi's voice betrayed his admiration for his handiwork. Brad realized that the deaths of billions of human beings mattered little to the man. The science was all he cared about. Such men sickened Brad. They had been the harbingers of death and destruction for decades from Nobel to Oppenheimer, blithely risking the future of mankind in the name of science. For every Louis Pasteur, Jonas Salk, or Albert Sabin, there was a Richard Gatling, Josef Mengele, or Gerhard Schrader, the inventor of Sarin gas. The pursuit of science for science's sake was to tread a path in a minefield with eyes shut, except that the innocent suffered as well as those stumbling blindly.

"There's always hope, isn't there," Brad said. "We'll find a cure."

Malosi's sneer surprised him. "Hope is a cancer that eats away at you until all that's left is harsh reality." He pointed to the floor. "Here or somewhere else, we're all going to die."

"Your time may come real quick if you don't shut the hell up," Deen challenged, as he jammed the barrel of his AK-47 hard into Malosi's stomach.

Malosi pushed the rifle's barrel to one side with a single finger. "Young man, I have lived with death for weeks. If you wish to kill me, pull the trigger and do so. If not, stop swaggering about and railing like a madman."

For a long second, Brad thought Deen might pull the trigger, but Hughes' voice barked out, "Deen!"

Deen lowered the weapon and stepped away from Malosi. He stared at Hughes; then strode angrily from the room. Until that moment, Brad hadn't realized just how tense he was. He relaxed his shoulders.

"Do you intend to join us or return to your hidey hole?" Hughes asked.

Malosi bent over to retrieve his identity card, and then shrugged. "I will join you. There is a measure of safety in numbers, but I must warn you that, although they are stupid creatures, the zombies are persistent. Given time, they will find a way to break in here."

Hughes' answer was somewhat petulant. "We'll deal with that eventuality when it arrives."

Brad hoped they didn't have to deal with it too soon. With Malosi's help, they uncrated and moved the generator and connected it into the building's power panel. They ran an exhaust line to a vent in the roof by connecting several lengths of fire hose. To prevent the noise of the generator from attracting hordes of zombies, they surrounded it with piles crates and stacks of supplies to muffle the sound, leaving ample room for air to reach the intake. Brad watched on as Deen purposely shoved a crate into Malosi while they worked in a childish attempt to provoke him. Malosi shrugged off the clumsy 'accident' with a smile, but Brad noticed a barely concealed look of hatred flicker across Malosi's face whenever he glanced in Deen's direction. Brad pulled Deen aside and warned him to stop, but he doubted Deen would heed his advice. From the twinkle in Hughes' eyes, Brad surmised that the conflict between the two men amused him. He considered Deen's actions contemptible and Hughes' deriving pleasure from them as juvenile. Brad began to suspect that Malosi was far more dangerous than he first thought and would bear watching.

They fueled the generator and cranked it. Next, they relit the fuel-oil boilers that supplied heat for the Biology and Core Pods. By closing off the two dock areas and any unnecessary rooms, they managed to raise the temperature in the loft to a comfortable fifty-five degrees within two hours, allowing them to remove their heavy outdoor gear. The opportunity to move around without the cumbersome anorak was a godsend to Brad who was beginning to think he was living in it. Later, as he was inspecting one of the labs that he thought Liz might need, he caught Malosi smiling at him.

"How much responsibility do you take in this disaster?" he asked Malosi.

The smile faded from Malosi's lips. "Responsibility? Why should I feel responsible? I did not create the nanites. That was Cromby's sin alone. My input into the project was minimal. I autopsied our failures to determine the cause of that malfunction and suggested a tweak here and there in a particular molecule to enhance the nanites' effectiveness with the endocrine system. General Scott pushed Cromby beyond his limits. If one can cast blame on an act of God, it falls on the military who so eagerly welcomed our failures as opportunities."

Brad was livid. "An act of God? How dare you bring the Lord's name into your unholy experiments?"

Malosi laughed. "I suppose you believe we did the devil's work."

"Not all evil derives from the devil. Men are evil enough on their own."

"Evil? You think me evil. Our goal was to coax damaged flesh into growing new, healthy tissue, a worthy goal, don't you think?"

"But you didn't stop there. Your new toys were too … useful."

Malosi shrugged. "They got out of control."

"You created a thing with no way to stop it from spreading." Brad chopped his hand in the air to emphasize his point. "That was unconscionable."

"Our failsafe …" Malosi stopped speaking.

Brad's ears perked up. "Failsafe?"

Malosi shook his head. "As you said, they got out of control."

Brad could see that Malosi was lying for some reason but figured confronting him now would serve no useful purpose. "A doctor is coming with the rest of our group. Will you work with her?"

Malosi smiled. "To find a cure? There is little hope for that, but I will assist her if you insist. I suppose my continued safety resides in my usefulness."

While Hughes and Deen patrolled the building securing the outside doors and windows, Brad and Malosi cleaned the labs and chose the open upper level as sleeping quarters. Later, they could convert individual offices into private rooms, but for now, communal-style living would suffice. Several times as they worked, the floor shook and glassware rattled as tremors caused by the volcano raced across the island. Brad stared at Mt. Erebus through the window with its summit crowned in a blood-red halo and recoiled at the monster on their doorstep. With inhuman monsters surrounding them and a gargantuan monster threatening to brush them off the island, he wondered at their chances for survival.

Later, they performed an inventory of supplies and discovered cases of food on the dock originally destined for a winter expedition, enough to feed the entire group for weeks if a bland diet of canned meats, vegetables, and tapioca pudding didn't kill them first. There were undoubtedly more supplies scattered around the base, but the army of zombies would make scavenging difficult. He hoped that they could find some way off Antarctica before that became necessary.

Before his trip to McMurdo and Amundsen-Scott, he had looked forward to exploring a new world. Now, he was hopelessly homesick for North Dakota. He realized the odds of reaching home were dismally small, but with luck, they might reach Australia. There, they might find ships and people who could sail them. He tried to push aside thoughts of what they might find in Australia or in the States. The Spanish Flu pandemic of 1918 had killed five percent of the population. This nanite virus could leave only five percent, but if no one was immune, it could eventually eradicate all human life from the face of the earth.

He caught Malosi staring at him and realized that he had been standing immobile in the middle of the room. Malosi dropped the bundle of blankets he carried onto the floor and said, "You strike me as a survivor. There are always a few in any disaster. I, too, am a survivor. People such as ourselves set aside our differences and work together. I know you hold me responsible for what has happened, but that is like trying to blame a hurricane for blowing. What occurred was inevitable. Many groups throughout the world are experimenting with nanite technology. Some of their goals were not as noble as were ours. What happened was an accident, nothing more."

"Some accident," Brad snorted. "Most of the world's population is dead or dying." He didn't mention that were also doomed.

"My point is, in situations such as this, group dynamics suffer. Friends become rivals. Acquaintances become enemies. This group coming – how many are there?"

"Eleven, no ten now. Why?"

"Eventually, some will grow tired of the group effort and rebel at any authority. Some will simply give up."

"So what's your point?"

"You, Hughes, and I are survivors. Perhaps a few others in your group."

"You discount Deen?"

Malosi frowned. "Deen is a fool. Without your guidance, he would already be dead. My point, as you so eloquently asked, is this. Shortly, an opportunity to promote survival for a few individuals might present itself. If this occurs, I would like to count on your assistance. Your female companion, Doctor Strong, would be a welcome addition."

"Are you planning a trip?"

"I'm planning on surviving as long as possible."

"Why? I thought you said there's no cure."

"*We* cannot develop a cure. That does not mean others might not have already."

"You forget that we're stuck at the bottom of the world."

"Once this plague began, word would have leaked of Project *Resurrection*. If someone were to seek to develop a cure, they would eventually seek information at *Resurrection City*. Perhaps they would send an expedition. If so, we should be ready."

"Why not all of us?"

"I would imagine that space for survivors would be extremely limited. My credentials would assure my place in any evacuation. My word could secure one or two more."

Brad was disgusted. "You would abandon the others."

Malosi frowned. "By the time help arrives, it will already have become every man for himself."

"You don't have much faith in mankind, do you?"

"None at all."

Malosi turned and left the room, leaving Brad to brood over Malosi's offer. Given what had happened at Amundsen-Scott, Brad realized that Malosi's prediction of chaos was not too farfetched. No one believed they could be capable of complete and total selfishness until their lives were threatened. Then, an innate sense of self-preservation kicked in, the thin veneer of civilization chipped and cracked, and the baser animal instincts took control. What were the zombies other than the basest part of a human fighting for survival? Was mankind in general any better? He liked to consider himself civilized, but would he accept Malosi's offer later if things fell apart?

Feeling the need for company, he sought out Hughes. He found him drinking coffee in the break room. Noticing the dour expression on Brad's face, Hughes scowled.

"Has Malosi been at you too?"

Brad didn't know why he was surprised that Malosi had been hedging his bets by making the same offer to each of them. "The man has no scruples."

"Maybe you should have let Deen kill him?"

Brad shook his head. "We might need him."

Hughes looked at him over the rim of his coffee cup. "I doubt it. Still, if you want to keep us civilized …"

"I don't trust him. It's just … he's the only one with any idea of what we're facing."

"If he's not lying, of course."

"Yes, there's that possibility. Meanwhile, we keep an eye on him."

"It'd be simpler to shoot him," Hughes replied, but Brad detected a hint of humor in his voice.

"What's left to do?"

"The building's as secure as we can make it, the zombies haven't found us yet, and we have supplies. Deen is … exploring. The only thing left is to wait for the others to arrive."

"Can we contact them on the radio?"

Hughes nodded. "When they get close enough we can use the walkie-talkie, or I can go back and bring the Sno-Cat. Its radio has a longer range."

"Bringing the Sno-Cat here would be too noisy. It would be better if we stopped the others a safe distance away. They would have to follow, more or less, the same route we did, right?"

"More or less," Hughes agreed.

"I'll go back to the Sno-Cat and wait on them, lead them in on foot."

Hughes grinned, "And leave me and Deen here alone with Malosi?"

"You won't kill him and I expect you to stop Deen from killing him."

"You expect an awful lot from me."

Brad stared at Hughes. "You're hard, but you're no killer. Deen's frightened. Fear changes a man. He might want to strike out at someone. Malosi would make a good target."

"I don't like Deen all that much, but I won't kill him to prevent him from killing Malosi. I don't trust the man."

"I don't expect you to. Just keep an eye on him, on both of them."

Hughes nodded and took another sip of coffee.

"I'll get some sleep and leave in four or five hours," Brad said. "If they didn't run into trouble, they should be here by then or soon afterwards."

Hughes said nothing. Brad realized he had gotten all the conversation out of him he was going to get. Hughes was a difficult man to read at times. He was cold and self-sufficient, but he lived by a personal code of honor, a line that he would not cross. Brad just wasn't certain where Hughes' line was.

* * * *

Brad awoke with a start as another tremor rattled the building. Outside the window, bright flashes in the darkness indicated that Mt. Erebus was once again coughing up hairballs of fiery phlegm. He was torn between hoping that a river of lava would sweep down its flanks and wipe out the zombies and the fear that he and the others would be caught as well. Checking his watch, he saw that he had slept only three hours, but knew he wouldn't be able to sleep again. Washing the sleep from his eyes, he went to the break room, made and ate a cold ham and cheese sandwich, washing it down with coffee that had been brewing all day. The strong caffeine helped perk him up. Hearing breaking glass, he sought out the source and found Deen in a storage room tossing empty glass bottles at the wall. He started to confront Deen for creating a mess, but seeing the look of rage on Deen's face, decided to let it slide. In the receiving area of Dock B, he interrupted a heated conversation between Hughes and Malosi.

"Is there a problem?"

Hughes pointed at Malosi. "Our friend here wants to go exploring outside alone. I suggested that he not."

Malosi scowled. "He threatened to shoot me if I left. Am I your prisoner?"

"Let's just say that it's dangerous to venture out alone."

Malosi was unconvinced. "Yet, you are making preparations to greet your friends."

Brad shrugged. "It's a one-man job. I volunteered."

"And leave me here with this man."

"I could take Hughes with me and leave Deen here with you."

Malosi went silent for a moment. "I see. In that case, I shall welcome Mr. Hughes' companionship." He turned and walked out of the room.

Hughes shot Brad a smile. "Touchy, isn't he?"

Brad noticed the stacks of cases in the receiving area. "Is any of this stuff useful?"

"Most of its scientific equipment – glassware, chemicals, etc. No food."

Brad thought of Deen's rampage in the storeroom. "By the time Deen gets through making a mess, we might need the glassware."

"Are you leaving?"

"Now is as good a time as any. I should be back to the Sno-Cat in an hour. You keep the walkie-talkie. I may need you to provide a diversion for our undead friends when I bring the others in."

"I could let Malosi go out alone."

Brad smiled. "Maybe something less harmful to the zombies."

Brad donned a used anorak that fit and a new pair of gloves he found in a closet to replace his bloody ones. He took his rifle and a curved blade on a four-foot-long pole that looked as if it someone had designed it as a pruning knife, though where anyone would have used it in a land with no trees was beyond him. He hoped it would make a good, silent weapon if he encountered zombies.

Exiting through the lower Aquarium entrance, he stayed close to the buildings to avoid zombies. He immediately noticed that the ground was spongy and the ice was melting. He didn't know if the continued rise in air temperature was from the volcanic activity or a worldwide phenomenon. He wished for a moment that he had Bain's Geiger counter to check for increased radiation, but then realized it didn't matter. He would have to venture outside and breathe the air, even if it proved fatal. He doubted it would prove deadlier than the nanites infecting his body. He considered removing the heavy anorak, but decided that though uncomfortable and unnecessary to protect him from the cold; it would provide extra protection against zombies.

Zombies were everywhere. It was as if the rise in temperature had made them more mobile. He avoided them as best he could and when spotted, made a circuitous route to divert them from following. On the last leg of his journey, between the last buildings and the edge of the island, two zombies prowled the shoreline in search of penguins. He watched one of them chase down and begin to devour a male Adelaide penguin. A fight ensued as the two zombies fought over the carcass. The creatures were starving. He wondered if they would devour one another in their hunger. He tried to sneak past the two creatures as they pushed each other and growled like awkward teens arguing, but they spotted him and forgot their differences. He could have outrun them, but they would have simply followed him out onto the ice. He confronted them with the pruning knife to avoid noise.

One managed to reach him ahead of the other. He stepped aside as it lunged at him and swiped at its neck with the knife but managed to embed it in the creature's shoulder. It jerked the weapon from his hand. He pulled his hunting knife and faced it, desperate to dispatch it before the other joined its attack. It raced at him. Brad ducked its outstretched arms and plunged the knife into the creature's side with an upper stroke that should have gutted it. It paid no attention to the gaping wound spilling dark blood on the ground. Within seconds, the wound stopped bleeding. The pruning knife dislodged from its shoulder. Brad shoved his bloody knife in its scabbard, picked up the pruning knife, and delivered a two-handed overhand chop to the zombie's skull, splitting it almost in half. The creature groaned and dropped at his feet.

He had no time to rest or to admire his handiwork as the second creature took up the fight. This one was more wary, staying just out of reach of the pruning knife but not allowing Brad to move away. Brad heard the growls of more zombies in the distance and knew that they had caught scent of the blood. He had very little time before they would spot him. He rushed the creature, feinted with a blow to its midsection, ducked out of reach, and planted the blade in the creatures back. Using the long handle for leverage, he turned the creature and grabbed his knife. Facing the creature, he stepped inside its reach and jammed the knife into the creature's neck and upwards into the brain, twisting it for maximum damage. Blood ran down his hand and arm, making the knife slippery, but he held on knowing that to release it would mean his death. The creature pawed at him futilely with its claws. He was glad for his decision to keep the heavy anorak. Finally, the blade did enough damage to kill the creature. Its red eyes rolled back into its skull, revealing no white at all. It slumped into Brad's arms. He dropped it to the ground, and, for extra measure, lopped off its head with the pruning knife. He raced down the beach, onto the ice, and into the darkness before the other zombies reached the beach. He hoped the odor of the dead zombies would mask his scent. He was too exhausted for another battle.

19

Sept. 15, Ross Ice Shelf near McMurdo Base, Antarctica

Liz sat beside DeSousa peering out the front window of the Kharkovchanka. They had seen the enormous ash cloud rising from Mt. Erebus, a black smudge in the dark sky, and felt its tremors. She hoped McMurdo still stood amid the earthquakes and ash fall.

Their own journey had not been without mishap. Crossing the ice shelf, they had detoured several times to avoid deep crevasses. The delays had added days to their trip and increased tensions until a fight had broken out between Charles Lester and Maurice Jernigan, one of the heavy equipment operators. They managed to throw only a few punches before the others broke it up, but everyone now walked on tiptoes to avoid further conflict. Worst of all was the fact that the other Sno-Cat bearing Wilkie, Shimoda, and Mullins was still missing. If Wilkie had encountered one of the deep crevasses, the tractor would have plunged hundreds of feet to the Ross Sea.

DeSousa almost lost control of the vehicle when the radio blared out Brad's voice. Liz almost burst into tears of joy knowing he was safe.

"Sno-Cat one to DeSousa. Come in."

"This is DeSousa," DeSousa answered smiling. "I see you made it."

"We're safe. We found one survivor."

"A survivor?"

"I'll explain more about him later. How far from McMurdo are you?"

"About seven miles. Why?"

"The Sno-Cat is parked about a mile out. I'll keep flashing my lights."

Liz turned to DeSousa. "Why is he meeting us out here if everything is all right?"

DeSousa shook his head. "I don't know." He keyed the microphone. "Have you contacted Wilkie?"

Brad's answer sank her heart. "No. Is he not with you?"

"We separated five days ago and haven't seen or heard from him. There have been a lot of ground tremors."

"Yes," Brad replied. "We almost fell into a crevasse on the glacier."

DeSousa looked at Liz. "He's thinking the same thing we are. If Wilkie was alive, he would have beaten us here."

"Maybe they're lost."

"Maybe, but the odds are against it." He pointed out the window. "Hey! I see his light." He spoke into the radio. "I have you in sight Niles, about three miles out."

"Good," Brad replied. "We'll have to leave the Khark here and walk in. Too many zombies are in the area."

Liz counted the minutes until she spotted the Sno-Cat and Brad standing beside it. The huge tractor had barely stopped moving when she jumped down, rushed to him, and let him envelop her in his arms. She had no thoughts of proper decorum or of what the others might think. She was overjoyed to see him. She hadn't realized just how much she had missed him until she caught sight of him.

"God, I missed you," he told her as he kissed her hair, then her mouth.

"I'm glad you're safe," she said when their lips separated.

He pushed her face into his shoulder and cradled it. "Who was with Wilkie?" he whispered into her ear.

She stiffened. She had briefly forgotten about them. "Shimoda and Mattie."

"They might make it yet," he replied.

She nodded. "Who is this survivor you mentioned?"

Brad frowned. "I'll let you meet him first. He worked with the group that developed the plague, here in Antarctica."

"At McMurdo," she said in disbelief.

"No. A secret base in Oates Land. He said it's caused by nanites."

"Nanites? Why would anyone ...?" She paused. "The military?"

"You guessed it. He also says there's no cure, but I don't believe him. He's fought awfully hard to survive knowing he would eventually die."

"Do you trust him?"

"Not for a second. He's already trying to divide us with offers of safe passage when rescue comes."

Her heart almost stopped. "Is rescue coming?"

"He said anyone trying to develop a cure would come to Resurrection City for samples."

"Resurrection City?"

"The name was their little joke for the base where they developed the plague."

She shuddered. "Some sense of humor."

"Wait until you meet him. You'll just love him."

"I can't wait. You've lost weight," she noted.

He had no time to reply. He looked toward the Russian tractor as Bain exited, walked up to him, and offered him his hand. "Good to see you again."

Brad clasped Bain's hand in both of his and pumped it several times. "Welcome to McMurdo."

"It's rather a pleasure to be out of that smelly tin can." He sniffed the air and frowned. "Though the air here has a certain unkind quality to it."

"Mt. Erebus is throwing a party. We're all invited."

The others began climbing down from the Kharkovchanka – Lester, DeSousa, Reed, Jernigan, and Kopenski. They stood in a small group and eyed the dark cloud and flashes of light over the volcano with vary levels of trepidation. Kopenski hugged herself with her arms and shivered. Liz knew it wasn't from the cold. In fact, she realized the temperature was above freezing. A thin sheen of water pooled on the ice in a few shallow depressions.

"Do we walk in?" she asked Brad.

Brad pulled the walkie-talkie from his pocket. "I'll see if the others can provide a little distraction."

He contacted Hughes. "We're ready to come in," he said.

Hughes replied, "When you hear the explosion, come quickly. I don't know how long we can keep the zombies busy."

They began the walk back to the base. Liz was dismayed when they drew close enough to see the condition of the small city. The last time she had seen it was in the daylight, and at that time, it was a thriving metropolis, a hive of activity. Now, it was a dark, empty collection of fire-ravaged buildings haunted by the stalking, fleshy ghosts of its former inhabitants; people she knew. The depression she had been fighting for days threatened to smother her in a fold darker than the night. She didn't know what she had expected, but it wasn't this.

They reached the rocky beach just as a pillow of flame lanced the night air east of the base, followed by the sound of the explosion.

"Come on," Brad urged.

For fear that she might recognize them, she tried not to stare at the occasional human skeleton or the desiccated remains of dead zombies. She had seen enough friends die to last her the remainder of her years. When Brad stopped suddenly and held out his arm, she almost collided with him.

"Zombies," he whispered.

Four of the creatures stood between them and the science building, which was their destination. They stared at the flames but did not move toward them.

"We can't go around them." He looked back at Liz, and then the others. "I'll lead the way. Stay close together."

He ran into the open firing his rifle. The zombies turned and came at the small group. Brad dropped two before they had taken three steps, but the steel tower of a weather station protected the remaining two. Brad waved the others on toward the science building, but Bain took out his pistol and joined him. Liz wanted to stay, but knew she had to help the others to safety.

"Move," she yelled, and shoved DeSousa who stood watching. Their goal was the second building on the small hill. After so many days of sitting, the jog up the hill was taking a toll on her. Her breath came in ragged gasps. She wanted to fling over the heavy, smothering Anorak, but knew she might need it again. She looked back over her shoulder and saw the two zombies break from behind the tower and rush Brad and Bain. The first one went down quickly, but the second, protected by the first one, was on top of them before either man could fire. The creature went straight for Bain, the nearest. Brad leaped in, grabbed it by the collar of its shirt, and swung it around to face him. Liz screamed when the zombie lunged at Brad's neck, but Brad ducked aside and slammed the butt of his rifle into the back of the creature's head. It stumbled far enough away for Bain to shoot it in the head. Relieved, she turned to face the building just as a man she didn't recognize waved them toward the door he was holding open. The group raced inside. She remained outside by the door until Brad and Bain joined her.

Once inside, the man slammed the door and locked it. She took a quick inventory to make certain that everyone had made it inside, and then she collapsed on the floor.

The stranger urged them to keep moving. She eyed him suspiciously, as he spoke in a clipped Eastern-European accent. "This building is not as secure as the Core Pod. I suggest you rest there. We have food prepared."

"Where are Deen and Hughes?" Brad asked him.

"They should be back by now. They used a propane tank as an explosive device and a gasoline trail to ignite it. The resulting explosion and flames seems to have served its intended purpose. The zombies were attracted to it."

"Not all of them," Bain said.

The man smiled. "You handled them easily enough."

Bain frowned. "Who are you?"

"Gregory Malosi. We don't have time to exchange pleasantries. Come."

They followed Malosi to the Core Pod. Liz remembered the biology lab from two years earlier when she had assisted one of the physicians with health checkups for the Dry Ice Valley team members. Upstairs, a pot of hot soup simmered on the stove and a large urn filled the space with the aroma of freshly brewed coffee. Blankets and pillows lay in piles along the wall. She wanted nothing more than to curl up and go to sleep, but her reunion with Brad had excited her too much for that.

While they were eating, Hughes and Deen returned from their expedition. Deen eyed the new faces and frowned. "Where's Wilkie?"

No one answered. Finally, Liz replied, "Wilkie, Shimoda, and Mattie Mullins are missing. We hoped they might have arrived ahead of us."

"What happened?"

DeSousa stood up. "I'll tell you what happened. Your buddy Wilkie ran off and left us."

Deen's face turned red with rage. He balled his hands into a fist. "Wilkie would never do that," he shouted.

"He did it, sonny," DeSousa countered, pointing his finger at Deen. "He cut and ran like a coward."

Liz had enough. "Stop it!" she shouted. They both turned to stare at her. "Isn't it enough that they might be dead? We don't know what happened to them or why they disappeared. Just leave it. We have enough problems to deal with."

Clearly, the tension between the two men had not vanished, but they backed away from each other. DeSousa returned to his cup of coffee. Deen walked to the edge of the stairs but didn't descend them. His eyes never left DeSousa.

"The ice was lousy with cracks," Bain said in way of possible explanation for their disappearance. "The tremors and the sudden rise in temperature made the glacier unstable." Then realizing that he had only heightened the possibility of their deaths, he added, "They may have been forced to take a long detour." He looked at the others gathered there. "None of us might be safe here."

Kopenski dropped her spoon into her bowl and gasped. "But we're on solid ground."

"With a great bloody volcano at our doorstep," Bain reminded her. "These tremors are growing stronger. As more ice melts or breaks away from the continent, the changes in pressure could trigger a major volcanic eruption."

"Where do we go?" Lester asked. "We barely made it here."

Liz saw Brad glowering at Bain as if willing him to shut up. "We have no choice but to remain here, at least for a while," Brad said. "No one is in any condition for another long trip. We have shelter, heat, food and water." He smiled. "As a matter of fact, we've rigged up working toilets. No showers for now though."

"Anything good on the telly?" Bain asked with a smile, falling into Brad's attempt to lighten the already dark mood.

"Just cooking shows."

Bain shrugged, walked over to the shelves of books and picked one up. "I suppose I shall have to read then, won't I?"

Liz was glad of the camaraderie between the two men. She had felt anxious while in the Russian tractor with all the tension in the air. At least here, everyone could have a little more space to themselves. She caught Malosi staring at her. He smiled.

"You are the doctor, Brad spoke of. It's a pleasure to make your acquaintance."

She glanced at Brad, who smiled at her sheepishly. "So you're responsible for all this?"

His smile faded. "I am not. The military hijacked and misused our project. They are at fault."

"But you worked on this nanite disaster," she accused. "Can you help me find a cure?"

"There is no cure."

His straightforward statement of denial angered her. "I refuse to believe that anyone would create such a dangerous machine with no off switch."

"Oh, it is possible to stop the nanites and perhaps the zombies they control, but we are each infested with the tiny creatures." He waved his hand about his head. "They are in the air we breathe. Anything powerful enough to render them harmless would be fatal."

She held her breath. Would he lie about such a thing? If there were no cure, why would he believe that help was coming? "You don't believe that."

His hesitation gave her hope. "It is a truth."

"But not *the* truth."

He said nothing. She was about to press him further, but Brad intervened. "I suggest that everyone try to get some sleep, or at least rest. Later, we have a lot to do to make this place secure and comfortable."

She nodded. Malosi used the lull in conversation to walk away.

Brad whispered in her ear, "Don't push him. I think he's dangerous."

She stared at Brad. "Do you think he's lying about a cure?"

"I believe he doesn't think we can find one, but I'm certain he hopes someone can. Otherwise, he wouldn't put so much effort into surviving."

Liz hoped that Brad was right.

After finishing her meal, Brad gave her a tour of the labs. She eyed the equipment with envy. Her medical clinic at Amundsen-Scott seemed so Spartan in comparison. She especially admired the *Tescan Vega* Scanning Electron Microscope. It would allow a clearer picture of her foe, the nanites causing the plague. She held out little hope that she could develop a cure on her own. Her expertise was as a physician, not a researcher, and she had no working knowledge of nanites, but Brad had faith in her and she couldn't let him down. At least trying was better than simply sitting and waiting for the nanite virus to strike.

"It's a beautiful lab, Brad," she told him.

He beamed with pride. "We tried to fix it up. I hope this is all you need."

"It's very well equipped. I'm sure that with Malosi's help, we can do some good work." His smile slipped for a fraction of a second before returning, just long enough for her to understand that her noncommittal answer didn't please him. "If it's possible to develop a cure or a vaccine, this equipment is up to the job. I don't know if I am," she admitted.

"I wasn't doubting you, Liz," he said gently. "I do have doubts about Malosi."

"Is he dangerous?"

Brad shook his head. "I don't know. I'm positive that he doesn't want to die, but I don't know how far he might go to ensure his own survival. Keep an eye on him."

*Great! She thought. Deen and DeSousa at each other's throats, Lester and Jernigan ready to throw punches again, and Malosi might be dangerous. As if an erupting volcano, a horde of hungry zombies, and facing imminent death from plague infection weren't enough problems to deal with.*

\* \* \* \*

Brad felt suffused with energy now that Liz had arrived. He wanted to race around the building singing and dancing, though he was good at neither. He felt like a kid again suffering the first pangs of adolescent romance. His separation from her had been the most difficult part of the long journey to McMurdo. He vowed never to part with her again. He had hoped that their reunion would have been more enthusiastic, but she had seemed tired and disheartened, distracted. He supposed that was to be expected. After all, their journey had not been without mishap. He didn't share DeSousa's belief that Wilkie had left them behind to fend for themselves. If that were the case, then he would have arrived already. He hoped that Wilkie and the others turned up soon. Their loss would place that much more strain on the group's fragile dynamics. The possibility of their rescue if necessary was almost nonexistent. It was all they could do to see to their own welfare.

He returned Liz to the loft area. Things there were winding down. Though it was only mid-afternoon, many of the new arrivals were settling down to sleep. He would let them rest as long as possible before tackling the remaining problems of setting up a safe base of operations. So far, they had avoided attracting the attention of the mass of zombies haunting McMurdo, but that could easily change. The first order was security. They needed more weapons than the three rifles and assorted pistols they now possessed. Hughes was certain they could obtain more weapons and ammunition from the main supply room. A scientific community such as McMurdo had no real need for weaponry. In fact, it was discouraged, but sports such as skeet shooting and the necessity of rifles for protection meant a certain number were stored for such eventualities. Arming and training everyone in their use could prove vital to their chances for survival until rescue arrived.

Food was no problem, but water was. The small tank in the loft above the labs would not last long. Melting snow, which was rapidly melting, would not produce enough for their needs. A larger water tank was needed and a pipeline to the base's main water lines. The third item on the list was a plan for rescue. Brad held out little hope for anyone searching them out. That meant that they would have to leave Antarctica under their own power. There were no planes adequate to meet their need. Until the ocean thawed, escape by ship was impossible, but it was their only choice. Building a boat capable of safely navigating the wild waters of the Southern Ocean would be laborious and possibly beyond their capabilities. The main thing was to keep everyone busy doing something. Once people gave up hope, they would give up cooperating. This would create a domino effect that would reduce everyone's chances for survival. In this instance, false hope was better than no hope.

On his way to the supply room to check on half-inch plastic pipe for a water line, he spotted Malosi exiting the building. Curious, he followed. Malosi moved carefully, avoiding detection by zombies. His circuitous path made his final destination difficult to judge. Finally, he stopped next to the communications building, checked to ensure that no one was observing him, and ducked inside. Taking a position just outside one of the windows, Brad watched Malosi pull a battery from beneath a table and connect it to a radio. He set the frequency and sat back to listen. Brad waited ten minutes, but Malosi did not move from his seat or make any move to contact anyone with the radio. After the ten minutes was up, Malosi disconnected the battery, hid it beneath the table, and went to the front door. He looked outside, saw that no one was around, and left.

Brad remained hidden from view to see where he would go next, but Malosi surprised him by returning directly to the science building. Clearly, Malosi had a hidden agenda and wanted no one to know about it. Brad's dilemma was, whom could he trust with this information? Had Malosi already recruited someone to help him, Hughes or Deen? If so, what could be his ultimate goal? Whatever it was, Brad was sure the rest of the group played no part in his plans. They were expendable.

As he was returning to the science building, Brad spotted movement on the roof of the Core Pod. Outlined against the glow from Mt. Erebus was the unmistakable figure of Guy Hughes. Brad wondered if he too was keeping an eye on Malosi. Hughes waved to him and pointed toward the edge of the base. Brad followed Hughes' hand and saw a moving light, a flashlight. He raced up to the end of the building. Hughes leaned over the edge of the roof.

His voice was fraught with barely controlled excitement. A broad smile graced his face.

"Someone's coming. I think it's Wilkie and the others. They're alive."

Like everyone else, Brad had given them up for dead. Their reappearance would raise morale, but they were in danger. "Don't they know the place is lousy with zombies?"

Hughes shrugged. "I tried the walkie talkie but got nothing."

"We have to go out and meet them before they attract a crowd. Find Deen and Bain."

As Hughes disappeared, Brad checked to make certain the safety was off on his rifle. He couldn't wait for the others. He could see zombies moving in the twilight all around him. Their chilling grunts and calls made him shiver. Many of them shuffled toward the beach. They had already detected Wilkie's group approaching. He hugged the side of the building, and then darted for the cover of an SUV. He spotted three figures stumbling up the beach. All three had made it, but they looked done in. When one fell, the other two helped the person to their feet and supported them as the three struggled forward.

He hated to give away his position, but the three were almost surrounded. He rose and called out, "Wilkie! Look out for zombies."

One of the figures craned his head to look around, finally spotting Brad beside the vehicle. "I lost pistol."

He had no choice now. He couldn't wait for the others. He broke from cover and ran toward the three stragglers. One zombie had surged ahead of the others. Brad stopped long enough to shoot it in the head. When he joined the others, he saw that he had been right. All three were on their last legs. Mullins was hanging onto Shimoda's shoulders, barely conscious. Shimoda didn't look much better as he held her up. One of Wilkie's eyes was heavily bruised and swollen and a cut ran down the length of his cheek. Brad realized they would never make it to safety without help.

He handed Wilkie the rifle and pulled out his knife. Wilkie refused.

"I can't see well. Give me the knife."

The nearest refuge was the SUV. He wanted to relieve Shimoda of his burden, but he needed his hands free for the rifle. "Come on."

Zombies came from all directions, closing in on them. Brad dropped two as he urged the others to move faster. A female zombie lunged at Wilkie. Luckily, she was much smaller than he was, and he swung her aside with one hand as he plunged the knife into the back of her neck with the other.

*Damn it! Where is Hughes?*

They reached the SUV just ahead of the zombies. Brad herded them in and slammed the door closed. Through a streak of dried blood on the driver-side window, he watched the zombies surround the vehicle. Their frustration became audible as they howled and grunted. They pounded on the windows and the sides of the auto with their fists. Brad knew the glass wouldn't keep them out for very long.

Shimoda's high-pitched scream startled him. He turned expecting to see a zombie inside the SUV. Instead, Shimoda stared at a severed hand in the floorboard clutching a set of keys. Barely considering if the SUV would crank, Brad pried the keys from the death grip clutches of the decaying hand. Inserting them in the ignition, he turned the keys. To his delight and utter astonishment, the engine turned over. Flipping on the headlights, he spotlighted Hughes, Deen, and Bain exiting the science building through the damaged aquarium. He gunned the gas and spun out in the mud, slinging zombies aside as he fishtailed. Hughes and Deen began shooting zombies while Bain motioned for him to drive up to the open door.

Brad drove the SUV like a snowplow, slamming into zombies and rolling over them with a sickening thud. He aimed for the larger congregations out of pure hateful spite. His rage at them burned hot. With less than twenty yards to go, luck failed him. The right rear tire hit something sharp and shredded, sending the SUV careening out of control. He fought the spin with the steering wheel like a kid in a bumper car and managed to keep the vehicle upright, but the rear end crashed into a lamppost.

"Everybody out," he yelled.

Zombies were everywhere, attracted by the noise and the smell of fresh meat. Hughes came out to meet them while Deen and Bain continued shooting as fast as they could. Keeping the three newcomers between them, Brad and Hughes whirled like dervishes, shooting at the closest zombies. One charged into Brad's back before he could take aim. He sprawled on his back on the ground as the zombie grabbed at his feet. Wilkie knocked it aside with his bunched fists, allowing Brad to regain his feet. He jammed the barrel in the zombie's face and pulled the trigger. Its head disintegrated as it fell backwards.

Hands grabbed at him as the zombies converged, but he fought them off. Out of the corner of his eye, he saw Bain grab Mullins and shove her inside. Shimoda followed. As Deen reloaded, Hughes covered him, but that left him and Wilkie alone with zombies all around. The rifle was useless in such close quarters. Wilkie slashed at faces with Brad's knife, but he could inflict no incapacitating wounds. Both men resorted to fists and feet simply to keep gnashing teeth away from them. Together they pushed their way through the throng of zombies.

Reloaded, Deen began firing. Only feet from the door, two zombies brought Wilkie to his knees. Brad kicked one in the back of the head, but the other one ripped into Wilkie's cheek with his teeth. Wilkie screamed in pain. Deen shot the creature three times in the chest. This didn't kill it, but it did push it away from Wilkie. The look of surprise on bloody Wilkie's face changed to one of horror as he realized what had happened. Brad offered his hand to Wilkie to help him to his feet. To Brad's surprise, Wilkie shoved him in the back with enough force to send him stumbling through the open door.

"Shut it!" he yelled.

As Deen started toward Wilkie, Hughes grabbed him by the arm and held him back. "It's no use."

Wilkie took one long look at the others before running away from the door, drawing most of the zombies after him. Fifty yards away, he stopped and stared at Hughes. "Do it!" he shouted.

Hughes raised his rifle, sighted Wilkie's head, and fired. Before Wilkie's body had dropped, Hughes walked inside and closed the door. Deen stared at him.

"Why?" he asked.

"He was a dead man and he knew it. He gave us a chance to get inside."

"We could have …" What he was going to say trailed off and he shook his head.

Brad looked at the horrified expressions on Shimoda and Mullins' face. His eyes cautioned them to remain silent. Hughes had done what Wilkie wanted him to do, but it didn't lesson the shock and the loss. Brad felt numb. Even though he had previously given the three up for dead, seeing them again had brought a brief moment of hope that things might change for the better. Now, he knew it wouldn't. Death surrounded them. Eventually, it would find them all.

Liz's examination showed that Mattie Mullins suffered from two broken ribs and a sprained knee, and that both she and Shimoda were severely dehydrated and undernourished. Liz shooed the curious spontaneous welcoming committee away while she tended to her wounds. While Mullins lay in bed recovering from her injuries, Shimoda related the story of their absence over a cup of coffee and two canned ham sandwiches. He ate with the gusto of a man who had given up hope of his next meal.

"We strayed off the Ice Road and missed our rendezvous with the Kharkovchanka. Wilkie decided it would be best to continue to the Ross Sea where he assured us we would wait for you." He directed this at DeSousa. "We were taking a break from the confines of the Sno-Cat, walking around to stretch our legs, when an earthquake hit. A crevasse opened up directly beneath the tractor. Without thinking, Mattie ran to it, climbed inside, and grabbed a backpack just as the tractor tumbled over the edge. She barely made it out. One of the treads caught her in the chest. Wilkie caught an edge of it in the face trying to catch her fall. We bandaged her ribs as best we could, but we had nothing except what was on us and what was in the backpack she had rescued. It contained a few packages of protein bars, a camp stove, and a can of chocolate. We had no shelter and no way to stay warm except by huddling together. Luckily, the unusual rise in temperature kept us from freezing to death, but we had to keep moving for fear of dying in our sleep. We walked toward McMurdo, but Mattie moved slowly because of her injuries. I thought we were lost, but Wilkie seemed to know the way. Eventually, we saw Mt. Erebus erupting and headed toward it." He looked at the others with tears in his eyes. "Wilkie saved our lives."

Brad recalled his near death experience when their vehicle had almost vanished into a crevasse. They had been lucky. Wilkie and the others had not.

"Let the man eat," Bain said, patting Shimoda on the back.

Shimoda smiled and shoved a second sandwich into his mouth. Brad slowly scanned the faces of those gathered around and noticed, with the exception of Deen and Malosi, a mixture of relief and sorrow. Malosi seemed on the verge of smiling, and Deen's face was blank. Wilkie was gone, another name on the growing list of lost friends and colleagues, but they were alive, and Brad hoped he could keep them that way.

20

Sept. 20, McMurdo Base, Antarctica

Over the next week, daily life at McMurdo slowly began to attain a degree of normality, at least as normal as it could in view of the circumstances. By converting office spaces into sleeping quarters and bringing in beds from the dorms, each individual gained at least a modicum of privacy. Tapping into the base water lines proved easier than expected, and now the group enjoyed the luxury of running water, showers, and working toilets. A schedule of duties posted in the lounge met little resistance. Everyone seemed glad to be doing something after the longs days of confinement in the Kharkovchanka.

Between nursing Mullins' injuries and assisting Malosi in the lab, Brad saw little of Liz for several days except at meals. Malosi was, if not pleasant, at least cooperative. Brad quickly realized that discovering a cure was not going to be easy. His rapport with Liz slowly passed beyond the awkward infatuation stage to a committed relationship. He realized that openly flaunting their relationship might create dissension among so many males, but decided to take that risk rather than chance losing her. As they lay together in her bed for the first time, they discussed her progress on the nanites.

"I don't know where to begin," she confided as she snuggled into the crook of his arm. Her smell enticed him, a mixture of freshly showered flesh and sex pheromones. His hand caressed her skin, enjoying the smooth silkiness of it. "Malosi can explain the endocrinological effects of the nanites, but that puts me no closer to understanding them. We've managed to deactivate them or destroy them with radiation, high voltage bursts of electricity, and strong chemicals reagents, but only in dosages that would certainly kill a human."

"At least they can be killed."

She nodded wearily while lightly tapping her finger on his chest. "Yes, they aren't indestructible, but we've just about reached our limit. Without more information on how they function, I'm stymied."

"And Malosi hasn't been forthcoming."

She hesitated before answering. "I get the impression that he knows more about them than he pretends. He spends more time listening to music on that damned Android of his than in research. When he's not listening to it, he's recharging it. Sometimes I think the only reason he helped you start the generator was to recharge his Android."

"Maybe he just likes music."

"It's like an obsession. His smile when he's listening … it's frightening. I don't trust him."

Brad nodded his agreement. "Neither do I." He had followed Malosi to the radio room twice since Malosi's first visit there. Each time Malosi simply sat in front of the radio and listened to his phone. He had confided Malosi's odd behavior to no one, especially Liz, fearing it might affect her working relationship with Malosi.

"I'm worried about Mattie?" she said.

Brad liked the normally energetic sous chef. She chaffed at lying in bed instead of cooking for the survivors. "Oh? I thought you said her ribs were healing."

"That's just it. Her injuries are healing much too quickly. She's been complaining of congestion in her chest. I haven't seen any black markings on her skin yet, but I'm afraid she's infected."

"Does she know?"

Liz shook her head. Her hair brushed against his chest, tickling him. "I don't think so."

"There's nothing we can do but make her comfortable." As an afterthought, he added, "Maybe we should keep her door locked."

Liz glanced up at him, but the anger in her eyes quickly faded when she saw the sympathy in his. She nodded.

Trying to navigate the conversation away from Mattie Mullin's plight, he said, "Bain says the temperature is almost five degrees above freezing, but he can't explain why."

"I might have the answer to that."

Brad looked at her in surprise. "Really?"

"An increase in $CO_2$ levels can create a greenhouse gas effect in the atmosphere and raise temperatures. How much carbon dioxide do you think billions of rotting corpses would emit?"

The thought of so many decaying bodies made him queasy, but her theory made more sense than his own pet theory of volcanic gases from Mt. Erebus as the cause.

"What did Bain say about radiation levels?"

Now, he was glad that she changed the subject away from corpses. "Steady. No increase. In fact, it might be dropping slightly. He and Shimoda are confabbing over it right now."

She had expressed her fear that rising radiation levels might create long-term health risks. He hadn't the heart to remind her that their long-term survivability was very low with or without radiation.

"Some good news," she agreed.

"More good news."

He smiled and said nothing until she punched him in the chest. "What?"

"I looked outside earlier. The horizon is glowing. The sun's coming up."

A smile softened the outlines of her face. "Thank God."

Brad traced her cheek with his finger. "The sun will be up all day tomorrow. No more darkness."

He leaned over and kissed her. She responded eagerly. His hand strayed to her breast and caressed her nipple. She moaned softly and pressed against him, grasping his hand in hers. She surprised him by pushing him over and climbing on top of him, straddling him. She pressed her breasts against his chest and moved his other hand to her hips. She guided him inside her and began to move, slowly at first but becoming frenzied as her fervor increased. Her new aggressiveness intrigued and delighted him. Earlier, she had been responsive but submissive, catering to his needs. Now, she was satisfying hers. Quickly, too quickly, he joined her in the throes of passion. Spent, she fell across him gasping for breath. He felt like a senior on prom night, sexually satisfied by his date and emboldened by his conquest, but unsure as to who had conquered whom.

As he regained his breath from his exertions, he caressed her back. She traced patterns on his chest with a finger.

"That was wonderful," she said. "I surprised myself."

"Dawn should come more often," he replied.

"It's more than just the sun coming back. It feels like we've turned a corner."

"Us? I think we might have rounded the edges off the corner."

She hammered his chest with her fist gently. "No, silly. All of us. We made it through the long night. If Malosi and I ..." She paused. "When Malosi and I figure out how to stop this nanite virus, we can find a way back home."

He eased her off his chest, kissed her breast, and sat up. "I have to go back to work. The temperature could start dropping at any time. Lester thinks we can rig a low-power electric heater into one of the aquarium tanks and fill it with fresh water. We're running an electrical line today."

He began dressing and then lacing his boots. Liz crawled across the bed and leaned her cheek against his back.

"We have to do this again. Soon."

He turned around and kissed her. "Very soon."

Just as he stood, someone knocked at the door. She yanked the sheet up over her body.

"What is it?" he snarled at the unwelcome intruder on their privacy.

"Sorry to bother you, but you might want to take a look at this."

Brad recognized Hughes' voice. He knew Hughes wouldn't bother him unless it was important. When he opened the door, Hughes discreetly turned his back.

"What's wrong?"

"Let's go to the roof."

Thinking that Hughes simply wanted to point out the sunrise, he followed Hughes up the ladder to the roof. The outside air reeked of sulfur. Bits of ash landing on his tongue tasted bitter and flinty. He gazed at Mt. Erebus belching out smoke and lava; then faced the eastern horizon, but saw only a faint smudge of light.

"Not that," Hughes said, "this."

He followed Hughes' gaze to the scores of zombies surrounding the science building and gasped. He quickly counted over a hundred. They moved in slow circles around the building or stood and gazed at windows and doors expectantly.

"How long have they been here?" Brad asked.

"I spotted them a few hours ago. There were about thirty then. More keep showing up. I decided I had better let someone know."

"Why now? Because of Wilkie?" A few zombies had seen them enter the building, but that was at the aquarium at the far end of the complex and happened almost a week earlier. These zombies seemed focused on the Core Pod.

"I don't think so."

Brad briefly considered their behavior to the rising sun, but their attention was drawn not eastward toward the sun, but toward the science building. Why was Hughes on the roof? When Brad had followed Malosi the first time, Hughes had been on the roof. Wilkie's unexpected arrival had prevented him from asking Hughes then what he was doing up there. What had brought him onto the roof this time? Certainly, the air inside was cleaner than the dust-laden air outside. There was no view to draw one's eye.

"Why were you up here?" he asked.

Hughes hesitated for a moment, and then said, "I've been watching Malosi same as you."

This surprised Brad. "Why didn't you tell me?"

"Maybe the same reason that you didn't tell me."

Brad smiled at Hughes' irrefutable logic. "You may be right. I guess trust has been in short supply."

"It is where Malosi is concerned."

"He's been sitting by the radio as if he's waiting for a call from someone."

Hughes nodded. "I figured as much. Bastard's been holding out on us." He pointed to the zombies surrounding the building. "I think he has something to do with these zombies showing up."

"For what purpose?"

"I don't know. While you were with Liz, I watched him sneak out again. He came back about twenty minutes ahead of the first zombies."

Brad felt a twinge of guilt at abandoning his tailing of Malosi for a few minutes alone with Liz. "Do we confront him about it?"

"No. He'll just lie. Too many of the others trust him more than they do you or me. He's been working them like a revival preacher – a kind word here, a pat on the back there, and that constant smirky smile on his face. He's even swayed Deen."

"Deen? That seems unlikely. Deen hates Malosi."

"They've had a few long conversations away from prying ears."

"About what?"

Hughes shrugged. "I wasn't privy, but Deen's smile frightened me. He looks like a kid pulling wings off flies."

"What do we do about these zombies?"

"We're pretty safe here for now, but when supplies run low, going after more might be dicey." He glanced at the horizon. "When the sun comes up, they'll be able to see us better."

Brad closed his eyes and imagined the sun rising over the Turtle Mountains in North Dakota. He could feel the first rays of warmth washing the nights chill from his face. He opened his eyes and saw only darkness. "I don't care. I need to see the sun again."

* * * *

Malosi enjoyed his time working in the lab with Liz Strong. She was a beautiful woman and it had been a long time since he had seen a woman. The military in its sublime wisdom had insisted on an all-male staff at Resurrection City to avoid 'erosion of morale', as they put it. This had delighted the half dozen gay staffers and had infuriated the remainder. Being so near a woman stirred him in ways he had thought forgotten.

She worked diligently and at times with bursts of inspiration that he admired, but she was no nearer a solution than when they had begun. He offered her his knowledge of the nanites, which was admittedly poor, and of the endocrine system of the human body, which for surpassed her own. For her, their work was a desperate attempt at a solution. For him, it was merely a way to pass the time in pleasant company.

Liz placed a tissue sample into the electron microscope and stared at it on the computer screen. The nanite resembled a horseshoe crab with two pair of tiny manipulator arms on one end. It operated much as did a cell, drawing nutrients in through the permeable membrane and excreting sugar for the host body and replicating target cells. A loud sigh escaped her lips.

"It looks so innocuous, almost beautiful."

"So does a plague virus," he reminded her. She angrily turned off the screen. Malosi smiled at her frustration. "I warned you there was no cure."

Her glare warmed him as much as would her caress.

"I can't believe anyone would create such a monster without a leash, some way of controlling it."

He shrugged. "Some monsters operate better with no restraints. The nanites lethality intrigued the military. We did not anticipate it becoming airborne."

"That's what I don't understand. How could it have become airborne? It was created to function inside the human body at certain temperatures, a certain degree of humidity – how could it survive outside the host?"

"We did not have time to search for an answer, but I do have a theory."

"Please explain."

She sat with her arms folded beneath her breasts, pushing them up and out. He longed to reach out and caress them, but knew where that would land him. Later, when her desperation for survival became a driving force, she would come to him.

"Our nanite is about 250 *nanometers* in size. The protective coat is not *capsid* as in most viruses, but a synthetic protein we called *acromase,* infused with molecules of zinc and selenium, which are present in the human body. I believe the nanite reduces its size by half, encapsulates itself like a spore, and spreads in the air."

Her mouth opened. "My God! It learns."

"Yes. Memory is after all chemical in nature. A simple molecular strand contains sufficient information to adapt to different conditions."

She shook her head in disbelief. "You created a thinking, adapting robot?"

He had a difficult time suppressing his smile at her insight. "Yes."

She closed her eyes and leaned back in her chair. "God help us all."

He doubted that God, if he existed, was concerned with the pitiful plight of his human creations or inclined to step in and correct man's mistakes. If the past was any indication, God preferred to wait until things reached a head and then wipe the slate clean.

21

Sept. 21, McMurdo Base, Antarctica

The sun rose slowly on the first day of spring, as if the icy land's grip on it was immune to the sun's heat. At last, it melted the frozen tendrils binding it to the earth and climbed higher into the gray, ash-hazed sky, a dull red blob of light. In doing so, it revealed the carnage and destruction of McMurdo Base. It also exposed the zombies surrounding the science building and infesting the base to the light of day. The creatures, born into darkness, had never seen the sun and stood mesmerized by its brightness, as if some kernel of memory, some spark of human joy remembered its beauty.

Brad, Hughes, DeSousa, and Bain stood on the roof looking out over the devastation. As much as the first faint rays of sun touching his skin delighted him, the sight below was disheartening. A hundred zombies circled the building and more patrolled the grounds between buildings. When Hughes leaned over the edge of the roof, a single zombie caught sight of him and began a loud wail that the others picked up until soon, a sea of growls, moans, and calls swept across the base. Their brief awe of the rising sun was gone, replaced with their thirst for blood and flesh.

"The natives are restless," Hughes joked.

Brad didn't share Hughes' sense of humor. The sight chilled him to the bone. "They're hungry, starving."

"We could toss them Malosi."

At this, Brad almost chuckled in spite of himself. "That would be cruel and heartless. The zombies deserve better."

In spite of their attempts at levity, the severity of the situation, brought home even more abundantly by the light of day, was no joking matter. If the creatures made a concentrated effort at breaking in, the barricaded doors and windows would not stop them. Their hunger was driving them to greater extremes. Brad had earlier spotted several zombies out on the ice chasing Adelaide penguins in an almost comical fashion, the penguins waddling and sliding on their bellies, and the zombies slipping and falling. The penguins had abandoned most of the local rookeries under the zombie threat, but a few still tenaciously clung to their territories.

The zombies were visibly starving. The ones without little or no clothing showed obvious signs of starvation – gaunt scarecrows of death. If not for the nanites inhabiting their bodies, trickling minute amounts of energy in the form of sugars into their black, viscous blood, they would be immobile if not dead once again.

Mt. Erebus rumbled for the second time that morning, releasing a cloud of ash and gas. The building trembled as a minor quake struck. Brad almost ignored it. Such tremors had become more frequent, some large enough to wake him from sleep.

"We need to find more weapons and ammo," he said. "Our few rifles and pistols won't be enough if they manage to get inside."

Hughes pointed to a supply building nearly a quarter of a mile away. "That's where they would be." He looked at Brad. "Any suggestions on how to get there?"

"It would have to be at night. Maybe a diversion like the one you used when Wilkie arrived."

Hughes winced at the mention of Wilkie. His sudden death had shaken them all. He shook his head. "Someone would have to wade through zombies. I'm not volunteering."

"We could start a ruckus on one side of the building," Lester suggested, "opposite the direction we're going."

"What about the return trip?" Bain asked.

Lester smiled. "I haven't gotten that far yet."

"No, that might work," Brad agreed. "We can distract them and slip through. We do the same thing when we return." He looked around at the others. "So, we're agreed?"

Slowly, they all nodded their assent.

"Okay, now all we need is a way to distract them."

"I still say we use Malosi," Hughes said.

Brad feared it wouldn't take much persuasion for him to agree with Hughes. Malosi had been paying far too much attention to Liz. He had caught Malosi's gaze lingering on her when he thought no one was watching. Malosi had offered no real help in the attempt at discovering a cure for the nanite plague, though he certainly knew more about the tiny robots than he pretended. He was intentionally withholding information. If not for the visible improvement in Liz's morale that the work produced, Brad would have insisted that they stop working.

"Maybe a Molotov cocktail would do the trick," Bain suggested. "They seem to be fascinated by fire."

Brad nodded. "That might work. Now, who's going?"

Hughes raised his hand. "I'm in. I need the exercise."

Bain shrugged. "I'm up for a spot of adventure."

Lester hesitated. "We need four," Brad hinted. "If we find weapons, we'll need a crate or something to carry them. I'd like at least two guards."

"Oh, hell," Lester finally said. "I'll come along. Maybe I'll find some cigarettes."

Brad hated to cajole Lester into coming, but he wanted people who could shoot and people that he trusted. He didn't trust Deen and wanted to leave DeSousa to watch Malosi and Deen.

"Good. We leave just after sunset."

The others left, but Brad and Bain remained on the roof. Bain pretended to survey the base, but Brad could tell that he was trying to come to a decision about something. He seemed hesitant to broach whatever subject he wished to discuss. Brad decided to help him.

"So what's on your mind?"

His question startled Bain. He jumped slightly, and then smiled. "Sorry, I was judging the benefits of mentioning something to you."

"And?"

"Well, I'm no volcanologist, just a highly paid weatherman, but I think we have a problem. Mt. Erebus is becoming more active. It is an effusive volcano like Stromboli, but these tremors worry me. Last night I saw a second plume of smoke. I believe the underlying magma lake is spreading, destabilizing the entire shield."

"I'm an astronomer, so speak slowly and use small words."

"At least one of the three previously inactive volcanoes is now erupting."

Brad knew the other three volcanoes – Mt. Terror, Mt. Bird, and Mt. Terra Nova. He had flown over them in a helicopter while training at McMurdo. Of the four, only Mt. Erebus was active. "What does it mean?"

"The entire lava chamber could erupt in a massive explosion, or a massive pyroclastic flow of tephra, hot volcanic gas and rock, could sweep over the island at a hundred kilometers per hour and at hundreds of degrees centigrade, destroying everything."

He stared at Brad as if expecting some reply, but Brad was at a loss for words. Their only refuge was McMurdo. Now, a threat even greater than zombies had arisen, this time one of nature's doing. It seemed that man had screwed up so badly that the earth wanted to eliminate all traces of its human infestation. Gaia was pissed. It suddenly struck him as funny. He began laughing. Bain gawked at him in utter astonishment. He leaned over the edge of the building and laughed at the zombies below.

"Okay, you dead bastards!" He thumped himself in the chest with his fist. "You'd better eat fast or you'll burn in the hell you deserve." He pointed to the growing ash cloud over Mt. Erebus. "That's your Mt. Doom calling you. Even Lord Sauron can't save your asses."

His tirade at the zombies flushed his system of the ironic humor at the plight of the survivors. He turned to Bain. "Tell no one else about this. They have enough to worry about, and, as you said, you're no volcanologist. You could be wrong."

Bain nodded. "That's why I waited to tell you."

Bain left Brad standing on the roof. Brad felt no urgency to rejoin the others for fear his face would betray his thoughts. He stared at Mt. Erebus spewing its burden of ash and volcanic gases into the air and silently cursed it.

\* \* \* \*

Liz could tell that something was wrong with Brad. He avoided her as he reinforced the doors and windows. She wanted to talk to him, but Malosi had promised to divulge some information on the nanites. She couldn't risk angering him. Any bit of advice might be all she needed to solve the problem. Malosi was waiting for her in the lab. His smile when she approached seemed genuine, but he had become an expert at smiling at the right time. His …

schmoozing was the only word she could think of … of the survivors was an art form with him. The fact that he was responsible for their friends' deaths seemed irrelevant to the fact that he made them happy. He cooked, he joked, and he listened sympathetically to their tales of woe.

His interest in her was not lost on her. His eyes followed her every movement. She was used to lecherous looks from men, but his eyes betrayed more than simple lust. She was afraid of him.

"Ah, Doctor Strong," he said. "Good to see you."

"Doctor Malosi," she returned, trying to keep her voice neutral. "What were you going to share with me?"

"First, an observation. Originally, our test subjects lasted 35-40 days without infusions of fresh blood. I had assumed that would apply to these creatures."

"They look as if they're starving," she said.

"Quite so, but they aren't dying. Something has changed."

Now, he had aroused her curiosity. "What has changed?"

He smiled but said nothing, as if coaxing her to guess. She didn't want to play games.

"I repeat, what has changed?" she said.

"Think about it for a moment. What conditions have changed since the outbreak?"

In spite of herself, she went over the options in her mind – weather, temperature, volcanic ash, volcanic gases … radiation. The thought sprang into existence like an explosion. "The radiation increase."

He nodded. "Yes. It isn't enough to affect humans, but the nanites are creatures of change. Even a minute increase in radiation could alter their programming, much as affects our genetic code. They have mutated. What might have been a simple pandemic, through man's folly at attempting to eradicate it with nuclear weapons, has altered it into an ever-changing threat."

"You seem pleased."

He shook his head. "Not pleased, surprised."

"This will make it more difficult to develop a cure. If …"

He stopped her and glanced around to make certain no one was listening. "There is no cure. There is, however, a way to survive. More specifically, there is a way for you to survive."

"Why me?"

"Isn't it obvious? I find you attractive and do not wish to see you become one of these filthy creatures. It will be a different world. I will have power. You could share in this power; have every available comfort."

"If I go with you?"

"Yes."

His audacity irritated her. His callousness made her furious. Before she knew what she was doing, she slapped him across the cheek. The blow surprised him, but he reacted quickly, grabbing her hand in a tight grip. His eyes went cold.

"You're an animal," she shouted. "If you know of a way to survive, you must tell me, tell the others."

"You had your chance. I will not make the offer again."

He released her and stormed out of the room. She didn't know if she hated him more for lying or for pretending to work for a cure just to be near her. She knew no one was immune to infection, so Malosi knew of a way to protect himself and her. She had to warn Brad.

\* \* \* \*

Malosi knew immediately that he had made a mistake. His infatuation with Liz had clouded his judgment. He had misjudged her dedication to her fellow humans. There would be no shortage of beautiful women in the world eager for the chance to survive. Of course, the pretty doctor would inform her insipid lover, Brad Niles. His refuge among the other survivors was no longer safe for him. He had briefly considered killing her both for her refusal of his offer and to cover his tracks, but that would only enrage Brad. With luck, they would welcome his exit and not attempt to search for him. He still had his 'hidey hole' as Hughes had so quaintly put it.

As he gathered his few belongings, a tremor struck the building, this one of a magnitude greater than any previous ones. Glass shattered and the floor buckled beneath his feet. Photos left by the original occupant of the office-turned-bedroom, scenes from some backyard garden filled with flowering plants and bird feeders dangling from shepherd's hooks, crashed to the floor. He braced himself in the doorway in case the ceiling came down. The tremor lasted almost a full minute. The steel support beams groaned as the building shifted. He could hear people screaming. He welcomed the diversion of the tremor. It would cover his escape.

The rumblings of Mt. Erebus were growing louder daily and the sky was hazy with soot and ash. If this most recent quake was any indication, time was growing short for those left at McMurdo. He didn't want to be in the vicinity when the volcano decided to blow its top and bury the island in ash and lava. He could wait no longer. His original plan of waiting for a radio call that might never come was no longer viable. He had to leave McMurdo. The remaining DeHavilland had the range to reach Resurrection City and was simple to fly. Though he had taken only a few lessons years ago, he was certain he could manage. If anyone had guessed the secret of the nanite plague, Resurrection City would be their destination. He would have to deal with Gilford when he arrived, but with any luck, the madman was already dead.

The biggest obstacle was in reaching the airplane safely. For this he needed help – Deen. Deen was a fool, frightened and easily led. He resented his relegation to a subordinate position by the others, but lacked the courage to assume responsibility for the welfare of anyone but himself. Malosi had carefully cultured his relationship with Deen, playing on his resentment and fear to erase Deen's earlier hatred of him. Now, Deen believed that only Malosi could save them, or more importantly, him. He located Deen in his usual haunt, the multipurpose area of the Atmospheric Sciences Pod in building two. Deen was eating a sandwich and drinking a bottle of wine he had found in one of the offices and stashed away for his use. A broken glass and a small puddle of wine lay on the floor, a casualty of the tremor. Deen saw Malosi coming and held out the bottle to him.

"No thank you, Deen," Malosi said. "I came to talk."

Deen took a long swig, draining the bottle, and then smiled. "I thought that last quake might bring you."

"Quite right. I believe it is time to leave."

Deen sat up and slammed the empty bottle on the floor. "Good! I'm ready to put this place behind me." He stared at Malosi. "You're sure about them coming back for you?"

"They will come. If anyone out there seeks the answer to the nanite infestation, they will realize that the answer lies in Resurrection City." He pointed a finger to his temple. "The answer isn't there; it's here, the proper code to deactivate the nanites."

Deen grinned. "I knew there was a cure. Otherwise, you wouldn't be so secretive about things. I'm glad I didn't kill you."

"As am I. We must leave this place quickly, now."

"Now?" Deen questioned. "Why?"

"Never mind why. Suffice it to say it is essential that we leave."

"Whatever you say, Doc. How and where to?"

"In the DeHavilland. I will fly us out of here, and we will wait for someone to come to us."

"The plane, huh? I should have suspected." He paused. "How do we get through the zombies?"

"There is a maintenance tunnel beneath the aquarium that leads to a sewer. We can follow it and exit a hundred yards from here, beyond the zombies."

Deen smiled. "You've got this thing all planned out."

Malosi returned his smile. "Yes, I have, right down to the last detail."

Deen waved his hand. "After you, Malosi."

"You meet me in the aquarium. There is a small detail I must attend to."

Deen shrugged, grabbed his rifle, and exited the atmospherics building. Malosi returned to the Biology Pod. Working carefully so that he would not alert the others, he removed the pile of furniture barricading the entrance near loading dock A. He opened it slowly and peeked out. Zombies milled about just outside the building. After weeks of near starvation, they resembled concentration camp survivors – gaunt, pinch-cheeked, and hollow eyes devoid of expression. They moved silently as if conserving their energy. They were hungry and eager for a meal. He would offer them one.

He flung the door wide and banged on it with his pistol. First one, then several noticed him. They growled and rushed up the stairs toward the door. He stepped back inside and rushed down the corridor. He looked back over his shoulder at the zombies entering the building and smiled.

He brushed past Charles Lester in the corridor separating the Biology Pod from the Core Pod, sending him staggering into the wall.

"What the hell's your hurry, asshole," Lester bitched.

He ignored Lester. The fool would learn the answer soon enough. He heard the first screams as he pushed through the door into the corridor leading to the Earth Sciences Pod and the aquarium.

*That should give the others something to take their mind off me.*

## 22

Sept. 21, McMurdo Base, Antarctica

Brad was cursing when Liz found him near the water station in the Biology Pod trying to redirect a water line. He waved his hand in the air trying to bring back feeling to his smashed fingers. In his other hand, he held a twelve-inch pipe wrench glaring at it as if it were the cause of his pain instead of his own ineptness with tools. If he were not angry enough, when Liz revealed Malosi's attempt to seduce her, he was ready to kill. Malosi's secretive behavior was one thing, but his admission of a cure and his refusal to share it was pushing his luck too far.

"Go find the others and get them together," he told Liz. "I'm going to find the bastard and toss him outside."

As he started to leave, she placed her hand on his chest to hold him back. "He's dangerous, Brad. Wait for Hughes," she pleaded.

He was too angry to wait. Malosi had committed the ultimate sin – he had messed with his girl. Whatever Malosi had been planning, whatever the reason for his trips to the radio, he would have to make his move now. He could disappear into the warren of buildings at McMurdo. If he had a cure for the plague, Brad would wring the secret from him before feeding him to the zombies.

"I think I know where he's going. I'll …"

A scream interrupted him. Instinctively, Brad knew it had something to do with Malosi. "Find the others and take them to the loft."

He picked up his rifle and made certain it was loaded. He pushed past her and raced toward the scream. He saw the first zombie outside the staging area by Dock A and knew Malosi's foul hand was behind its presence. The creature had the screaming Shimoda pinned against the wall. The much shorter Japanese climatologist was no match for the starving zombie. It sank its teeth into Shimoda's neck and ripped away a chunk of flesh. Brad aimed carefully and shot it in the head, but more zombies poured through the open door beyond. The creature fell as Shimoda sank to the floor holding his wounded neck, which spewed blood from a nicked artery. As Brad rushed to his side, Shimoda waved him away.

"Go," he shouted. "I'm a dead man. Save the others. Save Mattie."

Brad left Shimoda and rushed to the empty lab room to which Liz had confined Mattie to allow her injuries to mend. He was too late. Two of the creatures had smashed in the locked door. She stood in the center of the room naked. Black lines of infection traced across her heavy breasts, but she was still human enough to realize the danger she was in. She shoved at the first creature, but the second overpowered her. Her blood-curdling scream lasted only a few seconds. At the sound of her dying, Shimoda yelled in anguish and released his neck. Blood sprayed the wall behind him and the floor around him. Within seconds, he too was lying dead on the floor. Brad fired as quickly as he could as the zombies rushed down the corridor, trying to give everyone as much time as possible to escape.

As he passed the water station, he heard zombies in the opposite corridor. He couldn't stop them all. If they reached the main corridor ahead of him, they would trap him. He ran as fast as he could and reached the main corridor just ahead of the zombies. He pushed through the door into the Core Pod, grabbed a broom, and stuck it through the door handles. It wouldn't keep out the creatures for long, but every minute counted. He raced up the stairs and found almost everyone standing around. Hughes and Bain had their weapons trained on the stairs on each end of the room. Deen and Reed were absent. He knew Deen was probably in his quarters in the other pod. He had a rifle and could fend for himself. Reed was young and unarmed.

"Where's Reed?"

"No one knows," Liz answered. "I last saw him in the stockroom." She looked down the stairs. "You didn't bring Mattie?"

Brad shook his head. "She's gone. So is Shimoda."

Liz clasped her hand to her mouth. "No," she moaned. "I should have gone directly to her."

"Then you'd be dead too. That bastard Malosi let the zombies in. He's to blame for this."

"I just saw that asshole," Lester said. "I knew he was up to something." He glanced at the stairs. "Can they get up here?"

"Eventually. I barred the door but it won't hold long."

"What do we do?"

Brad thought furiously. They didn't have much time. "We cross over to the equipment mezzanine and up through the roof." He turned to the others. "Grab all the food you can carry."

"Won't the zombies be outside?" Jernigan asked. His fear showed clearly on his face. Brad noticed that most of the others mirrored his fear. The exception was Hughes. He appeared calm and ready for action.

"It looked as if most of them are inside now," Brad replied. "We can keep them off the roof."

"And do what?" Jernigan whined.

"We survive," Brad snapped. "That's what we've been doing for a month. We keep surviving. Now, get ready to leave."

A loud crash below meant the zombies had broken through the door. Time was short to make their escape. The stairs were narrow and only one creature at a time could climb them. While Liz propelled the others into action, he and Hughes shot each zombie as it showed itself. Bain and Lester took the other stairs case and did the same. Brad knew they couldn't hold out for long, but each dead zombie meant that the others had to climb over their corpses to come up the stairs, slowing them down.

Liz herded everyone through into the Biology Pod loft. He signaled for Lester and Bain to follow, and then took one more shot and nudged Hughes.

"Time to go."

Constructed of heavy wood, the door to the adjacent loft would keep the zombies out for a while but not indefinitely. To increase their chances, he and Hughes piled crates of stored supplies against the door. The seven remaining survivors climbed the ladder to the roof and locked the hatch behind them. The day was gray and overcast and the air stank of volcanic gases blowing toward McMurdo from the volcano.

"What about Deen and Reed?" Liz asked.

"The stockroom has a strong door. He's safe there for now. Deen's probably in the other building."

"Or with Malosi," Hughes growled.

That thought had also crossed Brad's mind. He and Deen had become fast friends in spite of Deen's earlier hatred for him. If Malosi had taken the time to cultivate his friendship, then it was for a purpose, probably one just such as this.

"Forget about Deen and Malosi for now," Brad said. "We need to concentrate on survival."

"Any suggestions?" Hughes asked.

"We can try to reach the Russian tractor," DeSousa replied. "We'll need fuel, but we can move out on the ice away from the zombies."

"Even with enough fuel and food, we'll be stuck out on the ice. If anything happened to the engine, we'd be right back where we started. No, we need a more permanent place."

"What about Scott Base. There were only a few people there. We can handle a few zombies."

Bain spoke up. "I don't want to unduly frighten anyone, but neither suggestion is safe."

DeSousa scowled at him. "What do you mean?"

"With the growing degree of tremors, the ice isn't safe. The same applies to Scott base. It's nearer the volcanoes." He glanced in Brad's direction. Brad knew what was coming and nodded. Everyone needed to know the truth. "Mt. Erebus is building to a major eruption. It would be unwise to be too near when that happens."

"You don't know that for certain," DeSousa challenged.

"No, I don't, but the risk of an eruption increases with each quake. Ross Island is a volcanic island. Volcanic islands can become unstable. I think we need a third option."

"The safest place is the Kharkovchanka," DeSousa insisted. "We load up on fuel and go west, maybe Casey Base."

"So we trade one dead base overrun with zombies for another," Lester argued. "Why bother?"

"At least it is away from the volcanoes," Bain said.

Brad realized that their arguing was getting them nowhere. "Look, our first challenge is getting past the zombies. Agreed?" No one challenged him. "Okay. We find Reed and Deen and decide as a group."

"What about Malosi?"

"Screw that son of a bitch. I hope the zombies eat him." Brad walked to the edge of the roof above the stockroom. Zombies roamed around the building below them. He yelled, "Reed!" One of the zombies looked up at him and snarled.

Reed opened the window just a crack and shouted. "I'm in here."

"We'll get you out. Just hang on."

"I don't have a gun," Reed said. "I hear zombies outside the door."

"The plane!" Lester yelled, smiling. "The DeHavilland Twin Otter. I think I can fly it." He pursed his lips and frowned. "But to where?"

Hughes shrugged. "Casey."

"No," Bain said, "Not Casey. I think I know where Resurrection City is. It's at Longitude 152.5 east about eighty miles inland." He looked at the startled faces around him. "I plotted its location using weather data from its telemetry station. I can get us within a few miles."

"Why the hell would we go to zombie central?" Hughes asked. "That's where everything started."

Bain ticked the reasons off on his fingers one at a time. "It was a small base, so there will be fewer zombies; it was military, so it will be well supplied; and if there is an answer to the plague, there is where we will find it."

Bain's suggestion made sense, but something in the back of Brad's mind was scratching away trying to get his attention. It worried him like an itch between the shoulder blades you can't scratch. Finally, he had it. *The DeHavilland.*

"The plane," he shouted, "that's where Malosi is headed."

Hughes looked perplexed. "Why?" he asked.

"His trips to the radio, his *tete-a-tete* with Deen – he's been planning a return to Resurrection City all along. He thinks someone is going to go there for answers. He was waiting for a radio call searching for survivors. He has the answers, and he wants to cash in on his knowledge." Hughes still seemed unconvinced. Exasperated, Brad said, "Don't you see? That's what this was all about, the zombies – a diversion like your explosion when the Khark arrived. He's making for the plane and needs Deen's help to roll it out of the garage."

Hughes shook his head. "That son of a bitch. He was willing to let us die to get away. When we find the bastard, I'm going to kill him."

"No," Liz said, "we need to learn whatever he knows."

"Then I'll slice off his fingers one at a time until he tells us, and then I'll shove a knife through his eye into his skull."

He made a jabbing motion with his hand. Liz's face paled at the extent of Hughes' vehemence. Even Brad thought he might not be exaggerating.

"We've got to hurry," he said. "The sun sets in a few hours. Taking off and landing in the dark won't be easy." He yelled down to Reed. "Reed, we'll create a diversion on the other side of the building to draw the zombies away. When you see us come down off the roof, break out the window and join us."

"Okay."

Reed sounded frightened. Brad didn't blame him. The prospect of racing through a bunch of zombies didn't appeal to him either.

To Hughes, he said, "We need something to draw the zombies below us to the other side of the building." He noticed the way the zombies were watching him. "I could walk along the edge of the roof. I think they would follow. Once they're gone, the rest of you scramble down the drainpipe. I'll follow."

"We could just shoot them," Bain said.

"No. That would bring more." He handed Lester his Winchester. "Take this. Let me have your pistol." He tucked Lester's pistol into his belt.

Liz, as he assumed, objected. "Why you? We can draw straws or something. I can probably climb better than you can."

He silenced her objections by kissing her. "I can run faster than you, that's why. Hughes is a better shot and Bain has the AK-47. I have the pistol and my knife." He looked at Hughes. "Keep her safe." Hughes nodded.

He walked to the edge of the roof and yelled at the four zombies in view. "Hey, you bastards! Want some meat?"

The zombies began a low keening, their eyes following his every move. He walked along the roof slowly making sure all three followed him, feeling much like a piece of steak on display at a butcher's meat counter. He watched Hughes lead the group off the roof. One by one, they disappeared over the roof's edge. By the time he reached the far side of the building, he had picked up a dozen zombies. He gave them one lingering last look at him, and then backed away from the edge. This produced a series of loud growls and hoots. He hoped the noise drew more zombies away from the others.

He raced across the roof, checked to make sure the coast was clear, and slid down the pipe. He hit the ground harder than he had intended and grimaced as his ankle sent pains shooting through his leg. He ignored the agony and hobbled away as quickly as he could. He saw the others, including Reed who had joined them, disappearing behind one of the damaged buildings. He had almost reached the building when he heard a loud crash behind him. Zombies poured through the smashed side door of the Core Pod. When they saw him, they began howling. He redoubled his effort, hoping his injured ankle didn't betray him.

He turned the corner and ran into a pair of zombies sniffing the air where the others had passed. He pulled out the revolver and shot both of them in the head at a run. Now, stealth no longer mattered. With zombies in hot pursuit and the probability of more attracted by the sound of the shots, the odds of reaching the plane seemed dismally low. For a brief moment, he considered leading the zombies away from Liz and the others; give them a better chance at surviving, but his sense of self-preservation kicked in. He had no desire to provide a meal for a pack of starving zombies. He had found real love for the first time in his life. He wasn't going to throw it all away until he had to.

He worked his way around and through a warren of buildings, some little more than standing charred timbers, on a direct path toward the garage with the Otter. Several times, he crouched or hid in the concealing shadows as a zombie lumbered by. The air thick with ash worked to his advantage, masking his scent from the creatures. They walked with heads held high sniffing the air for prey but walked right past him. His heart climbed his throat as he spotted two zombies devouring a corpse. He couldn't see the body well enough to identify it. His mind in turmoil and heart pounding for fear it might be someone he knew, he risked detection to creep closer for a better look. He sighed in relief when he saw that the creatures were eating one of their own. *I hope they eat each other until only one bastard is left.*

As he turned to leave, one zombie, a large black man wearing a ragged and bloodstained blue pinstriped suit, stood only a few feet away staring at him. A pair of dark-rimmed eyeglasses with thick lenses dangled from one ear. Brad wondered briefly if the creature could even see him. The zombie growled and lunged at him. *Good enough,* he thought. He dodged the first attack by stepping underneath the beefy arms that reached out for him. He wasn't as lucky the second time. The zombie shoved him in the chest with the flat of his palm and sent Brad stumbling backwards. He fell but scooted out of the way just as the creature pounced on him. He got to his feet and pulled his pistol, but before he could fire, the other two zombies that he had forgotten in the scuffle were on him. One of them knocked the pistol from his hand. He quickly drew his knife and fended them off as best he could, but his injured ankle limited his mobility and his slashes went largely ignored. Out of the corner of his eye, he saw the big zombie regaining its feet. Now he faced odds of three-to-one. He waited for the bite or the scratch that would doom him.

A shot rang out. The large, well-dressed zombie collapsed with half its skull missing. Brad shoved one of the remaining zombies into the second one, knocking them both off balance, and scrambled for his pistol. He fell to the ground, rolled over and fired twice, hitting one of the creatures in the left cheek and in the jaw, shattering teeth. Firing from the ground, the upward trajectory of the bullets assured that at least one of them continued into the brain. It fell across his legs dead. The second fell as his unseen savior fired again. He shoved the dead zombie from his legs and crawled to his feet. Hughes stood almost eighty yards away smiling. Brad waved and limped to him.

"Doctor Strong insisted I come back to help you," he said.

"Lucky thing she did."

Hughes stared at the three dead zombies. "The big black guy in the suit was Leo Macintosh, the senior advisor for Raytheon. I liked him. The others are waiting just ahead." Before Brad could thank him for saving his life, he turned and began walking away. Brad hurried to catch up.

23

Sept. 21, McMurdo Base, Antarctica

Malosi heard the shots in the distance and knew he didn't have much time. He dialed the radio to the Australian Defense Force military frequency he had learned at Resurrection City and began broadcasting.

"This is Mac Ops to ADF Woomera. Come in please."

He had waited patiently for three weeks for a call from anyone searching for survivors, but now his attraction to Doctor Strong had forced his hand. He had no choice but contact anyone listening before he made his escape to Resurrection City.

"Mac Ops to ADF Woomera. Come in please."

"This is Woomera. Who are you?"

He almost wept with joy. Woomera north of Adelaide was the center for much of the military satellite communication in Australia. If anyone had survived, Woomera would be listening. The signal was weak and filled with static, but it sounded like an angel from heaven to him. "I am Doctor Gregory Malosi at McMurdo Base. I worked with Doctors Willis Cromby and John Gilford at Resurrection City. I have the kill code for the nanite plague. Repeat. I have the kill code for the nanite plague. I will be at Resurrection City in four hours. Exact coordinates to follow."

"Are there other survivors?"

"No. I am the sole survivor. McMurdo is overrun with zombies. I am relocating to the following location. I repeat, do not land at McMurdo. My new location is Longitude 153.5 degrees 22 minutes 26 seconds, 72 degrees 42 minutes 15 seconds Latitude. Runway is five thousand feet. Repeat, five thousand feet. Copy."

The reply came quickly. "Copy, Mac Ops. You say you have access to the kill code?"

"I have the kill code. If you want to stop this plague, you must come to the coordinates I gave you and rescue me."

He leaned forward in his seat for the two minutes as some discussion took place on the other end. Finally, "Read you, Doctor Malosi. We will send a rescue party, but please tell us the information so that we can begin deactivating the nanites. We have been using EMP devices but their range is limited."

Malosi smiled. He expected just such an attempt to obtain the kill code from him. His trust of no one extended that far. "No. Once I am in the air, I will provide the information to my rescuers. Not before then."

"Read you, Mac Ops. We will have transport at your coordinates within forty-eight hours, repeat, forty-eight hours."

"I will be waiting."

He flipped the off switch before Woomera could reply. He had offered them the bait, now they must come to collect.

"I knew I couldn't trust you."

Malosi spun to see Deen standing in the doorway with his rifle pointed at him. Judging by the look of hatred on his face, Malosi knew that Deen had overheard the entire conversation. He would not be able to explain his way out of this one. He shrugged his shoulders.

"I never intended to share my escape with anyone. You would never be able to remain silent. The deaths of the others would weigh too heavily on your conscious. You would eventually let slip today's events. Once the military has possession of the kill code, they would not condone my actions as readily. I suspect their punishment would be rather harsh and immediate. Your usefulness is at an end."

"Brave words for a man with a rifle pointed at him," Deen replied. He nodded at the Android on the table lying atop Malosi's gloves. "Is that it, where you have the kill code?"

Malosi smiled. "It is. I need only play the recorded message and it deactivates all the nanites in a small area. Unfortunately, it does not prevent new nanites from infecting me. I must expose myself to the code repeatedly. The more power behind the broadcast, the greater the area of coverage."

Upon his arrival at McMurdo, he had toyed with the possibility of using McMurdo's Ham radio station KC4USV to broadcast the signal to kill all the zombies, but the fires had damaged it. With the unexpected appearance of the survivors, he had decided to keep the device for himself.

"You bastard!" Deen yelled. "You could have cured us. You could have cured me." He glanced at the Android. "Hand it to me."

"No."

"I'll kill you and take it from you. I don't need you."

"Really, Deen? How will you fly the plane to Resurrection City? Do you even know where it is?"

"You play that thing to cure me, and then fly us there and I won't kill you."

Malosi laughed. "Of course you will. You hate me, now more than ever. Once I fly us to Resurrection City, you will have to kill me."

Deen frowned. "Call them back and tell them to land here."

In reply, Malosi reached for the radio and spun the frequency dial. "No. You will never learn the proper frequency if I'm dead."

Deen raised his rifle higher. "You're pushing me, Malosi."

"Go ahead. Shoot. You had better hurry. I hear shots outside. The others, at least some of them, have escaped. I don't think they would be happy to see you."

Deen licked his lips in indecision. Malosi could see that Deen was wavering. Deen knew that even if he provided the others with the kill code, they would never allow him to live now that he had betrayed him. Brad might, but Hughes was more vindictive. He would surely kill Deen. Deen knew his only chance of survival was with Malosi.

"Hand me that phone and come with me. We're both leaving."

Malosi nodded. "I suppose I have no choice. He reached for the Android phone, but instead grabbed the revolver lying beneath his gloves where he had earlier placed it. Before Deen could react, he fired, striking Deen in the abdomen. Deen's own shot went wild and hit the radio. He stumbled backwards and dodged around the edge of the door before Malosi could fire a second shot. Malosi cursed and went after him. Deen was gone. A bloody trail led out the open door. Knowing that the shots would draw curious zombies, he decided to forget about Deen and go to the plane. The smell of blood would ensure that the zombies would pursue the injured Deen instead of him. He had to reach the plane and leave before the others discovered his plan.

* * * *

When Brad joined the others, Liz saw him limping and rushed up to help.

"Is it bad?" she asked as she placed her shoulder under his arm. He allowed her to take some of his weight.

"Just twisted it a bit. I'll live."

"We heard two shots a few moments ago." She pointed to a group of buildings. "From there."

The communications building was among those to which she pointed. "Malosi. I hope a zombie got him. At least that means the plane is still there."

He urged her to keep moving. Even with her help, his ankle throbbed with each step. The group encountered no zombies. He presumed the creatures pursuing them had stopped to dine on their dead companions, and the others had moved toward the shots. They reached the garage behind which the Otter was parked.

"Wait here," he said, but as he started to pull away, Liz stopped him.

"No you don't. You can barely walk." She looked at Hughes. "Can you check?"

Hughes said nothing but walked toward the back of the garage. He had taken only a few steps when Malosi stepped through the rear door. He was as surprised to see them, as they were to see him.

"Well, you survived," he said.

"No thanks to you, Malosi," Hughes said, drawing back the bolt to send a bullet into the chamber of his rifle. As he raised the rifle, Malosi raised the Android phone in the air.

"If you wish to survive, make certain that you do not hit this."

Hughes stared at the cell phone in Malosi's hand and hesitated. "Why, afraid of losing your tunes?"

"It contains the kill code that deactivates the nanites."

Hughes turned to glance at Liz, but didn't take his eyes off Malosi. "Is he lying?"

She shook her head. "No, I don't think so. I suspected he knew of a way to kill them. A coded message broadcast at the proper frequency would do it."

"It has kept me alive in spite of my injury." He pointed to Brad. "How long before the nanites begin changing him? I have contacted the Australians. They will arrive at Resurrection City within forty-eight hours. They are coming for me, but there will be room enough for all of us."

"Is that what you told Deen? You'd do or say anything to live, Malosi," Hughes said. "You tried to kill us once. I think we'd all be better off if I just shot you now. I know I'd sleep better for it."

"You doom us all if you do," Malosi warned.

"We'll have the kill code," Hughes said.

A look of anger morphed Malosi's face to something almost inhuman. He yelled and threw the phone across the room. Brad pushed Liz away and made a mad leap for it, his hands outstretched. He hit the concrete floor hard enough to knock the breath out of him, but he clasped the precious Android in his hands.

"Nice catch," Hughes said as Liz rushed to help Brad to his feet.

Malosi, seeing the danger he was in, began backing toward the door. He didn't see Deen enter the garage behind him. Deen's shirt was soaked with blood and he moved slowly. Hughes lowered his rifle. Malosi misinterpreted Hughes' actions as surrender. He smiled and turned around. When he did, Deen jabbed him in the stomach with the rifle he was holding.

"Got you now, you bastard," he whispered and pulled the trigger before Malosi could respond. The bullet tore through Malosi's stomach and upward through his chest, finally exiting his back near his spine. Malosi fell dead at Deen's feet. Deen glanced at Hughes and smiled; then, he fell across Malosi' body, dead from the wound Malosi had inflicted upon him.

As the stunned group stood there staring at the two bodies, a tremor twice as strong as any previous one struck the base. The ground shook like a pair of dice at a crap table. The concrete slab floor cracked with the sound of a dozen shotguns exploding, sending splinters of concrete flying through the air like shrapnel. The building shook and groaned as steel ceiling beams twisted. Dust and insulation cascaded from the ceiling.

The jolt knocked them all to the ground. Brad covered Liz with his body to protect her from falling debris, biting back his moans as the floor sent ribbons of pain shooting through his leg. His cheek bled profusely from a graze by a sharp shard of concrete. He could hear Liz's cries beneath him above the rumble of the earthquake. In the distance a report like that of a cannon split the air, followed by a shrill scream like escaping steam from a boiler.

"It's the volcano," Bain yelled, but Brad could barely hear him.

One of the corrugated steel wall panels fell away from the building, revealing the scene of destruction outside. Several of the nearby buildings had collapsed and others were following suit. To the south at the other end of island, three columns of thick smoke billowed into the air from Mount Erebus and two of its companion volcanoes. They met high in the atmosphere forming one dense black cloud that shrouded the sun. What appeared to be sparks shot from the volcano, arcing away in all directions, but Brad knew they were not sparks. They were deadly lava bombs, globs of volcanic basalt as big as cars. None reached McMurdo. After a few terrifying minutes, the trembling subsided but the rumbling continued.

"We don't have much time," Bain yelled.

Brad knew he was right. He wiped blood from his eye and helped Liz to her feet, ignoring the bolts of pain it brought to his ankle. "Everybody to the plane."

He hoped that Malosi had already prepped the Otter. They wouldn't have time to fuel it. As Liz helped him out the door, he saw Hughes and Lester ripping away the tarp. Ash fell around them like a thick, black rain. He wasn't sure the Otter could even fly under such conditions, but they had no choice.

"Everyone in," he yelled.

Lester took the pilot's set with Bain sitting beside him. The rear of the plane was half filled with crates and boxes. There wasn't room for all of them. Liz pushed him inside.

"Toss out some of this stuff," he told the others and shoved a crate with his shoulder. "If it's not food, get rid of it." Together, they dislodged enough freight to make room for all of them.

He waited impatiently as Lester familiarized himself with the controls. Finally, Lester cranked the engine. The propeller spun a few times and stopped as the engine coughed. He tried again. This time, it caught. There was barely room between the two buildings for the plane to move. The wings almost scraped the walls. After thirty harrowing seconds, the Otter was on the road headed into the wind for take-off.

"We have a problem," Lester called out.

Brad rose to look out the cockpit window. A wrecked truck blocked the road half a mile away. "How much runway do you need?" he asked.

"Twenty-five-hundred feet minimum, I think."

"You think?" Hughes shouted.

"I don't know," Lester replied. "I've never flown a plane this big before."

The garage they had just left collapsed. The Otter bounced as the road cracked.

"We don't have much choice," Brad said. "Gun it."

Lester looked at him, swallowed hard, and nodded. He pushed the throttle forward and the Otter's two engines roared into life. It rushed down the road toward the truck, which loomed larger and larger. Beside them, more buildings shook themselves to pieces. The Otter bucked and canted until the wings almost touched the ground, but Lester leaned into the wheel and held it straight. Two hundred feet from the truck, the wheels of the Otter finally left the ground, but only a few inches. Liz sought Brad's hand. He clasped it tightly and held his breath as Lester fought to bring the plane up. At the last moment, it rose, but the plane shuddered as the landing gear struck the roof of the truck. The Otter veered to the right as the landing gear sheared away, but Lester quickly corrected. They were airborne at last. Brad released his breath.

"We've lost the landing gear," Lester said. "I'll have to bring it in on its belly." His voice was a mixture of relief that they had taken off and fear that he would crash.

"We'll land in the snow," Brad said. "We'll be alright."

As they gained altitude, Lester kept Mt. Discovery to their left as he aimed for the Koettlitz Glacier to take them over the Transantarctic Range, beyond the Dry Valleys, and to the coordinates that Bain had provided. Behind them, one of the three columns of ash collapsed, and a massive pyroclastic flow raced toward McMurdo at a hundred miles per hour, wiping out Scott Base on the way. It swept over McMurdo less than six minutes later, inundating it with hot ash and boiling water from superheated snowmelt. Nothing remained. Where once stood a hundred buildings, the flow had scoured the ground of all ice and snow and any traces that man had ever set foot there. It was a patch of barren rock. With a mighty shudder, Mount Erebus finally relented to the growing pressure within its cone. The lava dome beneath it collapsed, allowing millions of gallons of seawater to pour in. The resulting explosion as water flashed to steam cracked the volcano's base, shattering the entire island. Shock waves rippled across the frozen sea for miles, radiating like a spider's web in all directions.

The concussion hit them a few moments later. The Otter dove for the ice as the air supporting the plane collapsed. Lester managed to bring up the nose as the ground rushed toward them at a dizzying rate. They passed over the ice so close that Brad could look into the frightened eyes of Adelaide penguins staring up at them.

"We made it," Bain said with relief.

Brad released Liz's death grip on his hand and reached into his pocket. He held out Malosi's Android phone and examined it. It looked no different from any other cell phone he had seen. He switched it on and scanned the song list until he came to one titled marked simply with an asterisk. He turned the volume to full and hit the play button.

"Let's see if this works."

Even over the roar of the engines, a shrill series of chirps and whistles filled the cabin. The sound vibrated Brad's chest. He felt as if his ears were bleeding. The sound lasted less than five seconds. He looked around at the others.

"Is that it?" he asked. He felt no different. Had Malosi lied to them again?

Liz leaned into his arms. "I hope to God it is."

Brad shoved the Android back in his pocket, leaned back against the fuselage, and let Liz rest her head in the crook of his arm. His leg throbbed, his cheek burned, but he was alive. They were all alive. If Malosi was right, they might remain alive.

24

Sept. 21, Melbourne, Australia

Val Marino stared out the upper floor window of the Crown Plaza Hotel at the Yarra River slicing through the heart of Melbourne like a dirty knife. Fires had burned away entire sections of the city and parts of the surrounding countryside. Runoff from recent rains stained the river brown. Things floated with the current, the flotsam and jetsam of a dead city. Some of them were human or had once been human, making the river a stinking cesspool, but as badly as the river smelled; the city itself reeked far worse.

The group had been in Melbourne for less than a week, little enough time to begin the long process of revitalizing a city so large. Securing Melbourne had gone much more smoothly and with less risk than they had encountered in Port Augusta. This time, they had used helicopters to place the EMP devices in the proper locations and had detonated them by remote control. Afterwards, the military swept the city for survivors and began the grisly task of collecting zombie corpses. An acrid black haze from the corpse fires burning day and night in parking lots and empty lots across the city hung like a dark rain cloud, reminding Val of the smoke covering the city of Adelaide when he and Elliot Anson had first arrived from Antarctica.

In Port Augusta, they had encountered the surviving remnants of the military that had grouped on the outskirts of Melbourne, and together they had swept Adelaide of zombies. Now, groups were working to clear both Melbourne and Canberra. As effective as the devices were against zombies, Val was disheartened at the number of survivors they had rescued so far – less than eight hundred from Port Augusta, two thousand from Adelaide, and just over twelve thousand in Melbourne, a city that once boasted a population of over four million. He knew he should have expected such numbers. Surviving the Demise was far easier than surviving the zombie onslaught that came afterwards.

He had a vague grasp of the science involved in the EMP devices, but mostly he did the grunt work, like Alex and Nicole. He was, or had been, a climatologist. Alex was an opal miner, as was Nicole. Jeffries, Ivers, and a handful of scientists working out of Camp Rapier in Woomera had developed the device. Their dedication had allowed them to continue their labors even as members of their own group turned into zombies, creating threats both inside and outside their labs. Now, the occasional treatment with EM waves kept them alive, but until they could develop a network large enough to sweep the entire planet clean of the nanite infestation, people would die.

Jeffries walked over to the window and stood beside him. In the fading light of day, the scientist looked much older than his fifty-two years. He stood stooped-shouldered and back bowed with the responsibility of his task. His gray eyes were weary. Val had noticed that Jeffries never smiled. At five-feet-six-inches tall to Val's six-feet, Jeffries had to crane his head to look into Val's eyes as he spoke.

"I had a report from Ivers in Canberra. They will be ready to begin operations in two days."

"How does Canberra look?"

Jeffries shrugged his shoulders. "Who can say? They saw signs of survivors, but the city and the surrounding countryside are teeming with zombies. We can only pray that it fared better than Melbourne."

"Or the rest of the world," Val added. He had heard nothing of his own home of Tucson, Arizona or most of America for that matter. A U.S. government still existed and Jeffries had radioed details of the EMP devices to them, but he didn't know how well they were managing to utilize the information. He removed his Stetson and stared at it, his only memento of his home. It had once been white, but now it was filthy from red dust, soot and blood. He wiped a smudge from the silver and turquoise hatband with the edge of his hand. He could always find a new hat, but continued to hold on to it like a dream that might fade if he opened his eyes. He would get a new one at *Cowtown Boots* when he returned to Tucson. He set the hat back onto his head and nodded at the smoke rising from dozens of fires. "We don't have enough people for this. It will take weeks to get rid of the corpses."

"What can we do? Many of the survivors are helping gather corpses, but to move them, we must first clear the roads of rubble. It all takes time."

"Corpses draw scavengers and disease. Hell, Doc, the smell alone will draw zombies for miles. They're like vultures. We can't keep zapping everyone with EM pulses. Hell, I light up a lamp when I walk by now."

"You must have patience and faith. We are making progress."

"Faith? That's in short supply around here. Elliot …" he stopped. It was too painful to continue.

Jeffries reached out and grasped Val's arm. "I didn't know your friend, but I, too, have lost friends and colleagues. No one has survived untouched by Death's whisper. If you have no faith in God, then have faith in science. In the end, we will succeed."

"I hope so."

Alex and Nicole had accompanied Ivers to Canberra. Though he had known them only a couple of weeks, he missed their company. Alex was hard and determined, like Anson had been, but without the extra years of wisdom to temper his rashness. Nicole was hard in her own way, but her pregnancy had softened her and thrilled Alex. Val hoped Nicole's impending motherhood would keep Alex out of trouble.

An explosion in the distance lit up the fading twilight and sent a dark cloud of smoke into the air.

"They are using explosives to remove rubble from the streets," Jeffries explained.

Val nodded. They had entered Melbourne by air, but he had seen the man-made barricades authorities had erected in a futile attempt to stop the advance of the zombies, little realizing that those standing beside them were infected as well. He could imagine the horror they felt as they saw friends and acquaintances die and come back to life as flesh-eating monsters. At least fate had spared him and Anson that gruesome memory. Marooned on the South Polar

Plateau, they had missed the orgy of destruction and death at Casey Base, had not witnessed friends turning zombie.

As the last rays of light spread across the carcass of the dead city, the lights in the room came on.

"Let there be light," Val said, smiling. Ironically, he remembered that today was the first day of full sunlight in Antarctica after six months of darkness. Part of him regretted that he had not been there to witness the dawn.

"Yes, the generators are working here, but it will be some time before they restore electricity to the city," Jeffries said.

"I don't think anyone will notice, do you, Doc?"

"I suppose you're right. We will concentrate our efforts on the airport and the docks along the river. The movement of supplies takes priority over raising the city from the dead."

"We don't need more zombies."

"No, I ..." Jeffries mumbled something inaudible and turned away.

Val realized he had touched a nerve. "I'm sorry, Doc. I'm being a dick."

"Eh?"

Val remembered the difficulties he had translating idioms from American to Australian. "You would call it a wanker."

"Oh, I see."

Still he brought no smile to Jeffries' lips. They seemed permanently pressed together from the hardships he had gone through and the deaths he had witnessed. "I find myself becoming morose lately."

"It's quite understandable. Some days it seems hardly to be worth the effort of rising from bed."

Val stared at Jeffries. "Why so glum? I mean, I'm trying to cope with the fact that everything I knew and everyone I cared for is gone, but you've created a device that can turn the tide on the plague. You should be dancing a jig."

Jeffries returned to his former seat on the sofa. An untouched glass of scotch and soda sat on the table beside him. Val had poured them both a drink earlier. He had quickly finished his, but even now, Jeffries ignored it.

"We have reached the point of diminishing returns on our EMP device," he said. "I thought that simply creating more powerful ones would allow us decontaminate larger areas. It isn't working out that way."

This was the first Val had heard of the problem. "What's the holdup?"

"The device seems to work well when covering areas a few kilometers in diameter, but the effectiveness drops off sharply. The frequencies we use are too muddled. Larger devices won't work. Neither will broadcasting the frequencies from satellites."

"What about Gilford's flash drive and Cromby's notes? Don't they help?"

"It gave us a starting point. In his notes, Cromby mentioned a kill switch but offered no details. It would seem that either they had no time to employ it, or it did not work." He sighed. "If we knew how to engage it, and if it were possible to disseminate the information widely enough, we could end the threat of repeated infection." He wrung his hands together and shook his head. "Without it, I'm afraid we can never rid ourselves of the nanites."

Val felt his stomach tighten. "Boy, you really know how to rain on someone's parade. Do you mean we're all doomed?"

"No, we can periodically subject ourselves to EM radiation to cleanse ourselves, but eventually it will take its toll on our bodies. More importantly, what about the millions we cannot reach. A civilization cannot exist with such a constant threat looming over it."

"What about setting up a research center? We could …"

"I'm afraid such a task would be impossible. No one alive knows anything about these nanites. I don't know where to start searching for a kill switch, if one even exists. It could be a certain frequency, a predator nanite, or some simple chemical harmless to humans."

Val returned to the window. Night had fallen and the city was a black smear. The dark band of the Ybarra River flowed silently past the hotel. Scattered fires throughout the city marked body disposal sites. His gaze turned south. He couldn't believe the path his thoughts were taking. After a few moments, he made a fist and pounded the windowsill three times.

"There's only one place where we might find that information."

He saw Jeffries' reflection in the glass as Jeffries stood. The expression on his face was one of disbelief. "You mean Resurrection City? That would be … suicidal."

He turned to Jeffries. "You said it yourself, Doc. We're all on a slow road to suicide now. We have to go back to where it all began. If there is an answer, it will be there."

"Such an undertaking would require the military's approval. It would require planning and an allocating of resources …"

"Hell, Doc. Elliot and I stole a C-130 that he could barely fly and made it from Casey to Adelaide. Returning should be a cinch, especially now that the sun is coming up there. As far as the military approving, what choice do they have?" He turned back to the window. Instead of a dark city, he saw an endless plane of dark snow and ice. "I'm tired of sitting around anyway. A vacation will do me good."

"Was anyone left alive in Antarctica?"

Val shook his head. Roger Basky had been near death when they found him at Casey. Anson had killed an insane John Gilford when he had tried to murder them. They had left Basky and Gilford's bodies at Resurrection City. "No, no one."

"What about the American base, McMurdo?"

Val shook his head. He tried not to dwell on the fate of his fellow Americans. "I don't know. They probably suffered the same fate as the others."

"Perhaps not. Perhaps someone survived."

Val thought about anyone trapped in Antarctica over the winter with zombies to contend with. "Then God help them. They're living in hell."

25

Sept. 22, Resurrection City, Oates Land, Antarctica

The flight from McMurdo had been a harrowing one. Lester was a novice pilot, unused to the vagaries of air currents of Antarctica. The warmer air along the coast, colliding with cold air pouring off the Plateau, produced pockets of disturbance that jostled the plane's occupants and eroded Lester's confidence in his flying abilities. Now, he would have to land them safely with no landing gear in the dark.

Malosi had been right about one thing – Resurrection City was dead. As Lester circled the base in the Otter at an altitude of two-hundred feet, he dropped a flare. Outlined in the ghostly glow were dozens of zombies craning their necks to search the night sky for the airplane they heard but could not find. The buildings looked intact, but the sprawled outlines of corpses on the ground told of the true horrors the base's personnel had endured.

"Just pick a spot and set her down," Hughes said on their third pass over the base. His irritation at Lester's procrastination was evident in his voice.

"She may flip," Lester warned.

"We can't stay up here forever," Hughes reminded him. "We have to take our chances."

Lester nodded, took a deep breath and reduced speed, lining the nose of the Otter with the runway. "I'll land us as far from the buildings as I can. There's a twenty-knot crosswind. It's going to be bumpy."

Brad grabbed the side of the airplane to brace himself. "Hang on," he urged Liz. He wrapped his arms around her and pushed his good leg against the rear door.

The engines changed pitch as Lester reduced power. Lester had explained earlier that the Otter had a stall speed of less than sixty miles per hour. That meant he could land at a lower speed without the plane dropping out of the sky like a brick. Brad was all for not dropping like a brick.

"Extending flaps," Lester called.

The Otter shuddered as the nose pitched down. The winds blowing across the runway dropped the left wing. Lester fought the controls to keep it level. He began pulling back on the steering column. The plane dropped suddenly. He pushed the column forward to bring it up slightly.

"Too much," he said. "I'm flaring now to raise the nose a bit."

The plane danced a jig in the air. Brad raised his head to look out the side window. Even in the darkness illuminated only by starlight and the spotlights of the plane, he could see that the ground was coming up quickly. The runway beneath them was a sea of half-frozen slush.

"Almost there," Lester warned.

The Otter hit the icy runway and slewed sideways. With no way to steer, that they didn't tumble seemed almost a miracle. The Otter's props struck dirt and bent. The engines screamed as gears ground against one another and teeth sheared away. Both engines died. They were now a three-ton toboggan hurling down the runway at sixty miles per hour. The Otter bounced into the air with each bump it encountered, but just as Brad believed they would become airborne again, the plane settled back onto the runway. The screeching of the remnants of the undercarriage tearing away as it dug into the ground became a high-pitched scream that resonated in his teeth. The Otter veered to the right and began spinning like a carousel, flinging passengers and freight against the walls. A large crate struck Brad's ankle. He suppressed a yelp of pain, though it would have been inaudible in the death throes of the Otter.

The silence came as a surprise. Brad was expecting a fiery end to their madcap sleigh ride. He glanced around the dark cabin trying to count heads.

"Is everyone okay?" he asked.

Liz mumbled something into his chest and pushed away. "I'll live."

One-by-one, they replied to his query. All seven of them had survived the crash. The Otter would never fly again, but they had made it.

"Good job, Lester," he said.

Lester didn't reply, as he slowly unbuckled his seat belt and pushed open the door. In the darkness, Lester's face was as pale as the moon. A few seconds later, the sound of retching reached Brad's ears. He smiled. He didn't blame Lester one bit. After any crash, there was always the possibility of a fire. Vacating the Otter as soon as possible was a priority.

"Everyone, make sure you have your weapons," Brad warned. "We'll have company soon."

The door was jammed. It took both his and Hughes strength to force it open. Brad helped Liz down and crawled out after her, being careful with his leg. He noticed zombies in the distance headed in their direction. Hughes kneeled on the ice and began firing his rifle. Brad remained standing, bracing himself against the side of the plane, and joined him. Lester recovered from his bout of the jitters, and he and Bain soon began firing into the approaching zombies as well. They reduced the creatures' numbers by half, but the zombies, near starving, continued their relentless advance toward them. They were now only twenty yards away and over twenty of the creatures remained. Brad fired his last bullet from the Winchester and pulled out the revolver. Beside him, Bain's AK 47 went silent.

Brad looked at Liz. "Take this pistol and make a run for one of the buildings with the others. I'll never make it."

Her eyes opened wide when as she realized what he was suggesting. "No," she said. "I'm not leaving you." She began to drag him toward the open door of the Otter. "We can shut them out."

He shot a zombie that had gotten too close and pressed the pistol into her hand. "We'll starve," he yelled at her. "Get out of here."

Hughes' rifle was now empty. Twelve zombies remained, too many to kill by hand, but Brad pulled out his hunting knife. Bain suddenly turned, grabbed Brad by the shoulders and shook him. "The kill code," he said.

At first, Brad was mystified, but then he realized they had Malosi's Android phone. He pulled it from his pocket, praying that the crash hadn't damaged it. He hit the play button and held it in front of him. The shrill coded message burst out from the tiny speaker, much quieter than it had seemed in the confines of the Otter. Suddenly, the nearest zombie stopped moving and its limbs began to twitch. Black fluid ran from its eyes and mouth. The creature's eyes rolled up until only the white was showing, and then it collapsed on the ground.

Liz grabbed the Android and walked toward the zombies. Brad lunged to stop her, but she was beyond his reach. He fell onto the runway spitting out a mouthful of dirty water and ice. Around her, the creatures stopped moving and began to repeat the first one's dance of death. Two literally shook themselves to pieces. Within seconds, all that remained were dead zombies.

Liz turned back and hugged Brad. He enfolded her in his arms and kissed her. "Damn, you're resourceful," he said. "I think maybe I'll keep you around."

"You just need a full-time nurse," she said.

"Baby, I need a keeper," he responded.

They passed several zombie corpses near the edge of the runway. Several of the bodies were crushed or had been chopped into pieces.

"Someone's been busy," Hughes commented. "Maybe it was that Gilford that Malosi mentioned."

Brad didn't care who had killed them just as long as it reduced the number of creatures they faced. Hughes took the Android from Liz's hand and began walking toward the nearest building. "Let's clear this place of zombies and make ourselves at home," he said.

* * * *

They chose the cafeteria as their base of operations, clearing it of dead bodies and lighting the propane stoves for heat, unaware that two of the bodies they removed were those of Roger Basky and John Gilford. Brad looked at the large row of stoves and ovens and wished that Mattie were there to appreciate them. She could whip them up a great dinner with a few potatoes and a can of soup. Liz refused to allow him to do any work. He lay happily on a bench and nursed his sore ankle. Once again, they were stranded with no transportation, but they now had a safe haven. If Malosi had not been lying, rescue was on the way, and they would in fact arrive in less than forty hours. It seemed too much like a dream after all they had endured, but Brad needed a dream to cling to. After the horrors of the Zombie Apocalypse, could things ever return to normal?

# 26

Sept. 22, Melbourne, Australia

The news had struck Val like a bolt of lightning from a clear blue sky. Someone had the kill code for the nanite plague. Woomera had received a message from a Doctor Gregory Malosi claiming that he had the code in his possession. His demand that they rescue him before he would relinquish it seemed less than altruistic to Doctor Jeffries, a man of immense conscience, but to Val, it made sense. If he had been stuck in Antarctica with no hope of escape, he too might hold the world hostage.

"If he's telling the truth, then our problems are over," he told Jeffries. The news had energized him. He paced the room with his hands clasped behind his back like an expectant father.

Jeffries was more sedate, sitting in a chair reading over some notes. He shook his head. "He may be lying; he's desperate to escape Antarctica, but we cannot afford to take a chance. He used an ADF emergency frequency. Not everyone has access to it. This lends some credence to his claims. He also mentioned Doctor Cromby and Doctor Gilford. Only someone who knew of Resurrection City would know them."

Val stopped and glared at Jeffries. He had encountered Gilford and had no desire to meet anyone else like him. "We have no choice, do we?" he said.

"No, we must rescue him. Even if he is lying, perhaps in Resurrection City we can discover more information about the nanites."

Gilford's attempt to prevent his and Anson's leaving by damaging the Hercules C-130 played through Val's mind. So did Gilford's attempt to murder them in their sleep. If Malosi was of the same ilk, he wasn't trustworthy.

"I don't want to go back," he said.

Jeffries cocked his head to one side and stared at him quizzically. "No one is asking you to, Val."

Val stared at Jeffries for a moment, noticing the changes in him. Since the message, the doctor had become a new man, more at ease. He looked years younger and moved with some of the determination Val had witnessed in Woomera. He had even smiled occasionally, though it looked as if the effort cost him.

"I have to," he explained. "I have experience on the ice and I've been there before."

Jeffries shrugged his shoulders. "If you wish. I will remain here. I'm too old for such a journey."

"I'll bring you back a penguin."

"Just bring back Doctor Malosi and the kill code. It's a chance to save the world."

"Will it work?" That was Val's biggest concern. He would walk through fire to end the plague. Since his arrival in Australia with Anson, he had lived among the destruction and the carnage until it sickened him. Thousands of corpses, tens of thousands of zombies, starvation, sickness, misery – it never ended.

"If such a code exists, we can broadcast a signal by satellite to every corner of the planet. In theory, we can kill all the nanites."

"What if it's a wild goose chase? Can we do it with EMPs alone?"

"Unlikely. We can clear individual cities, but not the atmosphere. Your original idea of balloons with the devices traveling the air currents was sound, but unfortunately, we are unable to increase the power of the pulse without increasing the danger to humans. Killing millions to save tens of thousands seems too much like slaughter. As you said, repeated exposure to the EMPs cannot be healthy. Without the kill code, mankind will slowly die out."

"Then it's decided."

Jeffries nodded. "The military is readying a C-40A jet for the journey. It has a range of three thousand miles, sufficient for the outbound journey. They are counting on refueling there."

"When we left, the fuel depot was intact, but anything could have happened since then." He turned to Jeffries. "Have they attempted to contact Malosi?"

"Yes, to no avail. If he has left McMurdo, there may be no radio at Resurrection City."

"Who's going?"

"A crew of four, Doctor Ivers, and a military detachment of ten men. And you, of course."

"Of course. Why should I pass up the opportunity to get stranded in Antarctica again?"

Jeffries sighed heavily. "Look, you don't have to go."

Val couldn't find the right words. He didn't want to sound mysterious, but he knew he had to return to Antarctica. The nightmares wouldn't go away, not even when he awoke. "I have to go. It's like coming full circle. I have to face my fears."

Jeffries nodded sympathetically. "I think I understand."

"When are they leaving?"

Jeffries checked his watch. "In about six hours."

Val clapped his hands together and smiled. "Well, I guess I'd better pack my toothbrush."

* * * *

Sept. 23, Melbourne, Australia

With usual military efficiency, the tower had delayed their departure three times. After five hours of sitting on the plane, Val was ready to either get moving or get off. He had more than sufficient time to come to regret his decision to return to Antarctica. Thoughts of closure seemed less appealing after hours of waiting.

Finally, the seat belt light came on and the engines revved. They were getting under way. As the C-40A lumbered down the long tarmac runway, its two General Electric CFM56-7 SLST engines struggling to lift it into the air, Val's mind drifted back to his last frantic takeoff from Resurrection City in the Hercules C-130, the quad props slicing through zombies. The plane banked right over the city, revealing the scars caused by out of control fires. He spotted a few signs of activity along the docks and two ships on the Ybarra River. He had never liked planes. As the plane gained altitude and leveled off and the roar of the engines reduced, he released his white-knuckle death grip on armrests. He looked around. At least the C-40A resembled a passenger liner instead of the massive, cold Hercules transport. He even had a call light, though no flight attendant accompanied them on this trip to bring him a drink.

"Nervous?" asked Captain Stewart Healy from across the aisle. Healy was in command of the small detachment of seven men and three women. Looking more like a surf bum than an officer with longer than regulation blond hair and his sun-bronzed skin, he didn't inspire confidence in Val.

"Only on takeoff," Val replied.

"I hear you've been to this place before."

He didn't know if Healy meant Antarctica or Resurrection City, but he answered, "Yeah, I've been there."

Healy leaned in closer. "What's it like?"

Val shook his head. The kid thought he was on a pleasure trip, a frigging adventure. "When I was there, it was frozen, stormy, and full of zombies and people trying to kill us. We barely made it out of there alive."

Healy looked at him for a moment and smiled. "Good. I'm tired of sweeping up dead zombies from the street and mowing them down from the air."

*Christ!* Val thought. *I'm on a mission with a thrill seeker.*

They had brought an EMP device, but Jeffries had advised against using it for fear that it might damage sensitive equipment. Val was all for dropping it from the air and taking their chances. He had enough of zombie killing to last a lifetime. His taste for adventure was sated.

"Maybe you'll get your chance."

Healy sat back in his seat smiling. Val looked at the troops, none over twenty-years old, and shook his head in dismay. *What have I gotten myself into?*

The trip would be long and boring, almost six hours long. Val had glanced out the window as they flew over Hobart. A few navy ships flying the flags of several nations were in the harbor, but once the island's evacuation was complete, the ships and the survivors would all return to Melbourne. Ivers, the only other person he knew on the jet, was so engrossed in his notes that conversation with him was impossible. When Marino had contacted Alex about the trip, only Nicole's strong objections and her threat to name their child after her Uncle Bartholomew had prevented him from accompanying Marino. To avoid any further conversation with Healy, Val dozed most of the way.

By leaving later than planned, night had fallen before the C-40 reached Antarctica. Below them, Val could see nothing but a dead, stark white landscape illuminated by the light of a crescent moon. Antarctica held none of the mystery and charm it once had. Now, it only evoked memories that he wanted badly to forget but knew he never could. He would be no more able to erase those dire, dark memories than he could memories of his first lover, his first job, or the sight of his first Arizona sunset. They would remain with him until he died.

"We're almost there," Healy announced, breaking into his thoughts. He nodded, but Healy was eager to talk. "We can't reach anyone by radio. With no landing lights, this will be a bumpy landing." Healy's smile evoked a vision in Val's mind of him riding a surfboard with a fifty-foot curler rolling over him. He was eager to test himself in a new environment.

"Malosi knows we're coming," Val replied. "He'll arrange something."

Fifteen minutes later as approached the base and no lights were visible, Val wondered if he had spoken out of turn. The base might be deserted. Malosi might not have made it there.

The C-40 lost altitude and speed and flew over the base. Several figures were outlined by light from an open doorway.

"Zombies," Healy said. He turned to his men. "We got zombies. As soon as we touchdown, break out in a standard pattern."

"They're not zombies," Val said. "They're people. They're waving."

"I'm taking no chances," Healy insisted. "If anything growls, I'm giving the order to fire."

"Christ Almighty! Are you that stupid that you can't tell they're human?"

Healy glared at him and checked his pistol.

"Lord, save me from a crusader," Val said under his breath.

## 27

Sept. 23, *Resurrection City*, Oates Land, Antarctica

"When are they coming?" Reed asked. His nervousness was beginning to affect the others. He jabbed the dial of his watch angrily. "It's been over forty-eight hours."

Brad nodded. He had expected their rescuers long before now. It was three hours after sunset. Had Malosi been lying yet again?

"I can tell time," he snapped at Reed. "If you're getting nervous, go outside and cool off."

Reed stared at him for a moment before storming out the door. Brad wanted to go after Reed to reassure him, but his swollen ankle prevented that. He could walk gingerly, but he felt weak and feverish. He had not broached the subject with Liz, but if Malosi had lied about rescue, he might have also lied about the kill code on the Android, a last minute attempt to save his life. If it was useless, then his fever might be the first signs of nanites inside his body furiously changing him into a zombie. He had a brief flash of himself, eyes dead and chest sprouting black tendrils of death, attacking Liz. His hand reached out to touch the pistol sitting beside him beneath the blanket. *Not yet*, he thought.

He had allowed the others to do most of the work of preparing their new abode at Liz's insistence. The first day, they had used a tractor to pull the wreckage of the DeHavilland Otter off the runway to clear it. They had also lugged the zombie corpses and dead bodies away from the base and built a funeral pyre to dispose of them. He had watched most of it through the window wishing he could help. As much as he loved Liz, her hovering over him nursing him like a sick child had been an affront to his manhood. With the major work finished, for most the second day they had all sat and waited. The waiting was worst of all.

Brad looked across the room at his companions. Liz leaned against the wall pretending to nap but knowing that she would spring up and race to him at his first sign of distress. Bain, Lester, and Hughes stared out the window into the darkness as if willing a plane to come as they played a game of poker using beers as poker chips. Jernigan lay sprawled on one of the benches snoring loudly, and DeSousa was busy wolfing down a bowl of stew. They all looked as tired as he felt. He didn't want to be the one to suggest that they begin making the base habitable, but if no one came soon, it was their only option.

In the silence, except for the scratching of beer bottles sliding across the table and Jernigan's snores, his mind wandered back to Malosi. His visits to the radio room, his grooming Deen to help him, his attempt to seduce Liz into coming with him, even letting the zombies into the Crary Building to cover his escape – if they had not been the acts of a madman, then he had a plan. A sound, slight at first, whispered for his attention. He raised himself to look out the window but saw nothing. He dismissed it as his imagination.

Suddenly, Reed burst back into the room. "I hear something!" he yelled, pointing at the sky.

Jernigan snapped awake. Beers clattered to the floor and Hughes banged into the table in his eagerness to reach the door. Everyone rushed to the door at the same time trying to get out. He held back until everyone had exited the room to avoid being trampled. Liz walked over and handed him the crutch she had found in the infirmary and insisted he use. She eyed him sternly. He hated the feeling of helpless it induced, but rather than argue with her, an argument he was sure to lose, he put placed it under his arm and hobbled to the door. The sound was still faint, barely discernible above the wind. Brad wondered if he and Reed were simply wishing a plane overhead. Then, he heard it again louder, the unmistakable drone of jet engines.

"It's them," Reed shouted. He hopped up and down on the ice in his glee. If not for his injured leg, Brad would have joined him in his Snoopy dance.

"They need lights," Lester said.

No one had thought of that, assuming the landing would be in daylight. There was no time to rig electric lights.

"Set some diesel drums on fire," Hughes suggested.

Brad had a better idea. He hobbled to the jeep and trailer they had used to haul away the corpses and cranked it. Thankfully, it was an automatic and had no clutch to negotiate with his injured leg. He yelled at Hughes, "Take the tractor to one end and leave the headlights shining. At least they'll know where the runway is and how long it is."

Hughes rushed to the tractor they had used to remove the Otter. Everybody else stood just outside the door of the cafeteria in the pool of light cast by the open door. The jet flew over the base almost low enough to read the letters on its dove-white wings. It circled twice as the two men raced to opposite ends of the runway. Brad watched as the big jet slowly descended, his heart was racing.

The jet touched down a hundred feet beyond the Hughes' tractor. The brakes screamed and the reversed engines howled as the pilot fought to stop the jet on the slushy runway. Brad watched the jet loom larger as it approached. For a brief moment, he thought it was going to overshoot the runway and crash into him. He held his nerve to give the pilot some idea of how close to the end he was coming. Finally, it came to rest less than twenty yards away. It turned and slowly taxied toward the buildings. Before the engines died, the door opened and men jumped down and spread out along the sides of the jet. They remained there as three men approached across the field. Brad pulled up in the jeep and limped out with the others to greet them.

"I thought there was just one man," an officer said. "Which one of you is Doctor Malosi?"

Brad barked out a sharp laugh. "Malosi's dead. The bastard tried to kill us." He held out the Android phone. "This is what you came for."

Another man, a civilian wearing a Stetson, spoke up. "That's it?"

Brad recognized the accent of a fellow American, but before he could reply, Bain pushed forward. "Val Marino? Is that you?"

Marino stepped forward for a better look. As he recognized Bain, a big smile swept over his face. "Ian Bain! What are you doing here? I thought you were in England."

"I wish I were," Bain replied. "I was at Amundsen-Scott." He waved his hand. "We're all that's left. Did anyone from McMurdo reach Australia or New Zealand?"

Val shook his head. "No one."

"Then they're all dead too. We're it."

Brad handed the Android to Val. "This is what you came for, but we'd like a lift back."

"Certainly. We'll refuel, search the lab for any pertinent papers, and leave tomorrow." He turned to the officer. "Right, Captain Healy?"

"Affirmative," Healy replied. He waved his men forward. "Let's get this show on the road."

From the darkness, a zombie appeared a few feet away from Healy. At Brad's yell of warning, Healy spun, drew his pistol, and shot the zombie in the head. The creature tumbled forward and collapsed.

"We thought we got them all. He must have been outside the base and followed the jeep in," Brad said. "Sorry about that."

Healy replaced his pistol and looked at Brad. "No problem." He turned to his men. "Sweep the camp. I want every damn building cleared before we refuel." He joined his men looking immeasurably pleased that he had finally gotten to shoot a zombie.

As the two groups mingled and walked back to the cafeteria, Brad felt Liz slip her arm around his waist and squeeze him. The weight of authority fell from him like chains of bondage, making him feel lighter than he had in weeks. Now, someone else could make the decisions and take the responsibility for their safety. He knew more hard work lay in front of them, but his days of giving orders and devoting himself to the welfare of others was over. Now, he wanted only to devote himself to pleasing Liz.

"We made it," she whispered in his ear. Her steps seemed lighter too.

"We were the lucky ones," he replied, "and I'm the luckiest of them all."

I would like to thank all my fans who demanded a sequel for *Ice Station Zombie*. I was happy to comply. I wish to dedicate this novel to you and to my wonderful wife, Kim, from whom all blessings flow. She allows me to kill for a living, even if it is only in my imagination.


J E Gurley

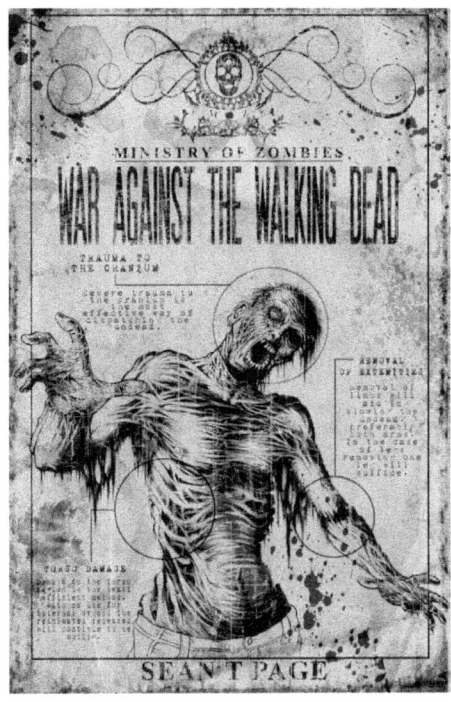

More than 63% of people now believe that there will be a global zombie apocalypse before 2050...

So, you've got your survival guide, you've lived through the first chaotic months of the crisis, what next?
Employing real science and pioneering field work, War against the Walking Dead provides a complete blueprint for taking back your country from the rotting clutches of the dead after a zombie apocalypse.

* A glimpse inside the mind of the zombie using a team of top psychics - what do the walking dead think about? What lessons can we learn to help us defeat this pervading menace?
* Detailed guidelines on how to galvanise a band of scared survivors into a fighting force capable of defeating the zombies and dealing with emerging groups such as end of the world cults, raiders and even cannibals!
* Features insights from real zombie fighting organisations across the world, from America to the Philippines, Australia to China - the experts offer advice in every aspect of fighting the walking dead.
Packed with crucial zombie war information and advice, from how to build a city of the living in a land of the dead to tactics on how to use a survivor army to liberate your country from the zombies - War against the Walking Dead may be humanity's last chance.

Remember, dying is not an option!

# Dead Bait

"If you don't already suffer from bathophobia and/or ichthyophobia, you probably will after reading this amazingly wonderful horrific collection of short stories about what lurks beneath the waters of the world" – *DREAD CENTRAL*

A husband hell-bent on revenge hunts a Wereshark...A Russian mail order bride with a fishy secret...Crabs with a collective consciousness...A vampire who transforms into a Candiru...Zombie piranha...Bait that will have you crawling out of your skin and more. Drawing on horror, humor with a helping of dark fantasy and a touch of deviance, these 19 contemporary stories pay homage to the monsters that lurk in the murky waters of our imaginations. *If you thought it was safe to go back in the water...Think Again!*

"Severed Press has the cojones to publish THE most outrageous, nasty and downright wonderfully disgusting horror that I've seen in quite a while." – *DREAD CENTRAL*

# DEMONMACHY
## Brant Danay

As the universe slowly dies, all demonkind is at war in a tournament of genocide. The prize? Nirvana. The Necrodelic, a death addict who smokes the flesh of his victims as a drug, is determined to win this afterlife for himself. His quest has taken him to the planet Grystiawa, and into a duel with a dream-devouring snake demon who is more than he seems. Grystiawa has also been chosen as the final battleground in the ancient spider-serpent wars. As armies of arachnid monstrosities and ophidian gladiators converge upon the planet, the Necrodelic is forced to choose sides in a cataclysmic combat that could well prove his demise. Beyond Grystiawa, a Siamese twin incubus and succubus, a brain-raping nightmare fetishist, a gargantuan insect queen, and an entire universe of genocidal demons are forming battle plans of their own. Observing the apocalyptic carnage all the while is Satan himself, watching voyeuristically from the very Hell in which all those who fail will be damned to eternal torment. Who will emerge victorious from this cosmic armageddon? And what awaits the victor beyond the blood-drenched end of time? The battle begins in Demonmachy. Twisting Satanic mythologies and Eastern religions into an ultraviolent grotesque nightmare, the Messiah of Death Saga will rip your eyeballs right out of your skull. Addicted to its psychedelic darkness, you'll immediately sew and screw and staple and weld them back into their sockets so you can read more. It's an intergalactic, interdimensional harrowing that you'll never forget...and may never recover from.

*Available at www.severedpress.com, Amazon and most online bookstores*

# BIOHAZARD
## Tim Curran

The day after tomorrow: Nuclear fallout. Mutations. Deadly pandemics. Corpse wagons. Body pits. Empty cities. The human race trembling on the edge of extinction. Only the desperate survive. One of them is Rick Nash. But there is a price for survival: communion with a ravenous evil born from the furnace of radioactive waste. It demands sacrifice. Only it can keep Nash one step ahead of the nightmare that stalks him-a sentient, seething plague-entity that stalks its chosen prey: the last of the human race. To accept it is a living death. To defy it, a hell beyond imagining

www.ingramcontent.com/pod-product-compliance
Lightning Source LLC
Chambersburg PA
CBHW071502170626
46811CB00007B/2685